THE HONEYSUCKLE
ROSE HOTEL

THE HONEYSUCKLE ROSE HOTEL

by

SHERMAN SMITH

]Elementá[

Sherman Smith

The Honeysuckle Rose Hotel

Cover image © Isaxar | Dreamstime.com

Published by]Elementá[– Sweden

www.elementa-selection.com

ISBN 978-91-7637-026-1

]Elementá[is a Wisehouse Imprint.

© Wisehouse 2014 – Sweden

www.wisehouse-publishing.com

ONE

NO ROOM AT THE INN

STELLA WOKE FEELING BOTH ANXIOUS AND CONTENT. SHE woke with a sense that something was about to happen that would be life changing—good or bad she did not know.

The only sound was the soft tick of the clock down the hall, and Earl's rasp and sputter snores. She suspected that in time she would come to despise that sound—Earl's snore—but for now she loved each note, each breath, telling her that he was there.

Last night had been New Year's Eve, 1948, and it had been delicious. She had never thought that she could be this happy. Was it a dream? Like most dreams, when one wakes, everything good just slips away, its sweet memory fading into star dust. That was why she was anxious—it was all too good to be true—yet, content, because it really was true.

She arose, careful not to wake Earl, slipped on her robe and slippers, and tip-toed down the stairs. It was a quarter to seven in the morning. They had not gone to bed until three. She was tired, but not in a hazy way. She knew that by afternoon exhaustion would be pounding on her temporal lobe with an unforgiving headache. *Shame on you girl*, she thought, *you are more than old enough to know better.*

She looked around the bar. Her eyes, dry and puffy, were not quite focused from lack of sleep, too much to drink, and tobacco smoke. She could feel that headache creeping up to meet the morning sun, but she was not about to let it ruin her morning—at least not yet.

This was their home and Earl's piano bar. The name might be hers, but it was Earl who gave it life. The dirty glasses, confetti, ashtrays, dishes that were going to be hell to clean, were all where they had left them when they had finally called it a night. The stench of stale tobacco smoke and spilled beer were the bar's own early morning hangover. The electric sign in the window quietly buzzed as it announced that this was Stella's Starlight Lounge, a place where music began, magic which she prayed would never end.

As she reached the piano her finger tapped down slowly on a key, its solitary note touching her heart as she remembered Earl's serenade. In a room full of people there had just been the two of them. He had gotten up from his piano, found her in his darkness, and took her in his arms. Henry played his clarinet while Brooks whistled, creating the illusion that Benny Goodman had stepped into their moment. Earl sang the lyrics to Moonlight Serenade as they danced, their soft steps were like walking on a cloud filled sky just short of heaven.

'I stand at your gate and the song that I sing is of moonlight.

I stand and I wait for the touch of your hand . . .

She hummed the song quietly in her head as she remembered his voice singing the same. The memory would have been perfect had it not been for Earl's dark glasses. Alas, she knew all too well that the eyes are not the window into a blind man's soul.

The coffee pot behind the bar quietly brewed the last night's left over coffee into a thick, black tar-like sludge. She smelled its bitter regret, but never-the-less poured herself a partial cup. She winced at the first taste, pouring the rest into the sink.

The song she hummed faded as her eyes settled on the space behind the bar where just little more than a year ago she had almost lost Earl. It was a dark memory, still hard to believe. Her eyes teared as she tried not to remember the ugly moment when Elroy Hawkes had shot Stub twice, nearly killing him.

Elroy had come for her, not Earl. He had thought that it was her when Stub came through the kitchen door instead. Dear God, it had all been that close. If it had not been for Ivory Burch they might all be dead.

She, Earl, Henry and Brooks had helped give Ivory back his will to live. Ivory had paid this debt by saving her life—more importantly saving Earl's. Of course, Ivory proclaimed that it was a debt that could never be fully repaid. She knew differently.

The electric sign, *Stella's Starlight Lounge*, sizzled in the window reminding her that this was not a dream.

"Where do you keep the coffee?"

Startled, her breath caught, as she turned, the empty coffee cup she held slipping silently to the floor where it broke sharply into three pieces. It wasn't until Henry had spoken, that she realized she was not alone. "Henry, what are you . . ."

"Doing here?" He finished the question for her. "Where

else better to be?"

She lit a cigarette, her hand still trembling, as she studied his face. His surprise return on New Year's Eve had been a most welcome surprise. For a Nisei, she supposed that Henry was a handsome man. She could look at most men and get a quick read on what was on their minds. Henry's Asian eyes always seemed half closed and she could never quite get a fix on where his thoughts were.

She could not tell if he had slept or not. It had been three in the morning when she had locked the front door. Henry must have been back in the kitchen. She hadn't thought to look, assuming everyone had gone home, leaving just her and Earl to climb the late night stairs in search of the sand man.

She had first met Henry when he had been assigned to her ward at the veteran's hospital. He had been an army medic with the Purple Heart Battalion—The 442nd Regimental Combat Team composed almost entirely of American soldiers of Japanese ancestry—Nisei. Most, if not all of the patients at the San Francisco Veteran's Hospital had suffered their injuries in the war against Japan. One of the most traumatic of the patients Henry had to face had been Ivory Burch, a former POW of the Japanese Empire. Ivory had once told his doctor at Oak Knoll Hospital that it had been an angel, a blind man, and a Jap that had helped him find his will to live again. Stella knew Henry to be a compassionate man who she had missed dearly.

Stella was a petite bottle blond, with a haughty, sultry, heart shaped face, who looked far younger than her thirty-nine years. Henry studied her for a moment remembering when she had befriended a lonely Nisei orderly struggling to care for angry broken men who hated the sight of him. The first thing he had learned was that Stella had heart. The second a deep unsettling sadness that was slowly eating away at her soul. It had been a distant two years prior when Earl had first sung his way into Stella's heart. Now, he could see, even at this hour of the morning, that there was a magnificent joy flickering in her eyes.

He did not know any better way to break the news than to just blurt it out. "I'm not going back to Stanford," Henry said, dropping the news as if it did not matter. The rasp in his voice suggested it did. He had not slept, and while not a cigarette smoker, he had not escaped the pall of the smoky bar. "It was a noble dream," he continued, "to think that I could become a doctor. I tried, but in the end it was not the hours, the studying, or the money, I found a simple truth within myself." He touched his chest. "I don't have it here. I haven't the heart to see anymore suffering—any more pain. God knows I saw enough in the war, and in that god awful place they called a hospital." His eyes shifted, a slight smile crossing his lips as he remembered a former patient, both enemy and friend. "Like Ivory I need to find my second chance in life and it sure isn't going to be in medical school." He paused, took in a long slow breath, and then let it out just as slowly. *That is it*, he thought, *nothing more needs be said.*

Stella's eyes said differently.

"I know what you are thinking." Henry's voice was edged in guilt. "A doctor is supposed to heal and give comfort. Hah, physician heal thyself, that is damned easier said than done. I can't because I transfer too much of someone else's suffering into myself and can't let it go. If the war had lasted any longer they would have shipped me out under a Section 8."

"Stella, I volunteered to become a medic because my dad wanted me to become a doctor. Medics received two weeks of basic training and six weeks of medical training, plus an additional two weeks of tactical training during which we learned how to set up aid stations and field hospitals. In combat we carried morphine, iodine, cotton swabs, bandages, and cigarettes. We were trained to provide first aid under fire, recognize and treat wounds, evacuate soldiers over difficult terrain. There was no training that can possibly prepare you to do this under fire—except from a medic who had been there and survived."

A tear ran down his cheek as he remained silent for a few very long seconds.

"Medic! The calls for help always seemed to be in the direct line of fire of a German sniper or machine gun nest. When you got there you found a soldier, often just a kid, with his guts exposed or a leg blown off. The look in his eyes as the morphine eased his pain is something you can never forget. You saved a few and lost too many. Their last words, simple and to the point, 'Why?'—or 'Mom'—then just as sudden as the bullet that had ripped through their flesh, they died. Medic! Another call, and you crawled or ran through a mine field as a hail of bullets buzzed around you risked your own life to save just one more. When my supply pack ran out all I had was a cigarette to offer them as I waited for another medic to show who might have something left that might do some good. The blood, their pain, is still with me." He held out his hands that shook with the memory. "Music seems to be the only thing that takes all that away."

Stella, who had spent too many years as a nurse at Oak Knoll Naval Hospital and then the Veteran's Hospital, had heard it all before. She had steeled her heart, but still felt Henry's anguish. She reached beneath a counter and found a number 10 can of Hills Brothers coffee, the aroma rich as she lifted the lid. "Are you sure about this?" Stella asked as she remembered how much it meant to Henry when he had first gotten his admittance letter.

He stared at the flickering sign in the window. "I've turned in the papers. My spot has already been taken by some other lucky bastard"

She filled the coffee filter, the cigarette glowing as it was clinched between her lips. "What now?"

Henry reached out and took the cigarette from her lips, flicking it into a nearby sink full of greasy cold water.

Stella batted an eye, annoyed that he had done that. It wasn't the first time, and it would not be the last. She was aware that he cared that she smoked too much. Back at the hospital, had someone seen a Nisei orderly be so forward with a white nurse, there would have been serious repercussions.

She placed a clean pot under the drip as the coffee began to brew. "Your folks, do they know?"

Henry turned his eyes away as he hesitated to answer. He had spoken to no one about this and was uncomfortable to even begin. She lit another cigarette. "Please don't," he said, his eyes watering either from the smoke or thoughts of his father.

"Pops, my dad," he finally said, his voice soft words coming from a place where they are difficult to come by, "is a proud man. Pop was born in this country and has never set foot in Japan. His father, who never learned to speak much English, encouraged Pop to become as American as baseball. And he did."

"When the war came and we were all taken away to the camps Pops' heart nearly broke when I enlisted in the all Nisei unit. In his heart he was born and raised an American. Now he was told that he was an enemy of America—that he was Japanese. He became a stateless man, who had no place in America or Japan."

"Our ancestors came from Japan. Pop could never understand how I could go to war against people who share our blood. That my war was fought against the Germans did not matter. My unit could just as easily have been sent to the Pacific. The war took from my father his land, his heart, and his son. My mother wrote that it would have been easier for him if I had been killed."

"I'm sorry," Stella reached out and touched his wrist letting her hand linger there for a brief but comforting moment. "Surely, your mother . . ."

"She does not write often for fear that Pop will find out. Her first loyalty is to her husband. Perhaps in time she will help my father find forgiveness. If not, I will ask his venerable spirit when his time has come to leave his earthly sorrows behind."

Stella poured their coffee. The joy of her morning had just turned as dark and bitter as the day old coffee she had poured down the sink. She could not find any words that would mean anything so she listened as Henry emptied a bucket of emotion.

"It is hard enough to be Nisei, to be here in San Francisco, and see the way people still look at us. My face is that of an island race against which this country fought a violent and ugly war. The war has been over for two years now and I am still not allowed to be forgiven for sins not of my own making." There were no tears in his eyes, just the pain of carrying too much weight for too long.

Stella poured a touch of whiskey in her coffee offering the same to Henry. He took his black. She was a magnet for broken men with big hearts. The only one missing from her deck was Brooks—at least she knew that he was nearby if he needed her. She had married a blind man which has its own unique challenges. She and Earl had taken in Stub and Ivory. Now, without asking, she knew that Henry had come to her for a reason. He needed a place to be himself—just like Stub, Ivory, and her Earl.

Stella remembered the day Henry had first arrived at the hospital. The war's end marked the beginning of his real battle with prejudice, self-doubt, anger, and shame. Like many combatants the horrors of the battlefield lay buried in the subconscious never letting the living forget the grim realities of their experiences. Henry had survived brutal combat alongside of men who shared a special bond, fighting and dying for a country they could no longer call their own, to prove they were loyal Americans. All the while, their families suffered humiliation and shame imprisoned in camps where they were often treated worse than America treated the POWs of Germany or Japan.

At the veteran's hospital Henry walked a lonely path amongst the patients who saw the color of the skin as the same as their former enemy. When riding the trolley to work he had to sit with his head down, his eyes cast to the floor with shame as the signs in the shop windows the trolley passed still read

'No Japs Allowed'. Henry had pushed his way through all of his personal pain to reach out and give part of his heart and hope to the man who hated him most for being alive; Ivory Burch.

Henry had been taken in by Gibby, a simple barkeep, who had once posted his own prejudiced sign. Gibby had put his own pain and anger aside offering Henry a room above the bar named Adam's Place after his son. Gibby, saw Henry for the hero he was, as well as a victim. If it had not been for Henry finding sanctuary at Adam's Place, Earl would not have found his own sanctuary there when he had been thrown out of the hospital, blind and penniless.

Life was what it was, not always easy, not necessarily fair. Stella was a magnet for broken men who seemed to follow some strange guiding light to her door. She too had been broken once. Had it not been for Henry she wouldn't have fallen in love with Earl. *What goes around . . . well,* she thought *. . . comes around, because everything will be all right.* She reached for another cigarette under Henry's watchful eyes. Everything will be all right. How, she hadn't a clue.

Henry had just complicated an already complicated situation. San Francisco had a housing shortage and was expensive. She could not afford to pay any of them a meaningful wage. She knew that her guys would all be happy just being there as long as they had their dignity, a few dollars in their pockets, a roof over their heads.

She and Earl had the apartment upstairs. There was a storage room off the kitchen, which if converted wouldn't be much better than sharing a bunk on a submarine. She knew from experience that Henry was going to have a hard time finding a room. Stub had a room in a single room occupancy hotel in a rough section of town where a person with Stub's disability became easy prey. His Tourette's had worsened since he had been shot and for his own safety he needed to get out of there.

Ivory could take care of himself. For a man who not so long ago had lost his will to live his recovery had been miraculous. While soft spoken, he was one tough nut, who did not take crap from anyone. Stella knew that with all his years of isolation as a POW he needed companionship to keep his ghosts at bay. Putting Henry and Ivory together as roommates would be a disaster waiting to happen. While she had come to love Stub, putting either Henry or Ivory with him might just drive them nuts.

"You stayed the night because you have nowhere else to go?" She asked matter-of-factly.

"I should have asked, but last night there just wasn't an opportunity."

"I know exactly what you mean. Henry, of course, you know that you are welcome. I hope your bar tending skills have improved because you are going to need them." As a bartender, he had never been great but compared to Earl or Stub he would be a winner. She chuckled within herself as she remembered Earl's first attempt to become the world's first and only blind bartender.

"I have the job?" Henry confirmed as his heart settled back in his chest. He had not expected the answer to be yes. It was a small bar that could produce only so much cash. His paycheck would come directly out of Stella and Earl's pockets.

"You can start right now by washing these dishes," she said as she eyed the dirty tables scattered about the room. "Ivory will be here around noon. "Right now I'm going to put some breakfast together, and then wake Earl. He and I have some hard talking to do." She poured a little more coffee in her cup, and then turned towards the kitchen door. "Eggs over-easy, if I recall," she said as the kitchen door swung shut behind her.

TWO

NOT AN EASY JOURNEY

EARL WAS NOT ONE TO SLEEP IN; IN FACT HE RARELY SLEPT. Learning to live in a world of perpetual darkness had not been an easy adaptation. Time, day and night are distorted.

He had been afraid of the dark since he had been a small child—terrified in fact. Deep within the dark malaise of his mind there exists a horrific dragon that has hunted him, hungry to devour his body, as well as his soul. The dragon that lurked in the dark confines beneath his bed, the dark recesses of his imagination, had hunted him since he had been a small boy. Now that he lived in perpetual darkness the dragon grew close. It would only be a matter of time unless he found a way to keep the dragon at bay. His music, his blues transfixed the beast. When he sang the beast slept.

When Earl slept, he remembered color and light. Through these dreams the dragon could see him, but he could not see it. His cloak of darkness became his shield as he struggled to push the beast, his terror away. Thus, Earl had grown accustomed to sleeping lightly, and only for short periods. Then he would wake, sing, and the music that had become his heart source, sent the dragon back to its own dark dreamscape.

Earl had been awake when Stella tip-toed from their bedroom; he often was. The woman was always busy, doing the things that he couldn't. She would start a project, and then another, as the little demands of life pulled her attention this way and that. Evening would come and the bar would fill with patrons wanting one thing or another. She met everyone's needs including his. She was an amazing woman who never complained, except to herself when she realized that earlier in the day she had started ten projects from her to-do list, and eight of them were unfinished at day's end. So Earl often pretended to sleep as she started her day with a few quiet moments for herself.

This morning Earl had heard most of Stella and Henry's conversation. He had not picked up on a thing the night before, but then again he had been too busy singing up a storm. There was one moment that gave him pause to think. That was when Henry played while he and Stella danced. He never cared much for Brook's whistling, even if he was a genius at it—but Henry's clarinet, that was music and he had missed Henry's magic in his life.

Henry is back, and oh how he had missed the man. That he now needed help from them was not something that Earl could say no to. He wouldn't even know how. That they could not afford to pay Henry anything close to his worth was a bad thing. That there was no room for Henry, Stub, and Ivory at Stella's was a heart breaker. He could not close the door on any of these men, nor could he stand to lose his home, his safety net, his comfort zone in a huge dark world that terrified him. He had not stepped outside the doors to Stella's in almost a year.

Now he was about to make the decision that they would

sell the bar and home that Stella had given him and find a new and larger sanctuary somewhere out there. Out there, were the two operative words that gave him the shivers. It wasn't the first time that he had taken a flyer and walked a tightrope, but its damned easier when you can see what is at the other end.

My poor Stella, he thought, *she will do anything to help Henry, Stubs, and Ivory. Anything but . . . but she's going to leave here screaming and holding onto the doorknob with everything she's got. This is not going to be an easy journey.*

Earl shuddered knowing that they needed to somehow make it happen.

After taking care of nature's duties in the bathroom he dressed and then found the upstairs phone where he carefully dialed a number. "Hope I didn't wake you Stub, but something's come up, can you come in for a couple of hours?" It was Stub's day off. If Henry and Ivory were going to be at the table then he owed it to Stub to put in his two cents worth. That done, he dialed again. "Operator, please give me a Mr. Thaddeus Mohler, the Alexander Hotel, here in the city. No, operator, I don't want the number, I'm blind and would appreciate you dialing the number for me. Thank you, I'll hold."

"I'm sorry Sir, there is no answer."

"Well it is early in the morning. Would you please keep trying and ring me back when he answers. Please tell him that it is Earl Crier calling and that it is important."

Earl came down the stairs with a painted on smile. "Hmmm, I'll have me some of that coffee, Henry, and make it black."

Henry looked over with a grateful smile. Earl had not said welcome back, he didn't need to, it was understood. Earl Crier was a man who touched him deeply. He was of medium build, average height, with salt and pepper hair, more salt than pepper. This morning he wore a dark brown smoking jacket. The red and purple, spider web scars that crept out from behind his dark glasses added character. At thirty-seven he had the beginnings of a drinker's double chin. His mellifluous voice and an uncanny ability to suggest rampant emotion beneath a face of absolute calm made him a fascinating performer to watch. Earl reminded Henry somewhat of the British actor James Mason. He was a piece of work, complex and as difficult as the day is long.

While waiting for his coffee Earl sat at the piano and began to play before Stella could stick her head out the door and say good morning—not that the morning was good, Henry's return was, the rest still had to prove itself.

'They call it Stormy Monday

But Tuesday's just as bad. . .'

Stella broke the egg over the counter rather than the fry pan. Darn it, pay attention girl. She reached for a towel afraid that the egg might slip off to the floor, caught her apron on the fry pan's handle, nearly pulling the pan full of sputtering grease to the floor.

Tell it like it is my darling, tell it as it is. Having sung into the wee hours of the morning Earl was in amazing form as he sang and played 'Stormy Monday'.

Henry delivered Earl's coffee with an earnest look on his face which Earl would have laughed at had he been able to see it. It was Earl's tone of voice and driving tempo that said it all.

The phone rang.

Stella answered, with one eye on the fry pan, the other on the egg as it made its way to the counter's edge. That the counter had never been exactly level gave the egg better odds on its escape. "Earl, it's for you, a Mr. Mohler?"

"Ahhhhh", Earl said as he ran his fingers across the keyboard and switched to a catchy Broadway tune. His fingers left the keys but he never stopped singing as he entered the kitchen and took the phone from Stella.

"Thaddeus Q here, the Q is for quality. What can I do for you Earl?"

"Thaddeus, I appreciate you returning the call."

"It is a bit early," Thaddeus yawned, "but how many people are lucky enough to get a call from the best blind bartender and crooner in all of San Francisco at this hour of the morning." There was an edge to his voice that suggested that his pleasant tone was a cover for something not as friendly. "What can I do for you?" He enjoyed bantering with Earl around his piano, a martini in hand. At the moment he was not fully awake and wished that Earl would just get to the point.

A few days back Earl had overheard a conversation between Mohler and a customer Earl did not know. Mohler had confessed with a drinker's confidence that he was thinking about selling his hotel. Mohler owned the Hotel Alexander, a forty-four room dust collector in the Tenderloin that had seen better days.

The Hotel Alexander had been passed down through his mother's side of the family, burned twice, lost once by his grandfather Samuel Anderson in a hand of faro in a perpetual game that ran in the cigar smoke filled basement of the hotel. Grandma Fedora won the hotel back with a sharp tongue and a cut of the cards. She had drawn a five of hearts, the former short term owner of the hotel a three of clubs. The hotel held a lot of family history. Thaddeus had been born there and now at sixty-seven he was reluctant to sell. Unfortunately he was fast approaching the point where he might not have any other choice.

The hotel was located a few blocks off Union Square, not far from the St. Francis Hotel. The old hotel had kept itself afloat during the early years of the depression as a speakeasy and dance club secreted in the hotel's infamous basement. That had been Thaddeus's moment to shine. Because of the club, the Alexander's rooms were usually booked. Thaddeus, dressed to the gills in a fine tux playing the perpetual host to the swells and a few of the barons of the city, who always had dough in their pockets and a girl in hand—frequently not the wife.

When Prohibition ended the speakeasy lasted another year or two, then the hotel fell on hard times. Thaddeus had been a great night club host, but he had never been a very good hotelier or businessman. The merchant mariners who started taking over the hotel's guest book, were hard on both the hotel and its reputation. These were tough men, and Mohler was not, they gave both the hotel and Thaddeus little respect, and few enough dollars.

God bless the war.

Through an old speakeasy chum, Thaddeus managed to land a contract turning the hotel into a Bachelor Navy

Officer's Quarters for the duration of the war.

Gentlemen and officers all, the hotel regained a little of its former class. Now, two years after the war had ended he had trouble attracting enough bookings to keep it afloat. That the Tenderloin had turned into a tough part of town didn't help.

"How much do you want for the place?' Earl asked.

Stella dropped the entire cartoon of eggs.

Clueless, Henry could only look perplexed.

At first take Mohler did not take Earl seriously. *How did you know? Never mind, I should have known, blind men have damn good hearing.* "How much are you willing to pay?" He asked.

"Not one red cent," Earl answered. "Do we have a deal?"

"Is this a joke?" Thaddeus had to stop and think for a moment. If this was meant as a joke, it was just this side of being insulting. However, Earl Crier was a man of character and not one to throw around insults casually. So, if this wasn't a joke, then Earl had just offered to pay him nothing for his hotel. "Earl, let me get this straight. You called me at an unreasonably early hour on New Year's Day. I say un-reasonable because I was there with you at Stella's Lounge until closing, so we both know how little sleep either of us has gotten. You called to say that you want to buy my hotel for nothing. You want to try it again, only this time with a few meaningful coins offered?" This time he sounded irritated, which he was.

"Thaddeus, you heard me right. Once you hear my full offer you might want to sweeten the deal by putting a little bit of cash on the table yourself."

The innkeeper laughed. He had not heard anything so ridiculous in a month of Sundays. "Earl, call me back after you've had some coffee and are fully sobered up."

"Stella's just put on the coffee and is about to throw together some bacon and eggs. Why don't you come on over. I'll buy you breakfast, and explain everything. I promise you won't be disappointed."

Thaddeus liked Earl and Stella, and Earl had indeed piqued his curiosity. "Alright, give me about thirty minutes. And Earl, this had better be good." Thaddeus laughed as he hung up the phone. "I have a feeling that is an understatement." He said to himself as he pulled on his trousers. *Who knows what Earl has up his sleeve, but I've got a feeling I'm about to find out.*

"Sweetheart, I'd better take my breakfast now. I won't have time to chew much between my words once he gets here."

"Who," Stella asked "and what is going on?"

Earl counted his steps as he headed back towards the stairs. "I'd best make sure I'm properly powdered and dusted before he gets here." Once he got his direction he began to sing. He could smell Henry as he passed. "Welcome back Henry, as long as you are here, I'm thinking about expanding our act. You still have your clarinet?"

'There's no people like show people,

They smile when they are low.

Earl was up the stairs before Stella could find the words to ask him . . . she asked Henry instead, "What was that . . ."

". . . all about?" Henry finished for her. "Buy a hotel?" They both looked at each other mystified.

24

Breakfast became brunch as the hands on the wall clock spun round and around. The negotiations between Earl and Thaddeus Mohler was straight forward and conjured by Earl from the ideas and exchanges between the two men. Each 'yes' and nod of the head was accentuated by a flourish of notes Earl peeled off the piano until finally at 11:30 in the morning the deal was sealed with a handshake.

It wasn't actually a purchase because nothing was put down, with no promise to pay a specified amount at any time in the future. There was in fact no contract, just a gentlemen's agreement. Earl made the deal for the hotel sight unseen. Earl's proposal gave Thaddeus Mohler everything he wanted for the hotel, and much more. He even lent them twelve hundred dollars, interest free, with no due date for repayment, to help expedite their taking over the hotel as soon as possible.

Stella sat there, stunned, awed at what Earl had been able pull out of the proverbial magician's hat.

Thaddeus promised to return the next day to give everyone a personally guided tour of the hotel.

Everyone?

The deal included free room and board for Henry, Stub, and Ivory. Ivory had missed the meeting but there was no doubt in everyone's minds that he would be on board. Stella's heart could not have been brighter, yet her angst fell just short of Earl's fear of stepping outside the front door of Stella's Starlight Lounge. How Stella was going to get Earl over his fear of the outside world she didn't know. Tomorrow he was going to have to do it even if she had to have Henry and Ivory carry him out the front door kicking and screaming.

"Are you sure about this," Stella asked. She was already suffering with regrets. She had bought the bar for Earl when he was lost to her, and she did not know if she would ever see him again. It had sat empty for months, the doors locked, with a lone sign in the window that had read: Closed Until Further Notice. The silence had been brooding, the monotonous tick of the clock, and the lonely clip clop of her shoes as she paced the floor, chain-smoking, waiting for word that he had been found.

Her eyes filled as she remembered the day he had come back to her. She had been upstairs taking a bubble bath when she heard the piano. At first she had thought it to be a wishful day dream, but when he began to sing, she knew that it was him. She had run down the stairs wearing only a cloak of bubbles. Now she was about to post a 'Closed' notice in the window again, just below the flickering sign that read Stella's Starlight Lounge- her home, her heart. "Are you certain about this?" She asked.

She sure as hell wasn't.

Certain? Earl thought. Stella's Starlight Lounge had been as comfortable as an old shoe. He knew every inch of the place, forwards and back, which to a blind man is pretty damned important. This new place he had gotten them into was huge. It had forty-four guest rooms; six were suites, spread out over five floors. The basement held shuttered speakeasy large enough to have hosted the Hollywood Canteen. It had two sets of stairs, a public elevator and a service elevator. *With any luck*, Earl laughed, *he'd get lost trying to find the john and do a header down an elevator shaft*. What the hell had he gotten them into—and was there a way out? It wasn't the hotel that scared him; it was walking out that damned door into the dark unknown. His world was always dark which was why he limited it to a space as he could. When he stepped out the door onto the public street the horizon held limitless terrors he could not or did not want to face.

"Earl," Stub said as he came through the kitchen door, "you shu. . . shu . . . sure don't loo . . . . look none too happy for a guy who juh . . . just bought himself a hotel for nothing. I just put this bottle of cha . . . champagne on ice. I thought we might cel . . .cel . . .celebrate as soon as Henry gets back."

"Where did Henry go?" Earl asked as he tapped a few notes on the piano.

Stella answered, "He didn't say where, just that he would be back as soon as he checked the laundry."

"The laundry?"

"That's what he said." Stella looked around the room wondering what to pack first. Most of the dirty dishes left over from New Year's Eve still lay scattered around the room. "Henry was supposed to tend to these dishes. Well, I guess they'll have to wait. Right now I've got to go out back and see how many boxes we have that haven't been broken down yet. Laundry? Why would Henry be doing laundary?

Stub could see that both Stella and Earl were in a quandary. Stella couldn't decide where to start on anything. Earl tinkered with the piano keys starting one tune then another making no sense of anything.

"Stella, you hear anything from Ivory yet?"

"Something about housekeeping, doing the laundry," Stella

answered as she started to do a bottle inventory.

"I'm asking about Ivory, not Henry."

"Why would Ivory be doing Henry's laundry?" Stella asked as she forgot about the bottle count and began to sweep behind the bar. "Do you think we should keep peanut shells on the floor at the new place? It'll take an awful lot of peanuts."

Stub, his arms loaded down with dirty dishes stopped to watch the crazy antics of his two employers. He shook his head wondering what other kind of craziness was headed their way.

The phone rang.

Stella answered.

Stub dropped the dishes in the sink, only there wasn't any water. *Damn it, there goes a week's pay.*

"Earl," Stella said, "It's Henry. He wants us all to take a cab down to the hotel to meet our new head of housekeeping." She hadn't thought about the house keeping. It was, after all, a large hotel, and they would need the help. Forty- four rooms is a lot to take care of. *How much is that going to cost us?* Earl is a great idea man, but he always left it up to her to work out the details. He could not see the numbers nor the value of one paperbill from another.

Earl stopped playing. "He, what? Go to the hotel you say? When?" He thought he had more time to get used to the idea. There had been a reason he had not left the bar since he and Stella had been married. His personal dragon waited for him out there, both terrifying and relentless.

28

"Now," Stella said. Her voice betrayed that she too was shaken. This was all happening too fast. She wanted to retreat into their bedroom and hide from the world. *I can't do this, it's too much to ask.* This was more a whine of self-pity than a scream of anger—a child without a parent to guide her. She started to move towards the stairway door.

"Stah . . . Stella." Stub reached out putting his hand on her shoulder.

She turned, shaking his hand off, her eyes wide. *God bless you Stub, I love you as if you were my little brother, but you are not my little brother. Go away.* This short little man with the stutter and the twitches was not the loving hand she needed right now. She needed Earl to reach out to her and tell her that everything was going to be all right—only he wasn't going to do that because he needed more reassurance than she did.

"Stah . . . Stella, you can't go there." Stub's eyes pointed towards the stairwell. Swa . . . swallow your hu. . .hu . . . hurt. You can . . . can't hide 'neath a blanket. Earl, can . . . can only run to where his dra . . .dra . . .gon is waiting." She continued to stare at him as he slowly turned her eyes towards where Earl sat at the piano.

Knowing that he had to leave his sanctuary had put Earl on the edge of a deep dark pit. When he was told that they were to leave now he had made the jump back to the disturbing memory of the abandoned well he had fallen into as a child.

𝒟

A bramble of tall weeds grew around the abandoned well.

Earl should not have been anywhere near there, but he was and did not see the well before stepping into it. Whatever he had fallen into was deep, the walls slippery, there was no way to climb out. He had been crossing through a field near an abandoned ranch where there was no one to hear his screams for help.

The sun set and fell. It became impossibly dark. The only way out was a dry stream bed that had once fed the well. He had discovered it just as the light had begun to fade. At first the entrance had only been a small hole no bigger than his fist. He dug until the entrance was big enough to crawl through. His only way out was darker than anything he had ever imagined—far darker than the bottom of the well from where he now cringed.

In the deepening dark he sensed that he was not alone, that something evil and hungry lurked in the deepest part of the dark. Waiting. He curled into a ball and hugged the damp side of the well as far away from the dry stream bed as he could. The dark seemed to snake out of the tunnel filling the well with its evil vapors until his only light came from a few distant stars that teased him before they too deserted him leaving him in a dark so dense its weight was crushing, making it hard for him to breath. He cried for the umpteenth time, and then tried to wipe his eyes with hands he could no longer see.

"Mom?" He had screamed until his voice failed him, as had his Dad. There had been no answers. Only when he didn't show up for dinner after softball practice would they grow concerned. He had taken a short cut through the woods and had never made it to softball; where no one missed him because he was frequently absent and not much of an asset to the team.

"Mom?"

This time his cry was barely a whisper as he listened for the silent slithers of the child devouring beast that lurked behind closed doors, beneath his bed at two in the morning, and in the bottom of abandoned wells.

There was the soft crunch of dried leaves, something was there, searching, looking down into the black depth of the well for its next meal. A small slide of dirt and a few loose pebble rained down on him. Wide-eyed, blinking in the swirling dark, he searched for the top of the well and found nothing.

More pebbles fell.

The beast, had found him. It was slithering down the slimy well walls, its razor sharp teeth and lizard like tongue anticipating the sweet taste of his flesh as it tore into him.

Terrified, he had nowhere else to go but into the pitch black tunnel that had once been a stream bed. Where it led he did not know. What he did know was that a horrific dragon was just behind him as he crawled into the narrow, twisting, darkness that led him from one nightmare into another.

The white and brown rabbit wiggled its nose. The dark hole smelled moist, if there was water, it was beyond its reach. It sniffed the air for danger, finding none and hopped on.

Time stopped as Earl crawled and crawled, determined that the dragon would never get him. The unbearable darkness possessed him as he began to sing just to hear his own voice and know that he was still alive.

"Twinkle, Twinkle, little star,

How I wonder what you are.

Up above the world so . . ."

🐉

Earl sat at the piano his hand perched above the keys, not touching, as he once again fell back into that well. He curled up against that familiar cold earthen wall staring into that pitch dark passage where the dragon waited. As long as he remained quiet, hidden within the comforting bed of dirt in his personal well of despair the dragon could not get him. He shivered. He had been in this place too many times and knew it well.

Stella pushed back her tears, "Hon, it's time to go. I told Henry we're on our way. Earl?"

Earl did not hear her.

She knew where he had gone and why.

She asked Stub to get her coat, and one for Earl. She lit a cigarette, took a long deep draw and then tapped the cigarette out. She hadn't the time. She had to get Earl out of his well, away from the dragon, and back to reality. She lovingly placed her hands and softly massaged his temples as she whispered in his ear. "Earl, I know where you are. The dragon can not get you as long as you reach for my hand. I'll lift you and guide you to safety. You don't have to crawl in the dark any longer." This was a promise she could not keep for he would always be in the dark, the dragon always lurking nearby.

At first he thought the voice was coming from somewhere ahead in the mindless black that lay ahead in the stream bed. No, it was coming from the top of the well, where suddenly appeared a few shiny stars twinkling above. "Mom?" No, it wasn't his mother. She couldn't reach him from where she was, just as she hadn't when he had first fallen into that well so many years ago. He recognized Stella's voice and smiled:

'Twinkle, Twinkle little star

How I wonder what you are . . .

My Stella by . . .'

He slowly reached and took her hands in his wrapping them warmly around hers as she lifted him from that place where his dragon lurked. "It's time to go. I told Henry that we are on our way. Just keep holding on," she rubbed her thumb on his palm, "and everything will be just fine."

Earl shuddered a profound sigh.

Stub hailed a cab.

THREE

PIE-EYED AND PISSED - OFF

IVORY SLUMPED OFF THE STREET CAR THAT STOPPED TWO blocks from Stella's Starlight Lounge Piano Bar. He had a world class hangover; his self-esteem had taken an even bigger shellacking. Last night, after closing, he had helped himself to a bottle of rye whiskey and taken it home to his small, single room in a boarding house full of losers like himself. There he had gotten pie-eyed, pissed-off, drunk. He tried not to drink, but sometimes he couldn't help but reach for the bottle. When he did he drank until there was no more, and then he would become angry. Life had been tough; he had been dealt every losing card in the deck, and often felt guilty about even being here. That was when the ghost of Sergeant Ware would pay him a visit.

A few days after his eighteenth birthday, Ivory joined the United States Marine Corp. A year later he arrived in China where he served in Sergeant Ware's platoon with the 4th Marine Regiment in Shanghai, part of the China Marines. The few, the brave - the men left behind. The China Marines felt that they had the finest officers, best athletes, heartiest drinkers, and sharpest regiment in the Corps. Before the

Second World War, the Fourth was the outfit that all Marines wanted to serve in.

Ivory Burch was damned lucky to have been selected for a billet with the China Marines. Back home, there was an economic depression. A PFC serving on the China station could afford luxuries that even a stateside bank vice-president couldn't. PFC Ivory Burch lived at the Privates' Club. His name and rank were emblazoned in brass letters across the door to his room where he had his own chink servant who pressed his uniform, cleaned his rifle, and just about anything else ordered. That had been quite the life.

As 1940 made way for 1941, the Japanese were just outside Shanghai's International Settlement's front gate. Life outside that gate was both dangerous and deadly. Anticipating war, the 4th Marines were ordered out of China in November, 1941. The Regiment was ordered to the Philippines, where on December 8th their war began ending. On May 8, 1942 the final death knell sounded with their surrender on Corregidor. Those that survived endured the Bataan Death March and long years of imprisonment by the Japanese.

Two hundred and five marines including Private Ivory Burch and Sergeant Ware were left behind in China to see that their remaining supplies and armaments did not fall into the hands of the Japanese. They had orders to be shipped out on December 10th. On December 8th, the remaining marines were ordered to surrender without firing a shot—something Ivory would never forget. In late January the entire group of 205 Marines was sent by train to the Prisoner of War camp at Woosung, outside Shanghai. There they joined the approximately 1100 Marines and civilians captured earlier on Wake Island.

In August of 1943 a group of about 500 POWs was sent from Kiangwan to camps in Japan near Tokyo and Osaka. Sergeant Ware and Ivory left Japan with 150 other men on November 11, 1943. There are no surviving records to show what happened to them.

There is only one man who knows.

Ivory Burch is the only surviving witness to their slave labor at a secret death camp high in the Philippine mountains. He lost a leg, came down with just about every tropical disease that can be lethal to man. Somehow he survived, that in itself is a miracle.

At a dysfunctional Veteran's Hospital in San Francisco, Stella, Earl, and Henry had helped him find his will to live again. It was was Earl's music more than anything else that had touched and found his soul.

Ivory Burch, at 27, still young, is an old China Marine, a survivor who by all accounts shouldn't be here. He is left with an artificial leg, nightmares that will never go away, frail heath always on the edge of getting worse, and an anger that boiled just beneath the surface. He came away from his military experience with a sense of shame, with a feeling he had not done enough. The Japanese had constantly told him that he did not deserve to live because he had surrendered. That he had surrendered without firing a shot is one of his most grievous wounds.

✿

It would not be overstating the obvious to say that alcohol is not Ivory's best friend—there is no friend to be found in that glass or bottle. Off duty Sergeant Ware had been a mean drunk which was usually followed with violence. Ivory had seen the Sarge bust up more than one slope chute or hooch house in China. The Sarge only stopped after the shore patrol left him with a throbbing hard-boiled egg on the back of his head and a night in the stockade. He should have been busted in rank a dozen times but he was a damned good sergeant with few enough to go around—he was needed at the China station.

It was a new year and Ivory had trouble letting go of the past, which made it harder to live in the present. Spurred on by the unrelenting ghost of the Sarge, and the unforgiving spirits of the marines he had left behind as slaves the Japanese had worked to death, Ivory had torn his room apart as well as the communal bath down the hall resulting in his immediate eviction.

He had hidden behind a dumpster in a nearby alley until the police had come and gone. He kept his distance as the building manager and a menagerie of ill-tempered tenants uselessly bellowed and bitched in the front lobby as a waterfall, caused by a broken pipe in the john, had cascaded down three flights of stairs. When he sobered up enough not to be a stumbling drunk, he snuck through a back door and up to his room to rescue what personals he had, the most important, his spare wooden leg.

With wet shoes, a splitting headache, and what little he owned stuffed into a threadbare duffel bag, he approached the front door to Stella's Starlight Lounge, rightfully afraid that he would be fired as he ought to be for stealing the rye whiskey.

The front door was locked. He tried it a second time before he noticed the sign in the window: 'Closed Until Further

Notice.' The ghost of Sargent Ware tapped him on the shoulder. Before the Sarge could razz him about how screwed up he was Ivory snapped at the Sarge's specter with a rage that drill sergeants reserve for each other.

The first day of the New Year had started out almost as bad as the day he had been ordered to surrender to the Japanese. Now, as he stared at the sign he thought about someone besides himself. Had something happened to Earl or Stella? He put the palm of his hand over his brow as he tried to see into the bar. "Stella? Earl? It's Ivory, open up." No answer. That was when he saw the piece of paper on the floor just inside the door. He recognized Stub's handwriting. Stub must have put it in the door window and it had fallen off. It was hard to read, but after a few minutes he figured out the address that Stub had left him. I hope it's not a god-damned hospital, he thought as he threw his duffel bag over his shoulder and went to find them.

FOUR

AWKWARD SOLUTIONS

HENRY WAITED AWKWARDLY OUTSIDE THE HOTEL ALEXANDER with his war buddy Yukio Hayashi. Awkward because the hotel was on the edge of the Tenderloin in downtown San Francisco where one did not hang out if you were Japanese, Korean, Black, Hispanic, anyone who wasn't vanilla. It wasn't posted, there was no law, that was just the way it was.

Stella's Starlight Lounge had been located in an area much the same. San Francisco had long been a racist city and still was. You had to be white in order to be welcome. Then there were your Italian neighborhoods, German, Jewish, and so on, each keeping to their own kind; distrustful of the other. Out on the avenues, where the fog crawled more often than not, folks would just look the other way, throwing perhaps a glance that suggested that you should leave before there was any trouble. No one wants any trouble here, really. And the eyes of the offending party would say: 'I'm sorry if we did anything to offend you, we were just passing through. I guess we had best be on our way' Only down here, a few blocks off Union Square one didn't just pass through, not if you knew what was good for you. It wasn't posted, there was no law, if seen, a friendly beat cop might find a law or two that you had just broken as further motivation to keep on moving—that is just the way it was. Henry and Yukio knew they were not just passing through. At least Henry did—sometimes you had to take a risk, and sometimes you had to do what one had to do, after all Earl and Stella were taking this risk for him—were they not?

The heavy glass double wide doors to the Hotel Alexander were locked. A sign read 'Closed for the Holidays.' Henry peered through a window and from what he could see it appeared to have been closed for quite a few holidays.

It was January and a bitter cold fog weaved its way through the streets of San Francisco. It was one of those days when the fog horn moaned until the sun set and rose again. Yukio rubbed his hands together to warm them, and then lit a cigarette. "One might think that folks around here haven't ever seen two Buddaheads before." He quipped.

Henry smiled quietly. "You always had trouble figuring out the difference between a Buddahead from a Katonk." Buddahead was a derogatory term that had been used by mainland Nisei soldiers for Nisei soldiers coming from Hawaii. It was play on the Japanese word "buta" which means pig heads. Yukio had been born in Hawaii, but had moved to Long Beach, California when he was twelve. Henry was 'Sanseis', third generation American. There had been a lot of animosity between the Hawaiian Nisei and the mainland Nisei at the start of the war. The Buddaheads island culture was too laid back, too soft and chummy. They didn't get the stricter line the mainland Nisei—Katonks—had to walk. White men's prejudice, blood, sweat, and sacrifice had changed all that and brought the Nisei together. War has a way of doing that, giving men a bond they could not have found in civilian life: that and a lot of sacrifice and the loss of too many good

Nisei—Americans all.

The two Nisei men could not help but feel the stares as cars passed by, the passenger's eyes turned towards them with disbelief tinged with a touch of anger. What were two Japs doing in this neighborhood? The hotels on and near Union Square were for white folks; blacks and Orientals were not welcome—especially the Japanese. The war had brought a great deal of pain and sacrifice and forgiveness was far from being found. The two men felt as awkward as feral cats caught on the race track as the gates opened for a gray hound race at Golden Gate Fields. Both men had to question why they were there—it was the same as looking for trouble.

Henry knew why.

The cold fog rolling over the hills felt more like a gentle tropical breeze compared to the bitter cold breath of prejudice he had felt when he had first returned home from the war. He had a job waiting for him at the veteran's hospital, but was denied transportation to get there and a simple room to call his own. Most of the patients had been injured in the war against Japan. Welcome home Henry.

The day he had stumbled on Adam's Place, a broken down old neighborhood bar had been one of the best days of his life. Gibby, the bar's owner, had given him a room and taken him in as if Henry had been his own son. It did not matter to the old man that Henry was Nisei. Adam, Gibby's son, had been saved by a Nisei medic when the 36th Army Infantry Division—The Lost Battalion—was given the assignment to clear a ridge deep in the Vosges, but had been cut-off by the Germans. This occurred because the flanking units received an order to withdraw that failed to reach them. Adam's unit, the

1st Battalion of the 141st, had been cut off since 24 October 1944. The all Nisei, 100th /442nd, was ordered to rescue the Lost Battalion. More men were lost in the 100th/442nd in the rescue operation than there were to save. Henry had no idea if he had met Adam. He had dealt with too many wounded and far too many dead. After recovering from his wounds Adam died in a jeep accident a few days before Germany surrendered.

After losing his job at the Veteran's hospital Henry stayed on at Adam's Place as bartender in training. Earl got booted out of the hospital and followed Henry where he turned Adam's Place into a lively neighborhood piano bar. It was Henry's clarinet alongside Earl's music that allowed Henry to gain some acceptance.

Earl's roommate, Brooks Weingarden, a blind, suicidal alcoholic, and his despised nemesis, had been left behind at the hospital with little care and only Elroy, a crooked orderly, and his rotgut moonshine for company. After ending Elroy's criminal hold over the hospital Stella brought Brooks to Adam's place hoping that Gibby would take him in. What Stella had asked was impossible because at the time no one knew that Gibby's heart was failing. Thanks to Earl the impossible became possible and that had been the beginning of Henry's heart felt oddball family. Those were the happiest days of his life, then he had made the mistake of leaving, which he never should have done.

After leaving Adam's Place for medical school the news of Gibby's death had touched Henry deeply, causing him to reevaluate which was more important, becoming a doctor, or his music. Now he had come full circle and his return was one of the reasons that Stella and Earl had made the bewildering decision to buy this old hotel.

Yukio had not a clue as to why he was standing in forbidden territory waiting for a white blind man and a nightingale. He wasn't sure about the nightingale part, but Henry couldn't say enough swell things about Stella. Henry had told him that there might be a meaningful job, which he needed to provide for his wife and young son. Yukio didn't know much more than that there might be a job for him, and best of all he could be working alongside Henry. Jobs were scarce, for a Nisei darn near dismal. He and Henry had been through a lot together. He had been with Henry when they had liberated a sub-camp of the Dachau concentration camp.

☙

He and Henry had crouched low behind the first of a long chain of wooden railway cars that led towards the large wooden gate at the front of Dachau concentration camp. At the first sight of the American troops, the guards dropped their weapons and raised their hands, but were gunned down without mercy. The dogs charged the advancing Americans only to be chewed up by machine gun fire. His platoon stepped out from behind the railway car and approached the camp with caution.

The first and the worst thing Yukio had noticed as they approached was the stench of rotting cadavers. There was a cry for a medic but the only casualties he had seen so far were the Nazi guards. He rushed forward to where a soldier pointed. The door to a weathered railway car was wide open, the car filled with hundreds of dead bodies the retreating S.S. garrison had simply left to rot.

A medic wasn't needed.

Inside the camp there were storage rooms filled with stacks of recently gassed prisoners; men, women, and children. A row of small cement structures near the prison entrance contained coal-fired crematoriums, a gas chambers, and rooms piled high with naked and emaciated human corpses. And there were piles upon piles of ashes, human ashes.

Henry was the only medic on scene, at least for the moment. There was nothing he could do. Yukio's eyes were locked on Henry as he looked out over the prison yard where dozens of dead inmates lay where they had fallen in the last few hours or days before their liberation. Since all the bodies were in various stages of decomposition, the stench of death was overwhelming—even in the bitter cold.

Yukio watched as Henry knelt, puked, and cried as he had never cried before.

Amongst the dead a hand had moved. The hand, skin clinging to bone, belonged to a man who should not have been alive, but somehow managed to hang on to that last grasp of life. Henry rushed over to him, knelt, took his hand, found a pulse, and as he did so he cried dry tears.

Yukio followed. As he knelt beside Henry he heard a frail voice as the pathetic man looked up, his eyes taking in Henry's face with profound curiosity. "Your eyes," he said in English with a pronounced Italian accent, "your face . . . are these the eyes of an angel?" He lay still as Henry once again struggled to find a pulse. Henry picked the man up, leaving some of his worn concentration camp gray-striped uniform stuck to the frozen ground. The man spoke to Henry in a whisper Yukio could not hear as the frail dying man was carried towards a deserted guard's barracks in search of a bed and some warmth.

Months later over cold beers and a few days rest Henry had told him what the frail little Italian had said before he died. "I don't think that you are an angel," he had whispered. "I think you are mortal like me. I've been waiting for you, what took you so long?" Henry had slipped in the snow never making it to the guard barracks. As he fell to one knee, the frail little man had looked into Henry's eyes. "Perhaps one day I'll tell you about the angel's eyes. I'm going to finally see them now; perhaps they will look like yours."

That was not the last man to die in Henry's arms, nor the last of death he would see in the war. It would not be the last Yukio would see having five of his Nisei brothers die before the war ended, two in his arms as he shared their last moments, wondering why they had to die.

Yukio and Henry shared a bond that could only be understood by other Nisei soldiers who had fought and had come as close to death as they had.

Thaddeus unlocked the doors from the inside. "You might be more comfortable in here, Henry," he said as he held one of the doors open. Henry had called saying that Earl and Stella were on their way over, that they didn't want to wait until tomorrow to see the hotel. It had been a small lie on Henry's part to both parties. He hadn't told Thaddeus that he was bringing Yukio, nor had he said anything to Stella or Earl. He wanted to get everyone to the hotel where he could present his idea.

At first glance Yukio did not like the Hakujin—the white man—who met them at the hotel. He had been told that Thaddeus Mohler owned the hotel. The Hakujin reminded Yukio of a bullying white G.I. he had met in Italy during the war. The G.I. had thrown a torrent of insults at him. The Nisei had orders not to get into fights with the white soldiers regardless of cause. The corporal, from a Georgia regiment, had reminded him of an English bulldog, short—not much taller than he—compact, incredibly muscular, with short legs that appeared to be bowed. He had a broad chest with heavy wide-set shoulders topped with a large bowling ball head. He wore a distinctly sour expression that was created by a seriously undershot jaw, large drooping jowls and weather wrinkled flat face, with dark eyes set low and wide apart.

Thaddeus had thirty or more years on that G.I., what muscle he once had now gone to fat. While taller than the memory, his thinning light brown hair only added to his own bulldog look.

Yukio and Thaddeus Mohler stared at each other with mutual distaste.

Henry saw that, slowly shaking his head. It was going to be a long day. He shook hands without making eye contact with the hotelier.

The first time Thaddeus had heard Henry play his clarinet at Stella's he had trouble seeing beyond the color of Henry's skin. Then, one night, Earl swept the ivories with an emotion that touched Thaddeus to the core. Stella had stepped behind Earl and began to sing:

'You'd be so nice to come home to

You'd be so nice by the fire . . .

46

It was gorgeous, but what stayed with Thaddeus was the depth of Henry's clarinet as the notes swept away the cigarette smoke, the clear notes harmonious with Stella. Towards the end Earl slid his fingers off the key board as Stella's voice faded leaving only the magic that Henry blew straight from his soul.

It had taken time for Henry to win his respect. Like most folks in San Francisco Thaddeus Mohler did not cotton to Asians, especially the Japanese. He did not think of himself as being a racist, one way or the other—it was just the way things were. Sure there were those who wanted to make a spectacle out of their prejudice, as if it were something to be proud of. He had once known a Jew-baiter, Reinhard Brandt, a Ukrainian butcher, who used to come into the speakeasy on the first Friday of the month. He blamed the Jews for everything wrong in the world. Then again, he didn't just hate the Jews, he hated everyone. Later, Thaddeus had heard that Brandt had returned to Europe where he could vent his rage against the Jews and be a hero to the Aryan race. Good riddance to bad rubbish, Thaddeus had thought. Prejudice is a hungry beast, the more you feed it, the more it demands. When he had been a kid growing up on this same street where he still lived it had been the chinks who had gotten the bad rap. Now it was the Japs. Time changes, not always for the best.

From Henry Thaddeus had learned, or at least he was beginning to look just a little deeper when it came to the color of another man's skin and heritage. What he didn't know was how much that was going to be tested as Earl and Stella changed his old hotel and challenged the status quo of just living. Time changes, people not so easily.

Still, Thaddeus couldn't help but glance up and down the

street concerned that he might be seen with two Japs. Having Henry in the hotel was going to be a challenge; that Henry was bringing with him more Japs was beginning to give Thaddeus serious second thoughts.

He pulled his coat collar tight against the wind. "Henry, care to come into the lobby? It is a bit warmer in there. The cab will deliver Stella and Earl straight to the front door."

At 5' 6", carrying an older man's earned bulk, Thaddeus still caste a fair shadow over the two men, who averaged 5'3" and were thinly built despite the years of combat. Henry bowed slightly. "Thank you. I'll wait here for Stella and Earl. Earl doesn't deal with change easily."

Lacking a winter coat, Yukio opted to wait in the lobby.

Thaddeus' eyes followed Yukio. The invitation was meant for Henry. He wanted to protest but something more important gnawed at him. It was what Henry had said: that the move would not be easy for Earl and Stella. He had been so pleased with the deal that it had not occurred to him that the move itself could be a deal breaker. *They're not having second thoughts are they*? He had hoped that the cash he had advanced to help with the move would have clinched the deal once and for all. The more he thought about this cockamamie scheme Earl had put together, the more he liked it. To have it fall apart at this point would be more than disappointing. "Anything I can do to help?"

Henry remained quiet thinking that perhaps he had said too much already. The awkward silence was broken by the sight of a yellow cab as it pulled up in front of the hotel.

This was the first time Stella had seen the hotel. She

squeezed Earl's hand as the cab rolled to a stop just in front. *Oh my*, she thought, *it's so big. How am I going to keep up with something like this?* A large vertical sign reading 'The Hotel Alexander,' attached to the front of the building, rose from the second to the fourth floors, there were five floors that she could see. A black wrought iron fire escape dropped down from the roof to the second floor. The building was brick, painted an unseemly egg yolk yellow that was fading and in need of a new paint job. It occupied two thirds of the block, including rooms that rose above a corner restaurant named Bab's Cafe. She could use a cup of coffee, but it was New Year's Day, and closed. The front of the hotel had large windows covered with heavy red drapes. *Those will have to go*, she thought as Henry slid open the cab's door.

It was the moment of truth for Earl as Henry opened the door. Earl stiffened at the thought of having to get out of the cab into the big wide unknown that terrified him so. He could smell the dragon as the door opened and Stella's grip on his elbow tightened. Stella gave him a firm but loving nudge out the door as Henry took his hand, guiding him out of the cab. Stella was out and had closed the cab door before his panic could get the better of him.

The look on Earl's face gave Thaddeus real concern. If he had ever seen a man who wanted to back out of a deal he would have looked like Earl Crier right now.

"Henry," Stella said, "get Earl inside while I pay the cab. Stub scurried around from the street side of the cab taking Earl by his right elbow, Henry taking the left, practically lifted him off his feet as he was hurried into the hotel.

"Here let me take care of the fare," Thaddeus said.

Stella did not waste time arguing. She was right behind Earl whispering to him that everything was fine and how swell the place looked. She hadn't expected anyone else and gave Henry a wide-eyed 'what the . . .' look when she saw Yukio. Once inside she slowly turned full circle taking in the hotel's lobby. The lobby had seen better days. Earl had told her that Thaddeus was having trouble keeping the rooms booked. What she saw suggested that the hotel hadn't had a guest for some months. The lobby was dim, smelled musty, with cobwebs beginning to take hold on lampshades and picture frames. The carpet was worn, with the pattern faded beyond recognition where the traffic patterns had been the heaviest. A dead potted palm stood forlornly next to the reservation desk. She wondered what else they might find dead as they explored the inner sanctum of their new home. "Home, oh dear." She said letting out an exasperated sigh.

"Ar . . .are. . .we in the ri. . right pla . . . place?" Stub asked as he still held onto Earl's elbow.

Henry let out a long low whistle.

Earl heard the comments and smelled the room. It took him a moment to collect his thoughts. Getting here had not been easy. Being manhandled into the lobby had been a second slap at his dignity. He sensed that everyone's first impression of the grand old hotel had not been exactly grand. He edged out of Henry and Stub's support standing alone for the first time in the Hotel Alexander.

The hotel had an air of expectant silence as if it were waiting to give its own appraisal of them.

"Boo!" He said breaking the silence.

Yukio stepped back. *This blind man is mad.*

Thaddeus joined them after locking the front doors behind him.

"Earl?" Stella asked, surprised at Earl's single utterance.

"No echo," he answered—then he said without pause, "Thaddeus, I think you under estimated your problem in renting out rooms." He paused for effect. "You just locked the front doors, is that to keep folks out, or lock us in?"

Damn, there goes the deal, Thaddeus thought as he struggled to not answer Earl's question.

Earl felt Thaddeus's discomfort, and understood for the first time why his plan to take over the hotel had been received without much need for negotiation.

"Stella," he said, "tell me what you see here. I don't care about the little things, give me the big picture. If I wanted to take a walk where can I go?"

"Well, let me see", she said as she moved toward the large drapes pulling them open to let in some January fog thinned daylight. She walked around the room peering into hallways, behind closed doors, finding a light switch here and there turning them on.

Earl listened to her footsteps, taking measure of distances as she explored their surroundings.

She looked up at a chandelier that hung in the center of the lobby. It did not add much light; half the bulbs were burned out, the cobwebs hanging from it glaringly obvious.

"Thaddeus, I'm still waiting for your answer," Earl said, his voice level and calm as he sought control of what was becoming an awkward moment.

"I let the housekeeping staff go about six months ago. Without the help I could no longer let out the rooms. Without enough rooms occupied I couldn't keep paying the staff. It had become a lose—lose situation."

"I can't fault you." Earl said, "I probably would have done the same thing had I been in your shoes. You might have been a little more upfront about it though. The fact that the place has been closed for some months without any housekeeping or maintenance paints a whole different picture regarding our prospects of getting the hotel up and running again." He turned in the direction where he had last heard Stella's footsteps. He was about to say that it might be best if they wished each other luck and he and Stella ought to go back to Stella's Starlight Lounge where they belonged.

"Earl?" It was Henry.

Damn, that is why we've gotten in this mess in the first place. Henry's come home and we have no room for him. Is he really our problem? Then there is Stub and Ivory, friends all, each with his own unique disability just like . . . he chuckled aloud . . . me. Well, hell, this ship isn't sinking; she's just taking on a little water. I guess we'll just have to find a way to plug the holes and dry her out. You can't beat the price. He sniffed the musty air. On the other hand . . .

Earl made up his mind.

"Stella, have you found the door to the lounge yet?" He rubbed his fingers slowly back and forth across his cheek as if he was pondering a deep question. Now he was playacting just long enough to be able to grasp onto some facts that hadn't reached the surface yet. "Perhaps . . . perhaps we should take this one step at a time. We should start with the bar and get some cash coming in and worry about the hotel later on."

Earl has a good head for business, Thaddeus thought, *but opening the bar won't bring in enough to save the hotel. Or can it? Earl is a showman. Just maybe? Forget it, I'm fooling myself.*

Henry nodded to Yukio.

Yukio had one foot out the door. If he did not trust Henry as much as he did he would have already skedaddled.

Buddy, Henry thought, *I wish you could read my mind. You are about to be clued in my friend, and your answer can make or break this deal.*

Stub headed toward a set of doors on the far side of the lobby that Stella hadn't reached yet. Time to explore.

A moment later Earl heard a short, poorly played rendition of chopsticks.

"Stella, let's go see if that piano can be tuned."

Henry and Yukio followed, Henry biding his time for the right moment to drop his plan right in the middle of everything. He glanced at Thaddeus. The man was trying but not doing a very good job of masking his prejudice. The hotel was still rightfully his and if he did not buy in the deal would blow up in their faces. If that happened, perhaps he should do the horrible thing and give Stella and Earl a break and hit the road. Something would turn up, it always did. No one promised me that I had a right to be happy—not in this world.

Stub finished dusting off the piano bench as Stella guided Earl to it.

"Well?"

Stella knew what Earl was asking. "It's a Chickering Grand," she answered.

"How old? What does she look like?"

Thaddeus answered, "Bought some time back in the mid-twenties. During prohibition we had a slick little speakeasy down in the basement. I had it brought up here when the hotel housed the Navy officers. They loved to sing around it."

Earl sat and tested the pedals, then lovingly each key. "It has been said that Chickering Grand pianos, built prior to the war, are considered the best, and that pianos from the 1880s until the 1925s have a rich and powerful sound, rounded and well-toned, with a clear and bright treble sound and a rich, deep bass. So they say. I have never had the pleasure of playing one until now." He smiled at Stella who had her hands on his shoulders. His fingers gently touched the keys as if he were making love to a woman for the first time as he began to play and sing:

'Maybe I should have saved those left over dreams

Dreams . . .

She needs a good tuning," Earl interrupted himself, "but she still has a good song in her heart."

'Funny, but here's that rainy day. . . .

"The room has good acoustics," Earl said when he finished. "What is the room's condition? Do we have tables and chairs, or is it empty?"

"The place looks great. The tables are set with off white linen cloths with little candle holders on each. It looks like we can seat around forty with another six at the bar. There are no seats around the piano, the way you like it."

He reached up and touched her hand, stroking it lightly. "That's fine . . . it sounds like we can have this place ship shape and ready to open in no time at all. Is there a front door, and heads separate from the hotel?"

Stub checked for the bathrooms.

Thaddeus answered yes regarding the doors, the restrooms off the lobby.

"Henry, you sure are quiet. You got anything to say?" Earl asked as he continued to play the piano softly letting the notes swim and dance in the air as if their presence would slowly pump life back to the room.

Henry directed his answer to Thaddeus. "You said that there are forty-four rooms, six of which are suites. What condition are they in?" How many have private baths? The basement, is it full of storage, or can the speakeasy be updated and reopened to the public? The restaurant next door, Bab's Cafe, is it any good, and have they ever done any catering for you?"

Good questions all, Earl thought.

Thaddeus was a little surprised at Henry's boldness. "The cafe is open every day of the week except Sunday. I eat most my meals there. Beulah—Babs—Fitzgerald does breakfast and lunch herself. Dinner is the best time to go. Her night chef knows his way around a kitchen. During the war we had a door put in connecting the hotel to the cafe. All it will take is a key, I've got it around here somewhere. Two of the suites I've kept up. One of them is mine, the other I've kept up in case of company. All the rooms are made up. A good dusting and clean sheets ought to do. Twelve rooms share three bathrooms. The rest all have their own. The suites each have two bedrooms, a full bath, small kitchen, and a central seating area. The heat is off on the second through the fourth floors. The carpet needs replacing throughout, but I haven't got the money."

"And, the basement?"

"That will take some work. It hasn't been used for anything but storage since 1935 or so. I brought in a cat to deal with the rats. I think the rats got the cat." Thaddeus directed all his answers to Earl and Stella. "Earl", he continued, "you and Stella get the suite on the top floor across from mine. You wanted three rooms for Stub, Henry, and Ivory. They can have any three rooms on the same floor as us.

I'll see that the heat gets turned on. The rest we'll leave be until there is a need.

I suggest they use the rooms with a shared bath, that will save us all some money."

It looks like this thing is finally coming together, Thaddeus thought. *Now if Henry will only mind his own business.* He couldn't help but frown when he eyed Yukio. *What the hell is he doing here?*

Earl thought about Thaddeus's string of answers. "No, Henry, Stub, and Ivory will each . . ."

There was a hard determined knock on the front door to the bar.

Ivory Burch peered in at them through a window. Stub, having found the bathrooms, waved at Ivory that he should go to the hotel's entrance. Thaddeus went with Stub to let him in.

Henry seized the moment to speak openly with Earl and Stella. "Please forgive my rudeness for not introducing my friend Yukio Hayashi. I have brought him here for a reason he does not even know yet."

Yukio bowed Japanese style.

Stella responded with a polite nod. Her grip tightened on Earl's shoulder. This had all become so confusing. She wanted to say, 'Stop, no more,' but she trusted Henry saying only "go on."

Henry wanted to get to the crux of the matter before Thaddeus returned. "Yukio and I served together in France. I want him to have one of the suites." His eyes turned towards Yukio then back to Stella and Earl. "Yukio is married. He has a young son, and a kid brother who is three years younger than he. In exchange for the suite, rent free, they will take care of the housekeeping until such time as it becomes too much for them. Open the hotel one floor at a time, reserving the rooms for traveling musicians—that was your idea and it is a good one. Yukio and his brother Teramato—Matt—can help in the bar at the same rate Stub, Ivory, and I get—plus tips." There he had said it. It hadn't been as hard as he had feared. He looked at Yukio. "What do you say, are you and Matt willing to give it a try?"

Yukio was caught speechless. *You bet*, he thought, his throat dry, the words not quite ready to come to the surface. His only reservation was that the hotel was on the wrong side of town for a family of Japanese Americans to be moving into.

Stella let out a quick laugh followed by a happy sigh.

Earl tinkled a few keys on the piano as he sorted out everything Henry had just laid out for them. He couldn't find anything wrong except for their working in the bar. Where would their payroll come from? It had been a struggle for Henry to be accepted, and that had been back at Adam's Place. The Hotel Alexander was practically uptown and there was still a big 'No Japs Allowed' mentality.

Thaddeus Mohler stood in the doorway. He had overheard most of it. "Earl, I hope you aren't thinking of buying into this? Why, if we allowed . . ."

"Shut up, Thaddeus. I was about to walk out, thinking that we were biting off too much to chew. This deal is only going to happen one way, and that is my way. Take it or leave it, 'cause that is the way it is going to be. If Stella and I walk out of here, we are not coming back, and you might as well burn the place down for the insurance money. You do have insurance?"

"The one person we have not heard from is Yukio," Stella said trying to cut the tension. "Pleased to meet you, Yukio. Any friend of Henry's is a friend of ours. You've got the suite if you can handle the housekeeping. One floor at a time and the common areas shouldn't be that hard. But what do I know, I don't even make my own bed." She laughed softly. "About you working in the bar, that will take some thinking."

Yukio understood, though he did not have to like it. The free rent would be a godsend. But he and his wife needed to have some kind of paying job, raising a toddler isn't cheap, especially without a grandmother living with you to help out. As a Nisei, finding a job in San Francisco is very difficult. To him the paying job in the bar was the deal maker. He remained silent; it was not up to him to say. He meant nothing to these people. He was grateful for Henry's friendship and would not jeopardize Henry's already fragile situation.

Thaddeus Mohler had never been spoken to like this.

It was one thing for a blind man to tell him to shut up. But, Henry, stepping into the middle of this with his cockamamie idea about Japs doing the house keeping in exchange for free rent. He couldn't let Japs live here even if he wanted to. Why, the whole neighborhood would be up in arms.

They had reached an impasse. No one wanted to be the person whose final words ended what had started to be a marvelous opportunity.

Ivory and Stub had also overheard.

Stub was tongue-tied. Working for Earl and Stella was the best thing that had ever happened to him—even if it had almost gotten him killed. He was having trouble living on his own. His room was in a rough neighborhood where anyone who looked vulnerable was. Moving into a swell place like this was all right by him. When he had first learned of Earl's plan his heart went all a flutter. Now it looked like the deal had just taken a flyer.

While Stub was tongue-tied, Ivory wasn't. Despite his hangover, and the shakes that were settling in after a long bad night's binge, he was going to put in his two bits worth. He gave Thaddeus Mohler one of those who the hell are you, and what business is this of yours, looks.

"Thaddeus, meet Ivory Burch, another member of our

odd-ball family," Stella said, her voice tinged with the first glimpses of regret. She was about ready to call a cab and take Earl back to their home where they belonged. "Ivory, this is Thaddeus Mohler, owner of the hotel."

Ivory had just heard enough to get the gist that somehow Earl and Stella had or were making a deal to take over the bar, also something to do with the hotel. He had missed the idea that free room and board was included—at least for him. He owed his life to Earl, Stella, and Henry, and would never forget it. He also knew that without them all he would have left was the Sarge; he did not want to go down that road. "Mr. C," he had taken to calling Earl Mr. C out of respect, "Stella, you all know how I feel about the fucking Japs. Henry and me have had our issues. We still do, but when I close my eyes, I can forget that he's a Jap. Hell, half the time I think Henry thinks he's white. Henry's a good man, and if called to, I'll stand beside him without reservation." He gave Thaddeus Mohler a hard look as he tightened his fist, trying to hold back his anger. This Mohler guy was beginning to piss him off. "The way I see it, most folks don't know the difference between a Jap, a Nisei, a chink, or a Korean. The war is over and things have to change. Too many have died kicking butt on those that thought they were better than the next guy— Nazis and the Jews, Southern crackers and the niggers, Custer and the

Indians. We all know Stub to be a good man and you are not about to fire him because some jerk has an issue with his twitches and stutters. I'm hoping that you are not going to fire me because I've got some serious issues left over from the war. If you decide to set up shop here I'm guessing that you are not going to fire Henry because it would make this asshole happy."

"Pardon my language, Stella, I don't mean no disrespect."

"What I'm trying to say Mr. C, is give it a shot. If I can handle working with them, then some lamebrain, who wants to come in here and have a drink, listen to some music, had better not show them any disrespect or I'll kick their ass right out of here."

Stella laughed out loud, her tension having drained with each word.

Earl ran a flourish across the piano keys. "Yukio, you and your kid brother can have the jobs if you want them." He assumed that the answer was given, with no further discussion needed. Except for one, "Brother Mohler, you got anything to add?"

Thaddeus studied the moment. Prior to today he had not thought himself a racist. Hell, his housekeeping staff he had let go had a couple of Filipino women. San Francisco had its ways of doings things and folks knew their place. Did that make him a bad guy? He looked at this motley crew he was buying into: a blind man, a ditzy blond, a couple of Japs, a guy with facial twitches who can't speak a straight sentence, and a broken veteran with a wooden leg. Was he prepared to trust the fate of his hotel, his home, to this cast of characters? Then he remembered what he had heard from Earl about Ivory's experiences. And what Ivory had said. "Things have got to change." *Starting right here with me,* he thought. *Yeah, I've had something to say, but if I do I'll only look like a donkey's ass.*

Yukio shook Henry's hand. "We'll take it."

"Not me, Boka—knuckle head—go over there and shake Mr. C's hand."

Yukio bowed.

From that moment on Henry and the rest of the crew adopted Ivory's term of respect, Mr. C.

Earl took Yukio's hand, holding it a little longer than Yukio had expected, taking measure of the man, and memorizing his pulse and the way Yukio's hand felt in his.

"Stella," Earl said, "why don't you check out our suite upstairs while I sit here and have a chat with this lovely piano and play a little. Ivory and Stub, you check out the bar and see what we need. Henry, I think you and Yukio ought to check out the condition this hotel is in."

Yukio freed his hand from Earl's from strong but friendly grip. His head high, eyes now locked on Thaddeus, he walked over, bowed, never taking his eyes off the old hotelier. "This is a good thing that you are doing. We will not embarrass you. One day you will be proud."

Earl squeezed Stella's hand, then let go to find the piano keys. Stella whispered in his ear as she stepped away. "Sometimes you amaze me, and other times you are just . . ."

"Amazing." Earl finished simultaneously. "Let's just say it's been an interesting day. Like the Master Chief on a ship I once served on used to say—Ain't no bad days, just some better than others."

Ivory had not moved since he had finished his grand speech. Stella took note of his duffel bag, state of dress, and pallor. It didn't take much of a guess to figure out that Ivory had met up with the old Sarge, got to drinking, and when they did they usually got . . . *what was it the guys at the hospital used to call it? Oh yes, 'royally pissed off'.* "It looks like you could use a cup of coffee and something to eat," she said as she walked over and gave him an appreciative hug. "And a shower," she added.

It was Stella's turn to take charge. "Thaddeus, is there anything open in the neighborhood where we can get some coffee and some toast perhaps?"

"Nearest place would be the restaurant at the St. Francis Hotel. No need to go there. I've got a small kitchen up in my place. The coffee is hot, no cream or sugar. I think I can throw together some ham and cheese sandwiches."

"Please," Stella said.

Earl turned the day over to Stella. He had done enough. He knew that it was not going to be easy moving into this place. He had loved 'Stella's Starlight Lounge'. It would always have a special place in his heart. Right now he needed to sweeten up their new home with some music. The old hotel and he needed to get acquainted.

'We meet, and the angels sing —

The angels sing the sweetest song . . .'

"Since Yukio and family will have one of the suites on the fifth floor everyone else should be boarded on the same," Stella said. Thaddeus, the room keys please- one for the suite and one each for Henry, Stub, and . . . of course . . . Ivory."

"Stub, why don't you join us and we'll get you settled into a room. Then you can do the bar inventory. Ivory, after you get a good shower, come back here and help Stub. Thaddeus will have coffee and sandwiches waiting. Henry, after you and Yukio do a tour of the hotel, why don't you help Yukio and his charming family move in. I can't wait to meet them.

Yukio, I hope that is not rushing you? We have work to do."

"I saw a pay phone in the lobby. I will give my wife a call and tell her the good news. Oh, boy is she going to be surprised." *You are not just whistling the Hawaiian War Chant,* he thought, *She is going to be delirious.*

"I . . . I might," with regret tinged with caution in her voice, Stella continued, "suggest for everyone's comfort you use the back service elevator, just for the time being. Does that meet with your approval Thaddeus? Good." She hadn't waited for an answer. "See that Yukio has a key to their suite."

' . . . We kiss, and the angels sing

And leave their music ringing in my heart.'

Now, what next, she thought. A 'To-Do' list a mile long was beginning to rampage across her mind. So much to do here, and so much to do back home. *Where to start? Where?* "Earl what do you think . . ."

Did I say ditzy? Boy did I get that one wrong. Thaddeus thought as he went for the room keys. He returned a moment later with the keys. The rooms for Henry, Yukio and family, were on the fourth floor, everyone else on the fifth.

"I never thought you'd ask," Earl chirped. Perhaps we should take a look at our suite. You can see if everything is ready for us to move in." He raised his eye brows until they showed just above the rim of his dark glasses. "You heard me right, I said move in. This afternoon I want you to take a cab back and put together an overnight bag or two. Enough to get us by until the movers bring everything else. You got me here, my love, and I'll be damned if I'm going to make that trip again. While you're gone, I'm just going to sit here and make some music. Henry, please make sure that all the doors throughout the hotel are propped open. My music needs to find and touch this old hotel's heart."

FIVE

THERE IS NO CHANGING MR. C.

STELLA LOVED THEIR SUITE. IT WAS LARGER THAN THE LITTLE apartment they had above the Starlight Lounge. They had a bath, but it had been down the hall near the stairs, which always worried her when Earl got up at all hours of the morning. Their new suite was painted parchment white with a green and rose patterned carpet that wasn't in bad shape. There were two bedrooms with twin beds in each. She would have to do something about that. The second bedroom she thought she would make into a sitting room for herself. That was one thing she had been lacking, a quiet space she could call her own. The kitchen wasn't much, it had a small fridge, stove, and an oven not quite big enough to roast a small chicken. That was all right, she didn't like to cook much anyway.

She opened the window and felt a pleasant cool breeze. The fog was lifting, and what a view. Being on the fifth floor she was one floor higher than the building across the street. When she looked down the street she imagined that on a clear day she would be able to see all the way down to the Bay Bridge. A fog horn sounded in the distance. There was little traffic noise, with few people out on the street because it was a holiday.

She left the second bedroom when she heard the music.— Earl's voice, the rapture of the keys, swirled throughout the old hotel, finding stairwells, and corridors alike. She touched the wall and thought for just a moment the old hotel's heart started to beat again.

"Mr. C," her eyes crinkled upwards as she smiled, "you have found yourself a home where there will be no bigots or dragons allowed." *Mr. C*, she thought as she left the suite door open and pressed the elevator button just across the hall, *I like that.* The door opened, she stepped inside and pushed the down button. Against the hum of the elevator she listened as Earl made friends with the Hotel Alexander.

Any prior reservations Thaddeus Mohler had melted away as easily as icicles at the first winter's thaw. As the coffee perked he listened to the new breeze as it rustled through the old hotel clearing the cobwebs and dust inch by inch from the once vacant hotel his parents had bequeathed him. He had never been much of an hotelier, and despite its location and reputation, he had managed to almost run it down to the auction block. He heard Earl's music echo throughout his home, thanked God for it, while feeling very much the fool for letting ingrained prejudices that weren't deserved almost get the better of him. He thought of Yukio's courage as the young man had looked him in the eye saying, "One day you will be proud."

Ivory's stomach grumbled as he found his room—#504. Stub was across the hall in 505. Earl and Stella's suite was just down the hall. Henry and the Jap family would be on the fourth floor. "Will you look at this," he said aloud as he took in his room. The room was warm and cozy, larger than the one he had just busted up. It had a real bed, a twin, not a cot, a closet, which he hadn't had since China, and his own bath, something he hadn't had, even growing up as a kid. Yes sir, this was the life of Riley. He set his duffel bag on the bed, set out some fresh clothes and stepped into the shower. The bathroom soon filled with hot steam as the spray gave him a good cleaning, which was more than he deserved after his antics the prior night.

After the shower he was going to shave, but he laid down on the bed to give the mirror time to clear. He hadn't slept since the night before he'd gotten shit-faced on rye whiskey, and partied down with the old Sarge. The one thing he needed was sleep—and he did.

"How long have you been planning this, and why the hell didn't you clue me in? Yukio asked Henry as they did a quick walk through of the hotel, floor by floor. Along the way they left each door open.

"About ten minutes before I called you," Henry answered. I didn't know anything about Mr. C's scheme to buy this place until this morning. It came as much of a surprise to me as it did Stella. The truth of the matter is that a couple of hours ago I didn't have a job or a roof over my head—now look at us." They laughed, each putting their arms around each other's shoulders as comrades at arms will do when the battles are over and the celebrating has begun.

All in all, the hotel was in good condition. All the rooms needed a good airing; the bathrooms a good scrubbing. All the windows needed cleaning. The hallway carpets needed a little more loving care than they could give. There were very minor signs of mildew, rot or infestation. The wallpaper was not peeling from the walls; at least that was something.

"I think I can tell Earl that we can have the second and third floors ready by the first of the week."

"You got it," said Yukio as he propped a stairwell door open. "Say, he's pretty good." This was the first time he had paid any real attention to Earl's singing.

"You don't know the half of it." Henry said as his mind drifted towards a question that had been chasing him throughout the tour of the hotel. *Who is going to run this place, Earl, Stella, or Thaddeus?* He had to think about that. *Thaddeus knows the business, but from what I've seen he's not very good at it. Earl? No way, you couldn't tear him away from his music for anything. Stella? Now this I gotta see. We need her in the bar with her winning smile. I guess it's got to be Thaddeus.* That thought gave him some real concerns regarding how he would interact with the Japanese American staff over the long term.

Yukio went to phone his wife.

Henry explored the basement - that it had once been a speakeasy had sparked his curiosity. There was no urgency in getting the basement up and running, if at all. He turned on the lights to what he presumed would be a big dusty storage room. "Holy-Moly!" The words burst out as soon as he had thrown the light switch.

Stella stood just inside the doorway as she quietly watched her guy pour his heart out as his fingers danced across the keyboard. She looked around the bar taking in every table and nuance. The only thing lacking were seats around the piano. Perhaps they could bring the barstools over from the bar? She studied them for a moment. No, they were too high, and there was no leg room. Most of the tables were four tops. There were two smaller tables, but they couldn't seat enough and would look out of place. *Earl would gladly trade this piano for his old piano back at Stella's. It had barstools that fit around the piano allowing for that personal up close audience Earl thrived in front of. On second thought, this is a better piano. Well, it's something to think about, we still have plenty of time.*

"Coffee?"

Thaddeus appeared next to her pushing a small room service cart loaded with coffee and sandwiches.

"Just in time, I have a feeling Mr. C has worked up an appetite," Stella said as she lit a cigarette, then poured herself a cup of coffee. She snatched a sandwich from the cart as Thaddeus rolled the cart over to the piano.

Stella served Earl. He sniffed the sandwich then laid it down on the piano top. "Butter, no mustard," he complained. "Provolone cheese, not Swiss, and a ham sandwich isn't worth speaking of without the pickle."

Earl's finicky attitude came as a surprise to Thaddeus. "This is what there is pal, take it or leave it. I'm not a short order cook."

"Never said you were. One of the benefits of being blind is that I usually get things my way—including a ham sandwich. It's too hard to pick them apart and put them back together again."

Thaddeus looked to Stella, who just shrugged her shoulders. "That's my Earl. You can't change him, so you might as well let him have his way. The return is bountiful."

"We'll send out for spaghetti and meatballs later," Earl said. "I like spaghetti. You ever seen a blind man eat spaghetti? No, well bring your raincoat." He laughed. "How about a spritzer on the rocks." He tapped a few keys on the piano as if he were about to play. "What day of the week is it?"

"Thursday, Thaddeus answered.

"How is the bar set up, Stub?"

Stub finished his sandwich and helped himself to Earl's. "The whiskey, bour. . . er. . . bon, scotch, gin, and vodka are good. We've got no beer, wine, or champagne. Ol . . . lives, onions, the mixers, we've got none."

Henry burst into the room with news of his discovery. He quickly fell silent thinking: *Ut oh, the boss is at it again.*

"Think we can pull this place together for an opening by Saturday?" Earl announced. While it was a question, Earl had already made his mind up. There would be a grand opening on Saturday and he did not care what they had to do to make it happen. "We've got a lot of regular customers and friends who are going to be disappointed when they show up at Stella's Friday night and we're not there. We can put a sign in the window letting folks know that we are now at the Hotel Alexander. Thaddeus, can you make a call and order up the beer and champagne in time? Whatever else we need, we can haul over tomorrow from Stella's."

"That's only two days," Stella fussed.

"That is why I didn't push for tomorrow night. I thought

that might be asking a bit much."

Thaddeus let out an incredulous laugh.

The word, NO, was still painted on Stella's lips. "Stella," Thaddeus said, "like you said, sometimes you just have to let Earl have his way."

It wasn't time for Henry to share what he had discovered in the basement. It was time to go to work.

SIX

A Secret Reveals Itself

THADDEUS HAD ALL BUT FORGOTTEN THE MUSICAL INSTRUMENTS that had been stored in the basement. The best days of his life had been when the speakeasy was rocking and hopping until the wee hours of the morning. After prohibition, the crowds thinned, the musician's union had bullied him for a larger piece of the action, while providing less and less talented bands, until finally the dance floor was empty.

After it closed he felt lost, unable to wrap himself around any one project, even running the hotel. The first few years he had secretly gone down into the basement at one, two, sometimes three o'clock in the morning. There he would light a small candle on a linen covered table towards the back of the room where he used to keep court—meet and great most everyone who was someone as they came into the room. Night after night he would sit there alone with his memories. He drank, never obsessively, and never more than one or two scotch on the rocks. Then one night he just blew out the candle, closed the door, and never went downstairs again.

Thaddeus's cobwebbed dust laden memories was what Henry discovered when he had first pushed open the doors to the hotel's dreary basement. When the lights came on, they dimly lit up a cavernous room. The tables were set for the Big Band dance years just as if they still the happening thing. At quick glance the linen covered tables could seat a hundred, perhaps more. These faced a decent dance floor and a raised stage where the instruments and chairs for sixteen musicians waited for their return.

The piano was an exact replica of the one upstairs. Next to it a gorgeous, stand-up bass and just beyond that, a drum set Gene Krupa might envy. One drum read 'The Hotel Alexander Orchestra'.

Dust-webs hung from chandeliers, where far too many lights had burned out. All the tables held new candles in small glass settings. The table nearest to him contained a candle that had long burned down to the end of its wick, alongside a bar glass usually reserved for scotch, its inside dry and dusty. The room echoed with its former glory.

The silence of the disused room was both sad and chilling.

Further exploration took Henry toward the back of the room where there had once been a full service bar. Further on, service doors led to a hallway with three doors. The first a storage room, the second and center door opened into a large kitchen, and the third to a second large room that had served as a small casino. He explored this, finding a discrete door and stairwell that led back up to the first floor where he could look out onto the smaller upstairs bar and the piano where Earl now played.

Incredible, Henry had thought as he retraced his steps to turn out the lights. Wait until Mr. C sees this. He chuckled at the thought.

Upstairs Earl had bigger news. They were to open in two days.

The basement discovery would have to wait. The bass, Yukio played, was the first hint of one of the hotel's deep secrets.

SEVEN

THE HONEYSUCKLE ROSE

SATURDAY AFTERNOON ARRIVED TOO SOON.

Much to Thaddeus's consternation, the Hotel Alexander had been transformed into The Honeysuckle Rose Hotel. The Hotel Alexander sign still hung high from the front of the building. But now there was a rose red, hand painted, sign on the front door reading:

The Honeysuckle Rose Hotel

A private residence reserved for people of the musical arts.

When Fats Waller first sang Honeysuckle Rose in 1929 it had caught Earl's imagination as well as his heart. It was at that moment that he knew that above all other things he wanted to be a crooner. The piano came natural to him, singing was something he had to learn.

He had been eighteen years of age, just missed the war to end all wars, had graduated from high school—just barely— and was done with schooling. He just wanted to get out of town. There was a big world out there and if he never returned that was all right by him. The Great Depression was a hot dry whispering wind, brooding, biding its time, until it would become a cyclonic storm that would affect everyone's lives.

Earl couldn't read or write music, but he had a good ear. Once he heard a tune he could play it, at least the melody, the words he sometimes had to make up. It wasn't the dance bands and cabarets that influenced him as much as it was the sounds that came from places like Memphis, Kansas City, and Chicago. He went to Kansas City with a small suitcase in hand, two bucks in his pockets, and the dream that one day his name would be on the marquee on the hottest joint in town. He never got to play in anything better than a second rate honky-tonk.

The war came and he signed on as a ship's baker in the merchant marine. A mustard gas explosion in Bari, Italy had taken his sight, but it had given him a magnificent gift, the ability to reach down deep within himself and sing and play as only a blind man who is terrified of the dark can. He migrated into jazz and pop, but deep down he was a blues man.

The little neighborhood bar Stella had given him he would always hold dear in his heart. Now, this hotel, this grand castle, he was determined to make into the hottest joint in town—The Honeysuckle Rose Hotel and Jazz Bar. He would have preferred a blues bar, but this was San Francisco, jazz was hot, just one step behind bebop. The bar he had renamed 'Stella's Starlight Lounge'; there could never be any other name for it.

It was four o'clock in the afternoon. They were to open at five. Were they ready? That was the question Earl had asked Stella all day . . . and Henry . . . and Stub . . . and Ivory. He hadn't asked Thaddeus, afraid he might scare the poor guy to death.

He hadn't asked Yukio or Matt either. Both were quiet

spoken men who kept a low profile still nervous about their very presence. Yukio would have to learn to speak up to catch Earl's attention. Working for a blind man was a skill they had yet to learn. Both followed Henry's lead as if they were seeing eye dogs in training.

The bar was in tip-top shape. Henry, Stub, and Ivory had rented a truck, hired four longshoreman who needed a buck, and had brought over everything they needed for opening night, including his old piano. It wasn't as grand as the one they had found at the Hotel Alexander, but his was designed so folks could sit around it, sing, and Earl could show off and banter with his fans. The hotel's old piano was tucked away nearby should a guest artist stop by. Earl was not one to easily share center stage or a piano seat.

"Are we ready yet?" Earl asked again as he sat at the piano waiting.

"Earl? We're ready, already," everyone chorused.

Earl flinched, shook his head properly chastened, as he laughed at his own expense. "What are we waiting for, open the damn doors and let them in." He said as he began to play the first notes of 'Begin the Beguine,' a popular song of the Big Band era.

"It's Stella," Henry interrupted. "We can't open until she gives the word. She's still upstairs getting dressed."

"And so it is written," Earl quipped as he moved into his new opening tune. To everyone's surprise it wasn't Stella's song. "I haven't played this one in some time. I've added a few personal touches which I hope Fats Waller won't mind."

'Honey, honey oh, honey,

You know I ain't got no money,

But honey, you got to listen to my plea . . .'

His voice was deep, passionate, and rich, full of heart and soul, making the song his own. Romantic and haunting, it made one shiver, as the melody reached out and touched the old hotel seductively reminding it that there was a new king in the castle.

' . . . Goodness knows

You're my honeysuckle rose . . .'

Stella dabbed at the makeup around her eyes. The mirror told all. She had a small breakdown, some good tears and a heartfelt sob, in her room where no one could see her. Sometimes a woman needs another woman to talk to, to empty her basket of stuff she can't share with a man because he is a man and just wouldn't understand. For now, she had to hold onto everything that weighed her down, because there was no way to let it go. She felt like she could cry a river, except for the emotional dam.

The move had all been all most too much—dizzying—everything happening faster than she could grasp. She had felt her feminine nerves begin to crack when Henry had returned and the decision was made that they were going to have to leave their happy little home. It hadn't been much, but it had been theirs.

There had been a lot of frustration and tears when she had lost Earl. When they had found each other, they built a home together and to give that up would take a special kind of love and courage. Earl was high maintenance. She only had so much to give and it was oh so hard to keep on smiling. They were taking on so much, so fast, and she was so afraid that tonight no one would show. And the night after that . . . and that. They were risking everything with so much to lose. Another tear sprinted down her cheek. She was afraid that this night would break Earl's heart, and that would break hers. She dabbed one more time, and then braced herself.

It was show time.

EIGHT

STORM CLOUDS GATHER

CLANG, CLANG, CLANG!

The cable car chimed as it came over the hill headed towards Union Square.

Al Louis put his hand to his hat to keep it from blowing away as he made a run for it. He had three blocks to go and that damned cable car had left him behind often enough he was beginning to take it personally. He had to catch that cable car, the street was too steep for him to try to climb unless he lost forty pounds. Good luck with that.

In his distraction he failed to take notice of a tall, thin man who turned away from him as he passed. It was January and the man was not wearing a coat, otherwise he took no notice. Unless threatened, Al didn't take much notice of strangers. They were after all strangers, no greetings exchanged, once out of sight out of mind, so why give one a second thought? He could taste trouble thirty yards out. If he did not get a whiff or taste of trouble it did not exist and neither did the stranger.

Les Moore was not blind to strangers; if anything he was acutely aware. He had seen men like this far too often. The pugnacious white man had the flushed face of a self-important cracker who always made it his business to be in everyone else's business. His whole life Les had been dealt low cards by these same self-made bosses. *Boy, do this, and nigger, do that, and boy don't you get in my way.* When a boss man said that you was in his way, you was, even if you wasn't, and he was sure to give you some grief just because he was white and you wasn't.

Les had found this to be especially true in the army where he found most everyone above a platoon sergeant to be color deficient—they weren't black. Most white soldiers didn't like serving with colored soldiers, thought that because they were colored they were naturally lazy and cowardly. When a colored stepped out of line they caught hell for it. The higher ranking white men leaned hard on the colored soldiers under their command to drive home the message that there would be no skylarking or cowards allowed.

Les could see the writing on the wall. You did not have to be educated to read it, you just had to be black. He was in a section of Frisco where colored folks were not supposed to be. Now, being that he was a black man, who wasn't supposed to be where he was, this white man coming his way would most likely be on his case like a bear on honey. It was night, the street lights left more than enough shadows, one of which he quickly stepped into turning his back as he pretended to look into a store window. *Lordy be, don't let this cracker spot a penny on the sidewalk or be wanting to look in this here window—just go on about your business and leave me be.*

It had been a long hot trip from Broussard, Louisiana. Les had been born and raised there and had barely ventured more than fifty miles away until the war broke out. He enlisted in

January, 1942 and was assigned to an all negro transportation company where he saw the world from the limited perspective of an all negro unit. Well, almost, the senior non-coms and the officers were all white, but they mostly left you alone as long as you did your job. If they felt the need to call you on the carpet they got on your sergeant's case. The sergeant then kicked your black ass until it was blue, he being madder than a mule chewing on bumble-bees.

Les learned that there was a whole other world outside of the hick share-cropping town he had come from. He had seen parts of North Africa, Italy, and France. He had seen London, Paris, and some of what was left of Germany. As the war wound down, he spent four months in a camp just outside of Paris where he had plenty of free time. He was a driver and the supply repo was full with nothing moving forward until someone made a decision that it was time to pack up and go home. He learned that the world was big, the music rich, and in a few places you weren't treated like a mongrel dog if you were black. Paris was the finest duty that could be had.

When he got home he found that Broussard hadn't changed, it was still small, hot, narrow minded, where he still could not drink from the same water fountain as a white man. And the unemployment weighed on you like the humidity; you couldn't get away from it.

The worst thing was that he couldn't play his music, not the music he learned in Paris, the music that came straight from his heart and soul. The best he could do in Broussard was the Beale Street Blues, Alexander's Ragtime Band and the Dark Town Strutter's Ball. Any nigger with a guitar or a horn played those same tunes, and they didn't have to be any good. You just had to sound like you was all beat down, which of course you was. If you showed ambition or drive you'ed be in the wrong town.

Now he played because playing was the same as breathing, something he just had to do. He had heard Harry James, Stan Kenton, Shaw, and Ellington, and they all breathed the same air as he did smelling of juleps, honey, and jazz -sweet.

In Broussard the air was no good.

Les made up his mind to get out Broussard. Playing was something he had to do, just like breathing. He had to go where his music coursed like blood through his veins. When he took in a breath, and blew it out, he became one with his trombone. With each note his soul sang: *I am, I am one with the universe, I am alive, and my music will echo for all time.*

He said goodbye to his pop, who didn't seem to care. It hurt him to see his old man aged well beyond his years from too many years toiling in the fields. When he could no longer work his heart and mind had become etched with the harder scars of idleness and moonshine. The old man no longer understood the words *I Am*. There were not that many black men in Broussard who had ever spoken or thought those words. It was a hard time for colored folk trying to etch out a living south of the Mason-Dixon—that was the way it was and had been for generations.

Les sought out his six brothers, and three sisters, who also didn't seem to care. He had been away for going on five years, and now that he was home he was just another mouth to feed. His mama cried, knowing she most likely would never see her second born child again. She'd knew that once a young'un left Broussard they never looked back. There's just not much worth looking back for.

He left with two changes of clothes, a bible his Mama had given him, a tobacco pipe his father had carved for him when he had gone off to war, his trombone, and the last of his military pay. He had thought about going north towards Memphis or Chicago. Instead he opted to head west where he had heard there was some new music brewing in the Jazz and the Blues clubs. Folks called it bebop. He had heard some on a record. It was a new sound, something he had to play. He didn't care about fame or fortune, although a little fortune he wouldn't shy away from.

Les Andrew Moore arrived in Frisco on the late afternoon train. The January fog chilled him quick the first moment he set foot off the train. Coming from the South he didn't own a winter coat. In the army one had been provided for him, it was still in fair shape, but he had opted to not buy it from the army for two bucks when he was cashiered out. He should have spent the two bucks. He shivered, rubbed his hands together, looked at a paper street map and headed off towards the Fillmore.

The Fillmore had drawn him clear across the country. With the influx of colored workers during the war the Fillmore neighborhood was now becoming known by word of mouth as the *Harlem of the West,* with its own churches, theaters, grocery stores, restaurants, newspapers, music and nightclubs. It was an all-black neighborhood surrounded by white.

A porter on the train had told him "You goin' to Frisco, then you gotta go to Jimbo's Waffle House. It's a new place, but everyone in the Fillmore will tell you that's where the action is. But I gotta warn you son, you get on stage you had better be good, damned good, or they'll kick your black ass right out of there. Those boys are the best there is and they're writing the book that is going to take us beyond bebop. Now if you can't get a chance to play at Jimbo's Bop City—that's what it's called now—there's the Plantation Club, Elsie's Breakfast Nook, Havana Club, the Long Bar, The Black Cat, the New Orleans Swing Club, the Blue Mirror, and the Booker T. Washington Hotel, to name a few. You want to make a name in music, then son, you be headed to the right place."

That is exactly what scared Les Moore. He had come all this way and he did not know if he was good enough. How good was good? Playing was like breathing, something he just had to do, and he did not want to have folks say "that Les Moore, he plays like a nigger from Broussard with a bad cold." *Maybe he should find a room and hold up for a few days*, he thought, *practice a little, work up some courage*. Right now he was on the white man's side of town and needed to keep moving.

He took a deep breath and caught a taste of honeysuckle sweet music. Whoever was playing knew his way around a piano, and that voice—the man could sing. The music was coming from a hotel just across the street.

NINE

As Ready as Breathing Good, Clean Air.

STELLA, WEARING A NEW ROSE COLORED EVENING DRESS, stepped into the room and was greeted with all smiles. She stopped just behind Earl, placed her hands lightly on his shoulders and joined him in singing 'Honeysuckle Rose,' making it their song. She nodded at Thaddeus, who, spell bound by their music, did not at first understand what Stella was saying: "Open the doors."

Stubs did, taking the front door keys from the old inn-keeper.

Thaddeus had decided to step back and not back seat drive the fun. He placed himself at a small two seat table near the front door to the street. Yukio brought him a scotch on the rocks and a clean ashtray. He didn't smoke, others did, especially Stella.

The doors to the hotel were opened with a certain level of expectation. Pins and needles turned quickly into hoar frost as the only thing that came in was bitter disappointment riding on the back of a cold early evening draft. All eyes moved away from the door. Henry eyed Thaddeus as he slowly turned towards Stella.

Stella knew what he was thinking—*had he just made a deal with a blind man whose dreams won't pay the rent.*

Stub returned to the bar where he picked up a glass and commenced to wipe it dry until he practically rubbed the shine off of it. The tension rose around him. "They will cah. . . cah. . . cah . . .ome." He whispered just above his breath, his stutter strangling his words.

Ivory, hands on his hips, marched out onto the sidewalk as if he were guarding against an uninvited hoard.

Matt looked at his older brother. "What's going on?"

Yukio shrugged his shoulders that he didn't know. He had never stepped foot in Stella and Earl's old place, so he did not know what type of crowd to expect. It had just been a couple of days since Henry had recruited Yukio and Matt turning their lives upside down. If the truth were to be said he was a little bit glad, though he couldn't show it, that they had no audience. Everything had happened so fast and he wasn't prepared to strut his stuff in front of an all-white audience, not yet.

Earl's fingers hung expectantly above the keyboard, his full attention absorbed by the silence of an empty house. Ting. A solitary note rang softly as his fingers slowly settled down on the slate of ivories. Ting . . . ting.

"Earl," Stella asked. Her heart raced down the sleeve of her dress as she reached out to him.

Ting.

Ivory slid back in. He looked first at Stella and then at Earl. "Mr. C, there ain't nobody there, and it don't look like nobody's coming."

"Now, don't that beat all," Earl said. "I didn't think we'd be busting at the seams, well maybe just a little, but I sure didn't expect a blowout. I guess we just need to give folks some more time. He played and sang two songs as if the house was filled with old friends and family. His heart bled as he sang as if every word mattered. After the second song his fingers stilled. "It's too close to New Year's Eve and . . . and . . ."

Ting.

He fell silent, there wasn't much else to say.

Henry couldn't stand the pained look on Earl's face. He elbowed Yukio, giving him a confident eye that said *let's do it brother,* as he reached for his clarinet where it sat in its case by his feet.

Henry took a position just to Earl's right, where the light masked his asian features. Yukio positioned himself just to Henry's left, where the light was the poorest. Henry had set the lights himself.

The piano music stopped just as Les crossed the street. A moment later the front doors to the lounge flew open and out came a muscular white man, with a slight limp, who looked like he was ready to bust someone up but good. Les ducked into the shadow of the hotel's entryway. He had seen the look the man carried too many times. *I'm mean, I'm bad, I'm looking for trouble—best not disappoint me, cause you won't want to mess with me.*

He didn't think the white man had seen him, but he sure didn't want to test his luck. That was when he saw the sign: 'The Honeysuckle Rose Hotel, A Private Residence Reserved

For People Of The Musical Arts.' *Do that mean black folks too?* He asked himself as he spotted the fat cracker that he had cautioned himself about earlier do an about face and come back up the street in the hotel's direction. "If it don't, it do now." He opened the door and edged himself in. One thing he had learned in the South, and it had paid off in the army, when you saw a white man who was looking for trouble, don't give him an excuse.

The hotel lobby was empty. A hand written sign was taped to the reception desk read: Please Register in the Lounge.

Henry and Yukio had practiced three numbers. Henry's first choice was Stella's song. Stella saw what they were doing and nodded her approval as she lit a cigarette. The swirling smoke rising from her cigarette changed his mind and he raised his clarinet to play the first notes of 'Smoke Gets In your Eyes.' Yukio joined in, his fingers plucking on the bass's strings

In a crowded room filled with tobacco smoke, Earl never missed the scent of Stella's particular cigarette brand. Tonight it was only Stella smoking. Earl sniffed, he did not smoke, but loved the aroma. Catching the scent he knew where she was, and began to play:

'They asked me how I knew my true love

was true . . .'

"Where did that gorgeous bass come from?" he asked. "Who?"

He got no answer. "Henry?" Henry was too busy.

'When your heart's on fire, you must realize,

Smoke gets in your eyes.'

Alfonso (Al) Louis, Assistant Secretary of the American Federation of Musicians Local #6, had taken a short cut through the Tenderloin. He thought it would get him to the Powell and Market cable car turntable which he needed to catch for a dinner appointment at the Mark Hopkins, atop Nob Hill.

The music that wafted out of the Hotel Alexander lit his curiosity. He knew that if he stopped, he sure as hell would miss his cable car—however union business was union business. The old hotel had not been under any Union contracts since before the war. There had been no requests for musicians to play there that he was aware of, and he made it his job to scrutinize most everything that came through the union for approval. If a musician wanted to work in San Francisco he had to be a union member in good standing. A contract between the union, the musician, and the establishment that wanted to provide entertainment had to be signed and approved by him or the Union President. He wrote down the name 'Honeysuckle Rose Hotel' that appeared to be newly painted on the windows of the hotel's front doors. He took out a handkerchief and mopped his brow. He was going to miss his cable car. He was too fat and out of shape to run any more. Frank Cambria, the Union President, his boss and dinner host, had been on his case lately about too many taverns and lounges working non-union bands. They needed to make an example of one or two of them. He was about to make the Honeysuckle Rose rue the day it had decided to skim on the union.

He followed street front windows until he found the front entrance to what appeared to be an active piano bar. Stella's Starlight Lounge was painted on the window. His breath fogged the window. He rubbed a circle in the window fog just enough to see through. Inside he could see a pianist backed by a clarinet and bass player. He could not see much and did not see that the tables were empty. It appeared as if the pianist might be blind. That didn't matter, it was his job to shut it down until a proper union contract was signed, delivering union musicians. He was about to go in and raise holy hell when the bass and clarinet players stepped back behind the bar appearing a moment later as waiters.

What the hell! No sir, the day had not come—yet—when Japs will be allowed in the union. It is one thing to try to cheat the union, it's altogether another thing when you add insult to injury. There will be no union contract allowed here. He would see to it that 'Stella's Starlight Lounge' would be shut down for good.

He wanted to storm in with his fists and voice raised in righteous indignation, scaring the customers out, while threatening the musicians with censure or worse. He had one foot set to go when he thought better of it. He knew his boss would want a few of the union guys to knock some heads together. It was good for morale when a few of the regulars got to throttle a few union scabs. If the hotel had anything to do with this it too would be shut down to. Nothing like a good old fashioned union picket line to make the union members feel of value; especially when the union was about to raise their dues.

Clang. Clang. The cable car left without him and there wouldn't be another for half an hour. Mopping his brow Al turned to face the hill. Cambria, his boss, would be on his third bourbon and water by the time he got there, and he would blame the extra drink on his tardiness. Flustered, excited, and angry, Al began the tedious climb, glancing back twice at the Honeysuckle Rose Hotel and Stella's Starlight Lounge.

Les cautiously opened the door to the lounge. At first glance it appeared to be as empty as the hotel accept for some idle bar staff and three musicians—two Japs and a blind, white piano player. Two Japs? Now this just didn't figure right. As far as he knew San Francisco was a racist city—always had been—mostly against Asians and Hispanics. It wasn't until the war started, when the shipyards needed workers that negroes had any real impact—out of sight, no harm done. A block back he had seen a 'No Japs Allowed' sign in the front window of a Chinese laundry. It hadn't been the sign that surprised him, it was a Chinese Laundry in this lily-white neighborhood that did. Now, here were two Japs playing in a white piano lounge, in a neighborhood, where colored folks, red, yellow or black, weren't allowed. *This here is something I've gotta see,* he thought as he quietly slipped in the door. He chose a small table to the left of the doorway. The table no one ever wants because it's got lousy lighting, near service doors that are always banging open and shut. Perfect for Les because no one would be looking to see just who might be sitting there.

Matt, Stella, and Ivory had their eyes on Henry and Yukio as they were about to stir up Earl's heart with a surprise of their own. Stub was a professional bartender and was always scanning the room for an empty glass or a new customer. Through the corner of his eye he caught the motion of the door to the lobby slide shut as a tall black man slipped into a seat at what he called the 'grouch' table; the worst seat in the house, a place where everyone complained, even if there wasn't anything to complain about.

He moved quietly over to Stella and whispered in her ear that they had a customer. He did this not because it was a black man who had just come in, it was because he was their first and only customer. He was colored, but Stub didn't care about that. When you have Tourette's Syndrome you learn early about the wrongs and pains of prejudice and being different. This wasn't his place and Stub wasn't sure if he could serve him; it wasn't his call. Frankly he was more concerned that Ivory would create a ruckus.

He had witnessed Ivory's explosive temper when he seemed to need to vent that volatile mixture at someone's expense, and he didn't seem to care who got hurt. He was a marine under attack, taught to never surrender—at least not again. Fortunately for Earl and Stella, Ivory always gave a clue when he was about to go off. It wasn't a twitch, or squared knuckles. He would get this distant look in his eyes, call in a subliminal character from his past -'the Sarge'- and then he would start swinging.

Shortly after Ivory had closed the door it opened behind him. Stella's eyes lit up when she saw two old friends and customers who had made the old 'Stella's Starlight Lounge' their favorite Saturday night stomping grounds. She greeted them, and wouldn't take no for an answer as she guided them to the barstools surrounding the piano. She told Earl who they were, took their drink orders, then returned to the bar where she needed to make a decision regarding the colored gentleman in the back of the room.

Their first customers knew Earl and were delighted to have seats that invited his personal attention and gift for gab. They told him there were two other couples that would be joining them as soon as their cab got here—that would fill up the piano side seats. The atmosphere in the room changed. Earl had an audience, small, but he had an audience. Earl pumped the energy back into what had been, for him, almost listless piano playing and began to sing:

'Oh, baby, baby . . .

A moment later, Henry's clarinet and the bass lifted Earl's music from magical to mystical.

'Oh, baby, you're my honeysuckle rose.'

The fact that a black man had slid into the lounge initially bothered Stella—just a little. As a former nurse, she had treated everyone equal. This was different. San Francisco had a history of racial and economic divisions. Everyone wasn't equal, or at least that is what the minority with the wealth and power wanted as the status quo. When she and Earl had accepted Henry, not just as a friend, but family, that had been out in the avenues, away from the crowd. It had been at Gibby's little neighborhood bar where they had first mixed Earl's piano and Henry's clarinet. Earl was blind, his music—color blind. At Adam's Place they had tested the social norms. Gibby's son had been saved by a Nisei medic in France during the war. For all he knew it might have been Henry. Henry couldn't say otherwise. One gig led to another, then once a month the bar was closed to everyone but Nisei veterans, friends and family. Stella smiled as she remembered how these men enjoyed the music and the dignity of being allowed their own moment. Yes, they had tested the norms. She glanced back at the couple sitting piano side. *What would they think? Dare she?*

When Henry had introduced Yukio and family into the equation, they put the hotel, everything they had, at risk. The Honeysuckle Rose Hotel was a gamble. It was on the edge of the financial core of the city where many of the grand hotels and restaurants made the city world famous. It was walking distance to where Sinatra, Como, Doris Day, Stafford, and Dina Shore filled the clubs. Where people, white people, danced to Benny Goodman and Woody Herman; where Count Basie played but was not allowed to stay. The social norms had to be upheld, appearances and tradition were important.

That was not the way Earl saw it. His music might be color blind, but he wasn't. "Stella,' he had once said, "a person ought not be color blind. If you ignore the color of a person's skin you are not recognizing who that person is and where they come from. Yeah, we should all be together as contributing human beings. The fact that we are different is part of the miracle of it all. You give someone the respect they deserve and they'll give it right back." He had paused thoughtfully for a moment. "There are those who do not deserve your respect, but that has nothing to do with their color on the outside." That was the way Earl saw people and one of the reasons she loved him so.

She studied the negro in the back of the room. He was tall, thin and had an intelligent face. He was dark, very black, no second guessing that he was colored. *Why would he come in?* She thought. *Is he looking for trouble? Perhaps.* But she doubted it. She tapped Ivory on the shoulder, curling a finger for him to follow her. By proxy Ivory had become their bouncer, their tough guy, if and when, they needed one.

Thaddeus spotted the negro tucked away in the back of the room about the same time as Stub. To him a colored on the premises meant trouble. *The boy was just looking for a few minutes out of the cold, but that wasn't his problem. If he stayed there would be problems. There always were when you let these people step above their place.* Look at what had happened to the Fillmore District after the negroes moved off the Southern dirt farms to find work in the shipyards during the war. They had turned it into a black ghetto. Especially now that the shipyards were no longer running and there were so many unemployed. The negroes had earned good wages at the shipyards, the working conditions and the dough far better than working in the tobacco or cotton fields down south. Most opted to stay—unemployed or not; in the Fillmore they had community.

Thaddeus never liked confrontation, he was a gentleman hotelier, not a bouncer, but someone needed to get his black ass out of here. It was important for the hotel to keep up appearances, not just anyone could come in. He paused for just a moment as he looked across the room at the two Jap musicians. *You make one exception and the whole world thinks they got rights that . . ."*

Stella caught Thaddeus' angst, giving him that look that only a woman can give that says: don't make an ass out of yourself, there is no problem here a woman can't handle. She was nudging Ivory forward as she was two steps behind.

Les Moore slowly stood as they approached. He had a habit of taking his trombone out of its case anytime he was around music. It wasn't a conscious thing. You just never knew when an opportunity to play might come up. He started to put it back in the case when the woman stepped up to his table placing herself in front of the white man with the pissed off expression on his face that he had seen earlier.

Stella smiled as she took a careful but measured look at the human being before here. She could see that while he tried not to show that he was scared, he was. He hadn't come in to make trouble, perhaps to avoid some.

Ivory wasn't helping the matter any. He was on the tipping point, ready to call on the Sarge—ready to explode. After five years of imprisonment and abuse his emotional threshold was practically non-existent. It had been Earl, Stella, and Henry that had helped him regain his will to live again, and like an over-abused pit bull, he was territorial, loyal and protective to a fault.

The problem was that he couldn't find his own value. *I am . . . what?* He didn't know. He could play a guitar, but he was a lousy musician at best. Music had been the tonic he had needed to heal physically, but he had no real music in him, at least when it came down to the talent of his adopted family with Stella and Earl He knew nothing about bar tending, and one drink brought back the nightmares and ghosts, both dark and ugly. He had an artificial leg; the rest of him was the muscle and steel of a prize fighter working on a comeback. When his temper flared he was visited by the Sergeant Ware – who he could never forget had given his life so Ivory could escape from the POW camp. Once again, he replayed how his unit of China Marines had been ordered to surrender without firing a shot back on December 8, 1941. His guilt was that he was still alive. Now he would not cower or give quarter to anyone. Here at the Honeysuckle Rose, everyone had his place—except Ivory. With nothing else to offer he had become their bouncer, their protective pit bull, which was was probably the worst use for him. One day he would likely hurt someone, and when he did that he would hurt Stella and Earl.

It was the way the dark stranger held his horn that finally made up Stella's mind. "Are you any good with that?" she asked with a welcoming smile.

A welcoming smile from a white woman? Les had gotten a few back in Paris, and London, but here in the States? *No Sir, she was setting him up for something.* He speeded up the repacking of his trombone as he braced himself for whatever the cracker with an attitude had on his mind. He glanced nervously around. His back was in a corner. The swinging service doors might just take him to a dead end storage room where he might be beaten within an inch of his life. He did not want to fight, even if he could beat this whitey it would be his sorry ass the police would be taking off to jail, not this bad ass boss who looked like he was about ready to take a swing at him.

Stella put her hand on Ivory's elbow, telling him that he and the Sarge could stand down. "Are you any good with that?" she repeated to the tall, dark man, nodding towards his horn.

"Yes, Ma'am," Les answered, showing neither vanity nor hesitation. "I can hold my own with the best, if that is what you be asking?"

"Well then, let's see what you've got?" The white woman invited as she stepped aside, her arms motioning him towards the other musicians. *Appearances be damned,* she thought, *Earl doesn't worry about it, so neither shall I.*

Ivory did not step aside.

Les wasn't quite sure who the boss was here and he wasn't about to push his luck. If he got thrown in jail, the beating he would most likely get would be the least of his problems. If and when he got out, he would find all his money gone, as well as his trombone. Sweeping up his trombone he quickly stepped past the woman seeking the quickest exit. "Sorry Ma'am, gotta go."

"Wait a moment, please. Wait." Her voice was kind and reassuring. "I'm Stella, and this is my place. And my husband Earl, he's the one at the piano. Take a good look at the guys who are playing our bass and clarinet. Here, your color doesn't matter if your heart is in your music. Please, I'd very much like to hear you play."

Les hesitated. Her words were sweet—too sweet—but damned if he didn't need a friend or two. He had never felt lonelier.

She turned towards Ivory. "Ivory, don't forget that this is a musician's hotel, and Mr... I'm sorry, I didn't catch your name, from all appearances is a musician. Don't worry about Ivory here, his bark falls a little short of his bite, and just as long as he doesn't call out his old marine platoon sergeant, he's harmless. I've been meaning to put a sign in the window, *'Warning, one pissed off ex-China Marine on premises.'*

Ivory did not like being called on the carpet, even indirectly. He nodded towards the tall, black man, but did not extend a hand of welcome or even minimal politeness. Instead, he motioned slightly, his arm weakly extended towards the musician's circle.

"They call me Les. Les Moore," he answered Stella, his discomfort still evident, his smile pasted on.

It proved to be a good thing that Earl had ordered all of the hotel stairwells and hallways left open. The music drifted upstairs where Katie Shigano Hayashi, Yukio's wife, and son Jake listened. She sat on a folding chair just outside the doorway to their new home. It was worlds above the small room she and her extended family had lived in the relocation camp during the war. Yet, her isolation made the suite seem very small, a new prison with invisible bars. Her husband worked all day and into the night. She had Jake, which for the moment was enough.

Jake lit up when he heard the bass. "Pop," he laughed with an affectionate grin. He had been allowed to stay up the night before just long enough to hear his 'Pop' practice on the bass. "Pop. . . Pop," he repeated pointing down the hallway where the music mysteriously came from.

"Ohhh, baby," Earl crooned as he leaned back towards where Henry and Yukio played. "Where the hell did that come from?" The bass had come as a complete surprise. Henry had found it in the basement, along with the instruments for a sixteen piece dance band.

Yukio had played before the war. While once accomplished, his playing was rusty, and it would take some time to bring his repertoire up to Earl's standard. He and Henry had practiced 'Honeysuckle Rose' late into the night. Henry's gifted clarinet playing only added to to Yukio's sense of inferiority.

Les walked quietly over to where Henry stood, his eyes asking if he was welcome. Henry nodded, just as surprised at the black musician's appearance as Stella had been. "Les," he said softly as he brought up his trombone readying it to play.

"Henry," Henry answered back. "You've got balls."

"Yep, got me two. Been told that Hitler only had one."

Earl overheard, didn't know who was on stage, but he knew the song.

> 'Land of soap and water,
>
> Hitler's having a bath.
>
> Churchill's looking through the keyhole,
>
> Having a jolly good laugh
>
> Beeee...cause...
>
> Hitler only had one left ball,
>
> Himmler had two but they were small,
>
> Goring lost his in the beer hall,
>
> And poor old Goebbels never had balls at all.'

Les responded with a chuckle and an honest smile. *These here folks are all right.*

"Earl is my name, son. My friends have taken to calling me Mr. C. Now, since you are standing in our music circle, I'm guessing you are here to play. You got a name? What's your sound?"

"Les Moore, Mr. C., and I play the trombone."

"You ready?"

"As ready as breath'en good, clean air."

The two other couples arrived taking their seats around the piano. Stella lit a cigarette as the sound of laughter, music, and good times filled the room.

Earl opened the set with another rendition of 'Honeysuckle Rose' followed by *'Lavender Blue', 'Sweet Georgia Brown', and 'Buttons and Bows,'* all from the latest hit parade. Earl played, but mostly he listened, bringing his piano in time with the bass. He could easily hear that Yukio needed help. Henry slid in.

Earl didn't know what Les could do or why he had chosen to grace their club, so he threw out a number, indicating that Les was to take the lead while he sang:

'We meet, and the angels sing

the angels sing the sweetest song I ever heard . . .

"Now just the trombone." Earl said. "Let's hear what you've got."

Les' music filled the room, swirling out into the depth of the old hotel.

Stella was immediately enamored. "Oh yes, you can play all right. You can play."

Earl jumped back in.

'Suddenly, the setting is strange

I can see water and moonlight beaming . . .'

As the tune wound down Henry joined Les in a haunting duet. The bass plucking deep and mellow, basic notes that always sounded good, but just falling short. In practice, Yukio had to push himself to keep up with Henry's clarinet. He was awed by Earl who seemed to be able to take his music

103

anywhere. This new man had just walked in off the street and, wow, he blew everyone away. As musicians Les and Earl knew how to soar bringing their music to where the birds fly. Henry, who had been comfortable in his playing, had to step it up which left Yukio trailing behind playing just some basic cords that sounded good, which in truth had little to do with the music that was actually being played.

At first it had been fun, now Yukio was giving serious consideration to earning his keep bar tending and making sure the housekeeping was top notch. He looked at Earl and wondered if he had picked up on the fact that he just didn't belong—his music not nearly good enough. A glance from Henry suggested that, *Hey brother, we've got to talk.*

"Son, let me shake your hand." Earl exclaimed, "and please . . . please, stick around."

Les set his trombone down, stepped forward, and took Earl's hand. "Les Moore, pleased to meet you." He looked at the customers sitting around the piano who were aghast at what they had just witnessed. When they had first arrived they hadn't paid any attention to the musicians. They all knew Earl, and Henry of course. Now there were two Japs and god forbid a negro.

Earl could tell by the way Les had shaken his hand, and a faint smell in his clothes, that Les was black. That didn't matter to him. What mattered was the way the man handled his horn. *Sweet and low.* He chuckled at the horn player's name. The night had started out with an empty house. Now that they had a small audience he found their silence disturbing. "Les, you need a room for the night? Thaddeus, take care of the man." He then paused, played a few attention getting keys, then said: "And folks when it comes to music here at Stella's Starlight Lounge, we are all color blind, more or less, if you get my meaning."

TEN

AS BLACK AS THUNDER MOMENT

THE TABLE IN THE CENTER OF THE RESTAURANT AT THE Mark Hopkins was reserved exclusively for Frank Cambria. While the dining room was crowded, the tables most immediate were empty. They were also reserved. Cambria did not like to be overheard unless he intended it that way. He was the President of the Musician's Union. San Francisco was a union town and the musician's union held a seat of prominent power—politically and otherwise. The famous Mark Hopkins Hotel did plenty of union business—not that it mattered, the prominent hotel had made the perhaps improper but prudent decision to not cross this particular union Boss.

Cambria entered and was seated with the propriety he demanded, nothing else would do. He wore a blue power suit, no tie, a starched white shirt that fit his portly frame like a sausage casing. His cheeks, pink and rounded, stood out against his alabaster skin. He bristled when he overheard himself being described as resembling the comedic actor W.C. Fields. His pale blue eyes were bright and kindly, though he was definitely not a kind man. He wore a set of thin spectacles that lent him a professorial look, which was what he wanted. His sight was nearly perfect, he rarely missed a thing.

Cambria was a man unto himself. Unlike many of the robber kings, gangsters, and power brokers who ran the city he had never married and did not attend those social gatherings where all the Greats gathered to stroke each other feathers. He held his cloak of power close and 'to hell to everyone else'.

He ordered a Hi-ball, Gilbey Sprey's Royal Scotch Whiskey, and a thick porterhouse steak, blood rare, with all the trimmings.

Ten minutes passed.

This was the second time in the last month that he had been kept waiting. Cambria did not like to wait for anyone. Why he continued to employ the lazy bum Al Louis was due to a favor he owed a member of the Board of Supervisors. The Musician's Union along with the Waiters and Bar Tenders Union padded the politician's war chests amply. Al was a cousin of someone who was owed a favor by a city supervisor. Cambria needed an obedient yes man who wasn't too bright. That favor had been paid back in triple, but one never knows when it comes to political favors how much payback is enough. Al was late, again. Tonight he had a good mind to say enough is enough and boot Al Louis out the proverbial door. He just needed a reason, and Al was handing one to him on a silver plate. Al was his enforcer who handled the trouble or gave some when so ordered. That didn't take any brains, just some brawn and a solid 'don't give a shit' attitude. He knew a dozen union bruisers, any one of which he could move into Al's job within an hour's notice. While Al was fat and slovenly, when it came time to push, he had a damn hard shove.

Cambria glanced towards the bar where four men were

bending their elbows, telling each other their woes, as they waited to plead their misfortunes to him. He had heard and seen it all a hundred times before. It was his practice to hold court over dinner at the Mark Hopkins once, sometimes twice, a week. Cambria did not like to be pushed around or bullied. He did the pushing. Dinner at the Mark Hopkins was a good way for him to enforce the power of the union: his power, his rules. If he ruffled some feathers, so be it, no one wanted to cause a scene in the middle of the dining room. So the issues that were most likely to raise a few tempers he brought to his dinner table. He enjoyed the game, and hadn't ruined one dinner that he could recall. If things got rough, he turned the dirty work over to Al, which was one of the reasons he was irritated by his tardiness.

He eyed the closest of the men waiting for their summons. The first was a beefy, former boxer, a guy named Jamison who owned a notorious saloon over on Broadway near the waterfront. The man had been holding back fees due the union and made no secret about it. Cambria was going to have to show him who was boss one last time. The pug-ugly had a mean temper, so Cambria preferred to wait for Al to show before he started business.

Jamison had his share of confrontations with Cambria and they always cost him a buck. Since V-J Day the profits at his saloon had taken a steep dive. He had laid off four good bartenders: if he let any more go he'd be cutting his own throat. Music was the last draw he had, and damn if he was going to pay the union before he paid the rent. Several of his competitors had realigned with topless dancers and sex shows. They seemed to be doing all right, but he needed time, and paying off the union would take away that margin. He had a good mind to grab that fat pig union boss and throttle him but good, but he knew better because whatever pain he might be able to dole out to Cambria, would come back to him in spades.

Walt Abernathy, the man beside him, had already closed his doors. The war had been good to him. His place had been a favorite watering hole for the ship building working stiffs. He did pretty good by the navy too. When whenever a ship's crew got liberty in Frisco his joint was standing room only. His saloon had two doors, two bars, the second for coloreds, their paychecks from the ship building yards were just as good as the good old white boys. Whenever an aircraft carrier came into port, he had made a bundle.

Now the navy had downsized big time. The ship yards had all but closed, laying off men and women, black and white. The blacks, mostly unemployed, still liked their liquor, only the race barriers had been drawn up tight, and they were no longer allowed on his side of town. He had already closed the colored's saloon. Now it looked like he had no choice but to close 'Abernathy's Saloon and Steak House,' at least until he found some investors, enough cash and a new draw to bring in the young drinking men. He had never made any good money on the steakhouse side of the business; the profit was in the booze. The Bartenders and Waiters Union had cost him his last dollar. Now the damn Musician's Union was demanding unpaid fees for the past six months. All he had was a small combo and a girl singer, they weren't very good, but who cared. In a noisy, drinkers bar, they were background noise. But, now he couldn't get his business going again without paying off the union.

Abernathy looked at the other men with him at the bar,

each with a drink in hand, each with a damn good reason to tell this union asshole to go to hell. *Maybe if we were to go in together?* When push came to shove one might try to stand up to one of the other unions in this town. No one stood up to Cambria and got away with it.

Cambria grew tired of waiting, his meal would arrive soon, and he had business to conduct. He eyed the room to see who might be friend or foe. Most were couples, middle aged, prosperous, most likely tourists. There were a couple of politicians five tables away, foes most days, friends when the union greased their palms. They were too far away to overhear anything he didn't want overheard. He recognized *the hat* sitting by himself across the room.

The hat, one Gavin Hoyt, a private detective who often worked with the district attorney's office, had become a regular, favoring the same table, the same nights, and times that Cambria reserved his tables. He always wore the same hat, a dark blue felt Trilby. Cambria chuckled. The man could no more hide beneath the hat than he could standing in the middle of an elevator. He nodded towards the man, who tipped his hat in return, the game was on and both men knew it.

The District Attorney was interested in finding a fight with one of the power unions. His re-election was coming up and he was looking for something sensational to get the working man's vote. Proving graft in the unions always raised a few hackles and plenty of press. The detective tipped the waiter well for whatever he overheard. Likewise Cambria tipped the waiter to keep his mouth shut.

Cambria called over the waiter and gave him instructions,

and then checked his coat pocket making sure his small Derringer was ready, safety off. With Al absent this was his backup. The waiter gave the detective a quick nod, letting him know that Cambria had just asked for his first meeting of the evening. The waiter went straight to the bar whispering to Abernathy that he would be first, bumping Jamison from his place in line. Abernathy protested, telling the waiter that Jamison had been first to arrive. He glanced over at Cambria who gave him a brief glance in return.

Abernathy approached Cambria's table reluctantly. He had nothing to offer, nothing to negotiate with. If he couldn't get a break on the dough he owed the union, he couldn't get an extended business permit renewed. His wife had her bags packed and both feet out the door. The only reason she hadn't slammed the door shut yet was that she didn't want to go home to her aging mother and listen to the repetitive 'I told you so' until the old woman croaked. If he couldn't get Cambria to give just a little, he was doomed, and everyone who knew Cambria knew that he had no heart.

Cambria signaled with his steak knife for Abernathy to sit.

Abernathy stood clutching his hat in both hands, knees trembling, nervous sweat forming on his brow. He was a small man with a Charlie Chaplin like physique. He looked harmless, and now with his riches to rags story he appeared even more the tramp. The waiter placed Cambria's dinner in front of him, standing back for a moment as Cambria sniffed and inspected his meal. With knife and fork he sliced into the steak, tasting a steamy pink morsel and then nodding his approval. The waiter stayed put. He had not been dismissed yet - he wanted to hear as much as he could.

"Mr. Cambria . . ." Abernathy whined, his confidence all but lost.

Cambria did not wait to hear what he had to say. "For a moment I considered giving you a break. If, and I say if, you get your business going again, you might pay the union what it's due. If? Then I came to my senses. You are a crook, a coward, and a loser. Nobody in this town is going to lend you one penny to open up shop again. There are good, honest, hard working musicians, who have families to support and bills to pay that will never see the wages you owe them. As President of the Musician's Union I just can't let that go . . . now can I?"

Abernathy's knees melted as salty sweat dripped down into his left eye giving him a twitch that only irritated Cambria more.

The waiter leaned in, whispered something in Cambria's ear, and then stepped quickly away. He made no pretenses as he gave the detective an urgent nod.

Cambria deliberately raised his voice wanting everyone to hear exactly what was said and by who. "Look at you, have you no pride? You are sweating like a common stevedore in a boiler room. You have nothing left to say that is worth hearing. Get out of my sight before you ruin my dinner."

Abernathy was backed into a corner. His eyes opened wide, his vision blurred from the sweat and the stress that clutched at his heart, as his hands shifted around his hat.

Jamison, who had strayed close enough to overhear everything saw what Abernathy was about to do. He shouted, "Abernathy don't, it's not worth it!"

Huffing and puffing from his steep hill climb Al Louis came into the room just in time to hear Jamison's warning.

The detective rose from his seat too late.

Abernathy dropped his hat where he had been holding a small hand gun which was now pointed directly at Cambria. When you point a loaded gun at someone your intent had better be to pull the trigger or you are a fool. Abernathy was a fool.

Cambria was a tyrant and a dictator, but he was no fool.

Abernathy hesitated a second too long and died a fool as a bullet from Cambria's Derringer, which had been tucked in his lap, pierced his gut. As he slumped forward, his face torn with pain and disbelief, a second bullet struck near his heart. Both shots were lethal.

A clear case of self-defense, Cambria showed no remorse as he gave Jamison a hard look, then quickly reloaded his Derringer. The gun seemed frighteningly small compared to what it had just done.

There were several screams, but mostly everyone stared in stunned silence.

Al Louis knocked over a patron as he strong armed his way through the stunned diners to come to Cambria's aid. Before Cambria could load the still smoking derringer Al's gun was pointed a foot away from Jamison's head who had rushed to try to stop Abernathy. "I wouldn't if I were you," Al whispered, his breathing still labored.

The detective did nothing. He was armed, but he was not a cop, and Cambria had clearly shot in self-defense. He watched expectantly, the moment dark thunder - someone had to step down before another shot was fired. With Al, gun drawn and trigger cocked, Cambria set the derringer on the table. He motioned for the waiter to order a new drink, his having been spilled. With slow deliberate actions he sliced into his steak and took a bite as he studied Jamison's face.

Jamison was not a coward like Abernathy, nor was he a fool. He was a big man who could easily swat Al Louis, if there had not been the gun pointed directly at him. "Easy there Al, you and me have had our differences, but that has nothing to do with what has happened here." His hands slowly eased his coat open to show that he was not armed. That done he extended both arms out in a cross position—a pose from which he could never draw a secreted weapon even if he had one. "As you can see I'm not armed." He addressed the room, not Al or Cambria. "I came here to ask for a little understanding from Mister Cambria, the President of the Musician's Union. I can see that now is not a good time, so I'll just be on my way."

The detective approached both men cautiously, his hands extended and open. "I'll witness that Abernathy drew first, leaving Mr. Cambria with no choice but to fire his own weapon in self-defense. Reaching Jamison he lifted the back of his coat to show that nothing was secreted there. He then patted down the coat pockets.

Al Louis lowered his gun to his side, never taking an eye off Jamison.

God damned murdering bastard, Jamison swore to himself as he lowered his arms, turned and nodded briefly towards Cambria. "I'll call your office to schedule a more convenient time. Good evening, sir. Enjoy your meal." Al still stood in his way.

Cambria pointed his steak knife at the chair across the table from him. "Have a seat Al. You are a bit late, but your timing somehow worked out. Waiter, bring Mr. Louis the blue plate special and a beer."

Jamison was ten good steps towards the door when he heard Cambria call after him. "Jamison, let's talk in sixty days. Don't worry about any payments until we have that discussion." Jamison did not turn or reply. The two other businessmen who had been waiting their turn at the bar met him at the door.

The detective returned to his seat. He wasn't going anywhere until the police came and ran him, and a few other witnesses, through the drill.

Cambria enjoyed his meal, regardless of the bleeding body that lay on the floor very nearby. The waiter brought a table cloth to cover the body which quickly turned red.

While he had arrived in time to get his boss out of a jam Al knew that he was still in Dutch for being late. The blue plate special that Cambria ordered for him was liver and onions. He hated liver and onions and Cambria would make sure that he ate every single bite with an appreciative smile on his face.

He sat there while his boss ate, then when Cambria put his knife and fork down, Al put his cards on the table. "Boss, on the way over here I found a piano bar and hotel that had a trio playing without union sanction. I know they weren't union because two of them were Japs. The piano player was white. He might have been blind."

Cambria thought about that and then smiled. "Perhaps the piano player doesn't know they're Japs?"

"Oh, he knows all right, their one big happy family."

Cambria's smile shifted to a hostile frown. "We'll see about that."

Detective Hoyt overheard just enough to make a note that he needed to find out where this bar was. If Cambria planned to give them some union trouble, he just might trip up and give the District Attorney something he could use. When it came to trouble the detective worked both sides of the street. The only problem was that he did not get the name.

ELEVEN

FINDING YOUR CHARACTER

SATURDAY REPEATED ITSELF ALL TOO SOON.

There was no denying that their opening night, the Saturday prior, had been a flop, except for their introduction to Les Moore, a black man whose musical skill was matched only by Earl—and sometimes Earl had to push himself to keep up with the young and unusually talented musician. When Earl pushed his own limits, Les demanded more, and more he got until they became kindred spirits breathing the same good air. All this left Henry and Yukio on the side lines.

Earl missed that.

Stella didn't.

Late that night, when Stella dragged Earl away from his keyboard, they had a talk as they took the elevator up to their room. Thaddeus was with them. Stella didn't mind, he had a right to know what was going on. He had after all an owner's interest. Thaddeus just listened. He was beginning to recognize that Stella was a pretty sharp cookie.

"He's very good, isn't he?" Stella said meaning Les. This was not a question but a statement of fact. Until that night, she had never heard anyone as good with a horn. Neither had

Earl. "Good. Why he isn't with one of the big bands surprises me. I just hope we can keep him around for a while."

"He is black," Thaddeus cleared his throat realizing that he was about to put his foot in his big mouth one more time.

"Oh, that." Earl paused as if choosing his next words carefully.

"Yes, that." Stella said. The elevator door opened.

"That young man is going to attract his own kind," said Earl. "There are a lot of good black musicians in this town. They are going to be a force driving jazz to a whole new level. Me, I don't want to be left behind. I felt and tasted that music tonight and realized that we are going to have to step up our game. If we want to keep Mr. Moore here, we are going to have to challenge him."

Stella caught that single word of respect: Mister. Earl did not see him as a black man, but as a musician who was his equal or perhaps, his better.

"If we don't, he's going to move on to the Fillmore where he can play with few limitations. He has to, it's in his blood." Earl continued, "If he goes to the Fillmore he won't be back. So we need to find a way to get some of those colored musicians to come here. This is a hotel that caters to musicians, isn't it?"

The hair on the back of Thaddeus's neck stood on end. The door to Earl and Stella's room swung shut, leaving him silent, with visions of terrible things to come.

"Remember the all Nisei nights we used to have back at Adam's Place? Henry says that the old speakeasy in the basement would make a great rehearsal hall or showroom."

Earl chuckled, "maybe we should bring back the all Nisei night? It would be our little secret."

"You wouldn't."

"It's something to sleep on." He said as they dressed for bed.

"What about Henry and Yukio?" Stella said. "If only you could have seen their faces. Yukio struggles, but there is no way he can play with you and Les. And I don't want to lose Henry, and we will, if you leave him as second fiddle."

"I hadn't thought about that," Earl said with a kind of quiet admiration.

"Music sounds different to the person who is playing it. It's the musician's curse. You're right, Henry can't play at Les's level, and I doubt that he ever will. I can't ask Les to play down—perhaps he'll extend a helping hand if Henry will reach up."

"Let's close the piano bar for a few days, give me some time to work things out. Sweetheart, we won't lose Henry, I promise. I love a good bass, but we both know that Yukio isn't good enough. As for Les, he'll move on one day. He's too good to stay here for very long. As soon as he understands his gift, he'll move on to better things. For right now I need to find a way to keep him here as long as I can."

A deep yawn broke up his thoughts.

Stella gave him a hug and a warm kiss, and then switched off the light. These late nights were hard on her; she doubted that she would ever get used to them—but that was life with Earl.

"Good night, sweetheart. I'll most likely be up in an hour or so and go down and play me some thinking music." He only needed two hours sleep, here and there, any longer and his nightmares returned.

Even though the train trip had been long and mostly sleepless Les could have played all night. He had not been able to play like this since he was in France and when it was that good, you just didn't want to let it go. He had been given a decent room with a private bath. The bath made him whistle, it was a far step from an outhouse or latrine. Yes sir, he was being treated all right. One question nagged him. Why? Did Earl know that he was black? If he didn't, what would happen when he did?

Stella and Earl had taken him in just as if he were family. Their man Ivory had other ideas. He hadn't figured out who the older white man was, Thaddeus somebody, but he could tell the man did not cotton to having no niggers around. Still, the old man had kept his mouth shut. For right now he had free room and board in trade for playing his horn. Sweet. But this here hotel was still in the white man's side of town and it wouldn't be long until he would have to move on down to the Fillmore. He'd been told the Fillmore was the Harlem of the west, dark town, where they played the sweetest jazz this side of Kansas City, and he had come to be part of it. For right now he had a nice roof over his head, clean sheets, and a place to practice. One thing he did know was that old Earl breathed music just like he did. The man was a musical instrument just reaching out to be discovered. They had a lot in common.

He lay down on the bed and fell into a deep pool of sleep as if he was an old bullfrog seeking the muddy bottom of a still water pond on a hot August day.

Earl woke two hours and twelve minutes later, threw a night gown on, and counted his steps to the elevator. After the second hiss of the elevator's door he made his way to the piano, where he played some thinking music until the sun rose. He knew that by the sounds of a city waking that seeped into the stairwells and corridors of the old hotel.

Stella slept in.

Time for some coffee, Earl thought as he pushed back from the piano and counted his steps one more time to the elevator.

Henry's thoughts had not allowed him to sleep. When he heard the elevator descend he followed a few minutes later. Henry spoke little first thing in the morning. He quietly made tea for himself and black coffee for Earl. After rice, and a hardboiled egg, he finally spoke. "Mr. C, the guy who came in last night, he's pretty damn good, isn't he?"

Everyone is asking the same question, Earl thought. He knew that Henry had more. The questions that Henry would ask as he worked his way towards the important one didn't need answering. More importantly, anything he might say would confuse the issue until Henry said what needed to be said.

The American side of Henry was waltzing around the question, afraid of what the answer might be. The Japanese side of Henry would find a way to phrase the question so as not to be offensive, showing respect, seeking a compromise that would save both sides any humiliation.

Earl sat at the piano, his coffee within reach, as he worked on a few tricky bars he had discovered the night before while trying to play alongside Les.

"Is he going to be here long?"

Earl played, saying nothing more.

"Last night, I realized that I might have been a little short sighted when I quit medical school. I have been thinking about going back, but I didn't want to leave you and Stella in a jam. Now that Les is here . . ."

Earl's fingers slammed down on the keys. "Bullshit, you no more want to go back to medical school than you want to re-enlist in the army. The truth is that you are intimidated by the man's character." Earl said.

"Character?" Henry asked, his face tight with confusion.

"That's what I said, character—his musical character—that is what allows him to play far above where you and I can. Well, son, that's going to change, and Mr. Les Moore is going to help us do exactly that." Earl played a soft rendition of *Autumn Leaves* as he tried to find the right words. "Henry, your character is a direct reflection of your personal conception of music. You have got to stop hiding behind your clarinet. Individual notes are less important than the way in which you deliver these notes to an audience. Your sound is unique to you and you alone. Just as an actor's voice creates his character, a musician's tone, touch and intonation create a unique personality. What is your sound and more importantly what is this sound you are conveying out there to the listener? Your sound is the first thing that a listener hears: a first impression with a powerful impact."

"Les Moore does not play a great horn. He plays a mean horn- his way, his sound, the horn expressing his music that comes from right here." Earl pounded his chest, and then returned to 'Autumn Leaves'.

"You've got to follow the sound you hear in your head and your heart and trust your original sound, but remember that when you hone your character, your instrument becomes an extension of you. You are the music. When you figure that out, that is when you will be able to play as Les does. Your music will become original, fresh, taking on a life of its own. Henry, you can't be completely original without first studying a model. Les Moore can be your model, as he will be mine. His horn is an extension of his inner self. He is music, and you and I are going to learn as much as we can from him, while we can."

Henry had been prepared to put his clarinet aside and limit himself to just helping out with the house keeping. He had no intention of going back to medical school. Earl had just thrown him a life line while showing him respect, kindness, and challenging him to become something he never dreamed he could be: to stop playing his music like he was a kid at home in high school. Good? Yes, but self-limiting. Now it was time to step up to become a musician in his own right, and that scared the hell out of him.

Stub had entered the room in time to hear everything. "Coffee?" he said, without a single stutter.

Doesn't anyone sleep around here, Earl thought. "Morning Stub, glad you are here. Henry tells me that the basement was once a hot speakeasy. I think it's time for us to go down and check it out. There are going to be some changes made around here, starting today."

Ivory was about to get off the elevator as they entered. "Mr. C, you look like a man on a mission."

Earl chuckled. *If Thaddeus shows up I'm on the wrong side of the clock.* "Grab yourself a bite and a cup of coffee Ivory and meet us below. I'll explain everything when you get there." Not one said a word as they guided Earl into the elevator.

"Here we are, boss," Henry said, "I'll describe everything as we make our way towards the bandstand. It once held a sixteen piece dance band and all the instruments are still in place. There are two pianos . . ."

Earl listened, taking it all in, and then let out a long whistle as he was guided to the first piano. He sat, gentling touching each of the eighty keys as if introducing himself to a new lover. His fingers flexed as he began to play and sing a powerful rendition of, 'And the Angels Sing."

The music floated all the way upstairs waking Thaddeus, who was still tossing with his nightmares.

Earl stopped as abruptly as he started. "The acoustics are fantastic. You said there are two piano? Help me over to the other."

The elevator door hissed open.

Once positioned at the second piano, he caressed the keys one by one, the same as he had done with the first piano. "This is the one," he said, without playing a note. "She's whispering a sweet love song." He touched off a single note letting it echo and fade across the room. "Ivory, glad you are here. We've got some work to do."

Half an hour passed as Earl played. Henry, Stub, and Ivory set about the tasks Earl had assigned to each.

Thaddeus followed the music, looked surprised, as he came down the stairs. "Earl?"

I'll be damned, Okay Stella, I guess you're next. Earl thought as he took a momentary break. "Thaddeus, top of the morning to you. I've done some thinking since we last parted. Stella tells me that you might have some concerns regarding our guest Mr. Les Moore. God, I do love that name, it amuses me. Fear not, my good friend, for Mr. Moore is surely sent by god, on loan to help make this place everything you have dreamed of and more."

You mean my nightmare, Thaddeus thought.

"No, I don't mean nightmares," Earl said as if he had read Thaddeus' mind. "Here is the way it's going down. If you don't like it say so, not that it will change a damn thing. Stella's Starlight Lounge is closed until further notice. We're moving everything down here where no one will hear or see a thing until we are ready. Les Moore is a genius on his horn and we are going to up our game in order to be worthy of playing with the man. When we are ready, we are going to need a few more musicians, waiters, bartenders, and a hat check girl. You are going to need a couple of desk clerks, and a bell hop or two, because the Honeysuckle Rose Hotel is about to get busy."

"Is that so?" Thaddeus was too overwhelmed to say much more.

"Oh, and Thaddeus," Earl said, "I wouldn't be too surprised if some of the new musicians are black."

Thaddeus rolled his eyes. "You are always so damn confident. Are you ever wrong?"

"I've done a lot of stupid things in my life, but I would be hard put to list them in order of stupidity."

"I give up. Have it your way," Thaddeus replied. "Let's give this cockamamie scheme of yours a try. I'm going to go back upstairs, have a heart to heart talk with the bigot in me, and then kick his ass out of here." He looked at his watch. *That's what I thought, time for a scotch. Earl, you are driving me to drink,*

Earl finished the song he had been playing. "There are three keys that are a little flat, but she's a beautiful thing. Henry, would you be kind enough to go upstairs and ask Mr. Moore to join us. He's in room number 406.

Henry returned saying that Les would be down as soon as he had showered. Henry was jazzed. He had started the morning bummed and disheartened. Now he was energized, challenged, and anxious to hear what Earl had on his mind.

Earl played some thinking music while he waited for Les to show. There was still one piece to his mental puzzle that Earl wasn't sure what to do with Yukio. The man had heart, but not enough talent, and Earl knew that he never would. If Earl suggested that he should tend to the housekeeping and some bar tending, he most likely would lose face. For what Earl had planned he needed everyone on the same page, all for one, and each one for all. More importantly, he needed musicians willing to challenge themselves. For Yukio, his mountain to climb was too steep.

Les entered with his trombone and a half eaten apple. Earl waited until he was piano side. "Top of the morning to you, you slept well I hope."

With his mouth full of apple Les nodded forgetting that Earl was blind. *Slept?*

Earl gave that no-never-mind look. "What do you think of the place, it used to be a pretty hot Speakeasy back during prohibition?" He did not wait for an answer. "I trust you have your horn?" That came as a request, not an invitation, as Earl began to play, 'Begin the Beguine,' Artie Shaw's rendition.

Henry was ready and jumped in with his clarinet.

Clearing his mouth of apple and too much saliva, Les quickly unpacked his horn and took the lead which Henry gladly passed over to him.

When finished, Earl brought down the cover over the piano keys with a deliberate clunk, something he rarely did. This caused everyone to jump. Whenever Earl did this Henry feared that Earl would catch his fingers and that would be the end of his music. Henry knew that this sudden action would lead to Earl making an announcement. He hadn't a clue what it was, but he knew it was going to be big.

"Welcome to Stella's Grotto which with your blessing will open one week from tonight, headlining Les Moore. Les, I can't pay you one thin dime, none of us gets paid for playing here. That will come in time, but by then you will have moved on, taking your place alongside great horn players like Harry James, Artie Shaw, Dizzy Gillespie, and Glen Miller—God bless his soul."

"I may be blind but I can see what you are thinking. Yes, you are good enough. As Henry said last night, you've got balls. It will take some to break all the rules. You are an unknown black man, headlining at a new jazz club in an all-white neighborhood, backed up by a Japanese-American clarinetist, and an odd ball blind piano player who knows more about the blues than he does jazz. If I could see you now

I would bet that your facial expression would be saying, *"You've got to be kidding me."* He gave a short barking laugh. I'm not asking you to play before an all white house because they will not come—not yet, and not for some time to come. It's going to take balls because we are going to do our best to fill the house with colored folks, including a few of Henry and Yukio's friends. I've heard tell that the Fillmore hosts some pretty talented musicians who are setting the new standards for jazz. That is why you came to town—am I right? Right now, the only folks you know in town are all here in this room. Well, we're going to pay a visit to the Fillmore, and invite a few folks to hear you perform on a stage better than anything they have there. The Honeysuckle Rose Hotel is a private residence for musicians and the management is color blind; as is this stage."

Les flexed his horn as if readying to play, but didn't.

"Damn!" That was Henry.

"You . . .you . . . got to be . . . be kid . . .kidding." Stub said to Ivory.

"Mr. C has gone over the deep end," Ivory said. "Now we know who has the balls."

"Gentlemen we have some rehearsing to do. Les, what is it you play best, and how do we lift it to the next level?"

Stella woke to what she thought might be a tough day. Their grand opening had been for naught. She and Earl had spoken about the sudden appearance of Les Moore and what it might mean. She worried about Henry, Yukio and his family, and Thaddeus. Earl had said that he would be playing some

128

thinking music, and that is what scared her when she first crawled out of bed. What was her husband thinking?

She couldn't make a 'to do list' that gave her any direction because Earl kept changing the 'dos'. With no guests other than Les Moore, the housekeeping was meticulous in Yukio and family's hands.

She followed the music and found everyone downstairs.

Thaddeus whispered something about Stella's being closed, the Speakeasy reopening, and the hotel going colored. He offered her a Bloody Mary, but it was far too early in the morning for that. She poured herself some coffee, a pot had been set up at a nearby service bar, lit a cigarette and took a seat where she could listen in. She hadn't a clue as to what was going on and for the moment was just along for the ride.

Thaddeus had told her that the upstairs lounge was closing. The Speakeasy was to reopen as Stella's Grotto. Stubs and Ivory were busy cleaning and moving furniture around while Earl held court with Henry and Les around the piano.

Finally, she couldn't hold her tongue any longer and had to ask. "What?" was the only word she could find?

Earl cocked his head as he leaned back towards Stella. "Finally someone has something intelligent to say around here. Stella, would you please repeat that one more time for the boys – ahhh, no offense meant Mr. Moore."

She did, and she meant it, "Would someone please tell me what the hell is going on here?"

TWELVE

SIZZLING INVECTIVES

THE MUSIC COMING FROM THE BASEMENT, NOW KNOWN TO a select few as Stella's Grotto, came at all hours of the day and night. For all the right reasons, Thaddeus Mohler had quietly decided to keep out of Earl and Stella's side of the business.

When he had made his deal with Earl he had rolled the dice, a gamble if there ever was one. Thaddeus had his regrets, but the truth was that he hadn't the dough or the heart to try to keep the old hotel going on his own. Change had come quickly. Now the old Hotel Alexander was not the same grand old lady she had once been. The Honeysuckle Rose Hotel, a private residence for musicians had replaced her. Only, so far, everyone in the house was staying free of charge. Worse yet, most were colored, and if word got out, he'd be run out of town wearing tar and feathers. But, oh damn, the music was good, and hour by hour it got better. So he hung out in the front lobby of the hotel reading an old copy of 'Gone With the Wind', listened to the music and waited for the phone to ring or the front door to open for someone who, for some odd—ball reason, might want a room at the Honeysuckle Rose Hotel.

The first couple of days he and Stella had chatted over

coffee and cigarettes -her cigarettes, and just to be clear, his coffee. He was still paying all of the bills. Earl's grand scheme so far had not produced a single Indian head nickel. Now Stella was spending more of her time back at their old place, sprucing it up for sale or lease. That was hard, at the hotel she felt lost and insecure, there she was packing up and saying goodbye to her home.

Enough was enough and it was time to put their instruments down and take a break. The elevator hissed as it took the musicians up to their rooms. It was 2:30 in the afternoon, Earl's nap time. They had been at it since seven in the morning. In half an hour or so Henry, Les, Yukio, Stub, and Ivory would all come down again and grab some lunch at the cafe next door, the price of the sandwiches and a cold beer each going on the hotel's tab. Then they would retreat back downstairs, brown bags and bottled beers in hand, where they would wait for their 'lord and master' to return to his kingdom in the grotto.

Thaddeus made a note that it was time to at least stock the beer downstairs. Paying the cafe price was killing him.

The phone rang, shrill and loud, breaking the silence.

"Hotel Alexa...sorry I meant this is the Huckleberry Rose Hotel. How can I help you?"

"Has a guy named Alphonso Louis been by there yet?" An impatient voice barked through the phone.

"No, can't say that anyone by that name has been by," Thaddeus replied. Of course, no one had come through the front door for several days, including the postman.

131

"He will, and when he does tell him that Frank Cambria needs to talk with him as soon as possible."

"Is there a number?" The phone clicked to a monotonous buzz. Phone still in hand, Thaddeus thought about calling up the cafe and ordering a ham on rye sandwich with a side of potato salad. His finger dialed the first number as the front door opened. He hung up the phone. "Good afternoon, welcome to the Honeysuckle Rose. Are you checking in?"

The man did not answer until he stood right across the counter from him. He searched the hotel like a nervous eyed ferret and seeing no one else he handed Thaddeus a business card: Alphonso Louis, Assistant Secretary, American Federation of Musician's, Local #6. "You are?"

Thaddeus glanced at the card, and then pushed it back to the man, as if what it said had no relevance. The man behind the card meant trouble. Unions in San Francisco played hard ball, often were corrupt, and unfortunately, far too often got their way. The man was most likely here to demand tribute to the union. Thaddeus planned on giving him a fast bums-rush. "I am, he answered, the former owner of the Hotel Alexander."

"I take it you have a name?"

"I do."

"Look, Bud, I'm asking nice, I won't twice." Louis took out a notebook and pencil, licked the lead end of the pencil as he prepared to jot down the name he was demanding.

"I don't see where that matters. Now if you will excuse me I was about to make a call."

"I was by here a few nights ago," the union man said with

132

an air of hostility, "and I saw that your lounge was open. There was a combo playing with a piano player who might have been blind, and two Jap musicians. You know the rules. You can't play live music of any kind unless it is approved by the union. All the musicians must be card carrying members of the musician's union. I looked in our files and found that the Hotel Alexander has been cited numerous times in the past for hiring non-union musicians. Hiring non-union scabs is one thing, but hiring Japs is something else altogether. I'm here to give you notice that I'm closing you down."

The threat Thaddeus had heard before, although it had been a few years since. Thaddeus did not like the unions, but he respected them because once you got on their black list they could make trouble—big trouble.

"Sorry you came all this way for nothing. The Hotel has recently changed hands. It's now a private residence for retired musicians. If you have any issues with the Hotel you will have to take it up with them. This is the Honeysuckle Rose Hotel now and I can assure you that the hotel has never hired or paid a musician to perform here. As for the lounge, if you had checked the front door you would have seen that it is closed for remodeling. I'm not sure what the new management is planning on doing with it, perhaps a nice little tea house or something."

"Look pal, I know what I saw, so don't try to give me the run-around." The union representative quick stepped to the door to the lounge. It was locked.

Matt, Yukio's brother, stepped off the elevator with a housekeeping cart and stopped for a moment to see what the argument was about at the front desk. The words 'union' and 'shut this place down' was all he needed to hear. He pushed the cart back on the elevator and pushed the down button.

Al Louis turned from the locked door just in time to see Matt's Asian face. "You there, stop." It was too late, the elevator's door hissed shut before Louis could reach it. He noted that the elevator had gone down.

"There, I caught him red-handed. He was the one on the bass."

"Yes, Matt is a Nisei. There is no law stating that one cannot hire a Japanese -American citizen to do common housekeeping. He's a very good worker, and comes at a rate the hotel can afford." Thaddeus couldn't believe his own ears. He was defending the hiring of a Jap to a bigoted union boss.

Louis' thumb punched the elevator's down button.

Matt had locked off the elevator as soon as the door to the basement opened.

Maintaining a straight face, Thaddeus continued. The basement is where the housekeeping supplies are kept. And if you must know, the young man can't play a note. He's a little simple minded. His older brother was a war hero with the all Nisei 442nd Infantry. My family knew theirs before the war. Now if you don't mind I was about to make an important call." He turned his back on the angered union boss." Please see your way out, the door is right over there."

Al Louis punched the down button three more times. He wasn't getting anywhere. He turned, screaming sizzling invectives, as he stormed out of the hotel leaving little doubt that he would be back.

Thaddeus turned towards the door as it slammed shut.

"Someone by the name of Cambria asked for you to call him as soon as possible." Of course it was too late. "I gathered it was something important." A slight smile crossed his face as the cafe next door answered his call. Thaddeus here, how is your corned beef on rye today?" He had changed his mind, corned beef sounded better.

Matt left the housekeeping cart in the elevator, pushed the stop button and hurried into the Grotto. Les was about to clear his trombone of spittle and play a few notes. "Stop, no one make a sound." That being said, Matt ran to the stairwell locking the door from the inside. Turning, short of breath, he gasped, "There is some union asshole upstairs giving Mr. Mohler a hard time. He says he's going to close the place down."

Yukio looked at his younger brother. "You sure?"

"Yeah, I think he heard you play the other night."

"Musician's Union?" Henry guessed.

"There is a union for musicians?" Les asked.

"White musicians," Henry added. No yellow faces allowed. No blacks."

"What do we do?" Yukio asked.

Henry opened his beer. "We wait until Mr. C wakes, then we see what Mr. Mohler has to say.

The phone rang, stirring their anxieties.

It was Thaddeus who confirmed that yes it had been a union boss from the musician's union. The man had trouble written on his face and cursing every other word he said. He was trouble personified, and there was no doubt that he would be back.

Thaddeus locked the front door leaving a note that if anyone needed in to push the night bell. He had located the key to the service door between the hotel and the cafe which they now used thinking it better to keep their colorful personalities off the street. Thaddeus grabbed his sandwich from the cafe, locked the service door between and used another key to unlock the door to the stairwell that led down to the Grotto.

Thirteen

Throwing Caution into the Wind

EARL HAD SLEPT BRIEFLY. THE QUESTION, *WHAT,* HAD BEEN disruptive to his sleep. He would have chosen a different word than what. *How? How were they going to be able to pull it off.* That was the question. He rose in little more than an hour, mildly refreshed, but he couldn't quite shake off his premonition that his dragon was waking too.

It was so damned quiet. His sense of foreboding grew as he stepped onto the elevator. He expected the boys to practice after they had eaten and were refreshed. His foolish thought was that, while he slept, they had some of their best jam sessions without him.

He couldn't quite get a handle on Les Moore. The man lived and breathed music. If the score called for his horn to take the lead—no problem. The problem was that he stopped short when it came to stepping into the role of a teacher. He had tried to give Les the baton, hoping that his natural gift and passion for music would carry them all forward. Unfortunately he was still insecure in his own abilities and kept handing the baton back to Earl, which was understandable because he was the biggest white man in the room. With his dark glasses and cane he was not exactly intimidating, unless you were a black man from the south, where the white man was boss, even if he was blind or in a wheelchair. Les was having a hard time grasping the fact that Earl didn't give a rip about color. The good city of San Francisco did, which made it that much harder for Les to accept the baton from a white man, even if he was color blind. They were making some good music, but nothing like they could if Les would just let go.

As the elevator descended Earl listened to the sounds within the hotel. A small child cried from the fourth floor. A phone down in the lobby rang, and rang, and rang. There was no music. It wasn't the lack of music that disturbed him, but rather the clamber of voices, as you might find in a crowded bar on a contested election eve.

Thaddeus had played down the union boss's threats. It had all been shallow bluffs on his part. Everything hinged on getting the Grotto open to paying customers and for that they needed the music, the same music the union was determined to deny them. Stella's Starlight Lounge was one thing—to fill the Grotto with thirsty cash paying customers was another, and Earl swore that they needed Les to do that. Once they became a hot club, there would be plenty of talent wanting their time on stage. What a grand dream, but you can't put *if* or *when* in the bank. The union boss had seen Henry and Yukio but not Les. Maybe, he didn't know that for sure. If he had seen Les, he would have played that card hard and doubled down. Earl had made a good call closing Stella's and moving everyone down to the Grotto. Now the question is how will they fill the Grotto. Thaddeus chewed on that thought with mounting gloom as he listened. The more he heard the gloomier it got.

Yukio argued that his playing wasn't worth putting everything at risk and that he should pack the bass away and stick to housekeeping and waiting tables until the trouble blew over.

In his gut Henry had no choice but to agree, however, he knew that if Yukio dropped out now he most likely would never play again. They had been through too much together to allow him to quit now. That, and Henry had truly bought into Earl's vision. He had drunk deep from the doubt bucket and had almost quit. Now he was the evangelist selling Earl's vision of paradise.

Les appreciated Earl's courage and his talent. Still he did not trust any white man to follow through on his word to a black man, that was the way the world worked, and it wasn't about to change anytime in the near future. If this so called union man wanted to make trouble then all he needed to see was some horn playing nigger playing without a union card. Earl was right; he should go to the Fillmore—by himself—no harm done, thanks for trying.

The elevator door slid quietly open allowing Earl to count his steps to the piano, the only path he ever took back and forth in the Grotto. This time it was hard to count, angst had replaced the music, the air around him tasted bitter not sweet. He couldn't make out a word as everyone talked, actively bellowing, none listening to the other. If this had occurred on any of the merchant marine ships he had served on the Captain would have feared a mutiny or worse.

Her arms full of bags, Stella found the front door locked. She pushed the night bell and got no answer. Using her key she found the lobby empty as well. She had double parked and needed one of the guys to help unload the car. She used the house phone to call downstairs. No answer. She dialed the house phone one floor at a time before trying the Grotto for the third time. Ivory answered and came right up. *I wonder where everyone is,* she thought, *not really putting much mind to it.*

Ivory unloaded the car, then took it on the journey that everyone hated. Street parking was limited, and so far they had not been able to find a garage to rent.

After the end of WWII, with San Francisco's population swelling, the streets had become snarled with traffic. The City also was in need of a cash infusion in order to continue to provide services and a decent quality of life for its 125,000 new residents. The Mayor put two and two together, and the first parking meter in San Francisco was installed at Bush and Polk on August 21, 1947. God bless them all. The cost was only one cent per hour, however the parking in the Tenderloin varied from one to four hours and a parking ticket was a buck fifty. With the average wage at thirty bucks a week that was costly. The streets were snarled during peak hours, which meant finding a meter could take anywhere from ten to twenty minutes, sometimes longer. The journey that everyone hated was parking Stella's car. There were some handicapped parking spots but no permits were issued to the blind. Permits were issued to licensed drivers who could prove a limiting handicap. Driver's licenses were not issued to the blind, thus no handicap permit.

With the elevator loaded with the knickknacks Stella had brought over from their old apartment she was about to punch the up button when the voices rumbling up from the grotto snagged her curiosity. She punched down. When the door slid open she understood the tension she had been feeling since she first returned to the hotel. "Earl, what on earth?"

Earl sat at the piano, his hands crossed as he listened to the baying hounds. So far he hadn't been able to put enough of the pieces together to figure anything out. He looked annoyed and short for words, which was something that just didn't happen very often to Earl Crier.

No one noticed Stella, they were all too busy defending empty words. She went over to the piano and whispered in Earl's ear "cat got your tongue?" She then proceeded to pound the G-sharp key hard and repetitiously until everyone had shut up. She rolled her eyes and said with a tone that mothers use on children and bartenders use on belligerent drunks, "Gentlemen, that is enough." She put her finger to her lips. "Shush, do not speak unless spoken to."

Mohler looked like he was about to speak, as if being the elder gave him dispensation. Her finger moved from her lip to point. "Thaddeus, not . . . one . . . word."

"But . . ."

"Now who can explain what this is all about?"

Earl smiled, a low chuckle rising in his throat.

"Earl!" she warned him with the same tone.

She eyed each man in the room searching for the one who she would allow to speak. All eyes moved in unison. "Him."

Mohler stood, his mouth opening and closing slowly as he tried to hold back the worlds that had been shushed a moment before.

"Well, I've got an elevator full of things that need putting away, so please don't keep me waiting." Stella softened her voice and smiled. Treating grown men as if they were children rarely works and it wouldn't now. She needed to get to the heart of the problem and that usually takes a little something men don't understand—a woman's heart. "Henry, please help me out here."

"I think it best that Mr. Mohler tells you. He was there, the rest of us are only stoking second hand information." Henry's lips then grew silent as he tapped his clarinet looking to get off the hook.

"Thaddeus, you were there? Where? What is all this commotion about?"

Earl followed Stella with the same question "That's what I'd like to know- what is this all about?"

Thaddeus told Stella and Earl about the irate union boss, his threats not so idle, and his threat to close down the hotel. He had seen Yukio, Henry, and Earl playing. The union gangster, that was what he was in Thaddeus's mind, had said nothing about Les Moore. After the gangster had left Thaddeus had closed the hotel down and had come down to the Grotto to alert everyone to what had just happened. The news had brought on a verbal donnybrook, with each wanting to accept or pass the blame or visions of doom. He paused as he let out a long slow breath, the tension giving way to some hope for reason. "Guys, you can't quit, I've got—Earl and Stella—we've got everything on the line and it is all hanging on your music. Yes, I know this union gangster is going to do his best to shut this whole place down. He very well may beat us into the ground. That we know that he is coming is a point in our favor. I sure as hell will not unlock the front door and roll out the red carpet for him."

Thaddeus almost laughed at what he was about to say. It had only been a few days ago that he had been called a bigot. It had taken some soul searching for him to admit it to himself. "Les, you are the brightest light in this room. I don't care if you're black, yellow, or come with stripes, God has gifted you with a talent everyone in the room wishes they had. We need you. I know you don't know us from a barn yard of white chicken farmers . . . damn it, we need you." He looked around the room, catching Henry and Yukio's smiles. "Nobody here but us chickens."

"He's right, son, we do need you." Earl said. "Stella and me, we've bitten off a bit more than we can chew here. Each of these other guys has a good reason for why they're here, and why they'll fight to stay. Henry, am I right?"

Henry nodded as he put a reassuring hand on Yukio's shoulder.

"You...you bet, Mr. C," Stub said. "I'm not lea...leaving here, even under the threat of a l...loaded gun." Stub had been shot twice back at the old bar, when a neurotic former medical orderly from the Veteran's Hospital had come to settle accounts with Stella.

The elevator delivered Ivory too late to hear much of the substance of the problem. He did not know it but this crisis was exactly what he needed. He was desperate to feel of value, to earn his keep. He was one ex-marine who would never step down if Earl and Stella were threatened—and now they were.

Earl wished he could see Les Moore's face and look into the

man's eyes to get a read on what he was thinking. He did not want to ask the question because he was afraid of the answer. Les Moore had no reason to stay, not with this type of trouble coming down on their heads. "Anyone have any ideas?"

Each looked at the other.

Thaddeus gave Ivory a short whispered description of the situation.

"From here on in, nobody leaves this building without me at their side." Ivory said. "You need me? I'll be camped out in the front lobby. No one comes in without me checking them out first."

Stella listened. Putting the hotel under martial law wasn't going to change anything. If the union was determined to shut them down, one ex-marine guarding their front gate would not stop them.

Henry, Yukio, Katie, his wife and baby Jack, and Brother Matt were Japanese American, working and living in a part of San Francisco that still had not forgiven them for the war against Japan. There was no doubt they would be used to rally the angst of the union bullies.

Stub still had not healed from his wounds and she doubted very much if he could be of much use in a fight. That the union might resort to rough tactics if needed, she had no misconceptions.

Ivory was more likely to start more trouble than he could stop.

Thaddeus Mohler was a gentleman, not a boxer. He was getting up there in age and she had noticed that the stairs were beginning to make him huff and puff more than he ought to.

When it came to handling trouble, Earl had amazed her more than once. His face had once been splashed all over the newspapers when he had stood up to an armed gang, intent on beating Henry and Gibby to death. He had found a gun behind the bar and taken out two of the hoodlums. The paper had declared that the remaining hoodlums had gotten off lucky because Earl was blind. He had shown uncommon courage backed with a good measure of luck. She knew that there was only so much luck to go around. Until the union showed their hand there wasn't much they could do and time was not on their side.

"Earl's right," she said. "Les, we do need you. There is nothing here to hold you except for a little free room and board and our friendship, whatever that might be worth to you." She leaned forward putting her arms around Earl's neck affectionately. "Closing the upstairs bar and moving everything down here is the right thing to do, for now. Locking the hotel down is also the right thing to do for now. Going over to the Fillmore with Les to find a few more musicians who just might want to take a risk to open this place up to good jazz, and more opportunities for musicians of color is the right thing to do; only we can't wait until next week or the week after that. People all across this country are beginning to appreciate bebop and jazz. San Francisco is beginning to be recognized as the jazz center this side of the Mississippi. The sound is coming from the Fillmore and it is more black than white.

There are a lot of white people who are willing to step over the color barrier because they like what they hear. We have got to throw caution to the wind and reach out to the Fillmore this afternoon—now. We can stand down this union if we can make a large enough spectacle of ourselves. Grab some headlines that will shake things up a bit."

"What you are saying is that this here battle between the union and you all has to become an attack by this here so call musician's union on music itself." Les said it and that was the turning point." I've never been down to the Fillmore, but I've got a hunch that there are more than a few black musicians that breathe the same air as I do- as you do, Mr. C." He pointed. "Henry, you once said that I've got balls". His eyes dipped shyly at Stella. "If you would pardon me for saying so, what good is they if you don't use 'em."

Stella felt Earl's shoulders brace. Once this idea was out on the table she knew that he would agree that it needed to happen today. There was no time for procrastination. It would be a mistake to give the union another minute to figure out their plan of attack. The tension that rose in Earl's shoulders was there because he was terrified of leaving the hotel. He hadn't left the little piano bar and apartment they had for months. The move to the hotel had been traumatic, and he hadn't stepped out of the hotel since the first moment they had met Thaddeus Mohler at the front doors.

Les saw the pained expression on Earl's face which added one more question to his growing pile. It just didn't figure. He had given the man what he wanted.

Instead of happy, the man looked as if he was adrift in a sinking boat with no life jacket. "What gives?" He asked Henry in a low voice.

"Earl is afraid of the great outdoors," Henry answered in a clear voice. He made no pretext about Earl's paranoid behavior. "Earl is in control here because he knows how many steps there are between one place and another; what obstacles are in his way. One step out that door is where he loses that self-control and confidence that attracts all of us, and it scares the hell out of him.

"Gives a guy some cause to think," Les said as he tried to put himself in Earl's shoes. "Still, it's worth a try."

Stella squeezed Earl's shoulders. "What was that?" she asked Les.

"I said, it's worth a try."

There was some good news, Ivory had found a monthly parking garage with a vacancy just two blocks away.

FOURTEEN

LOOKING FOR A FIGHT

"IF YOU ARE LATE ONE MORE TIME YOU MIGHT AS WELL JOIN the janitor's union because your name won't be worth shit to me." Frank Cambria snarled, which was his usual greeting to Al Louis.

Al nodded as if he heard and gave a damn. He heard it alright, every morning since the first day he got the job. After a while he just nodded, not hearing one word the tyrant snarled. If Cambria really wanted to fire him he would have done so a long time ago. The truth was that Cambria had a big bark, but didn't like to get his hands dirty, the dirty work was Al's job.

Cambria knew Al Louis wasn't listening. If he was in his shoes he'd have shut it out a long time ago too. Bitching at Al Louis was a habit, just like smoking, you started your day with a cigarette, and you started your day with a few choice words for Al. It felt good. "Sometimes, I think the only reason I keep you around is so that I can practice being an asshole. Today started out as a sweet day. I rolled out of bed, had a good cup of coffee, a regular Mr. Merry Sunshine. I get to the office and I find a dozen problems with their ass ends hanging out to dry, and they all point back to you. Why the hell didn't you return my call?"

There it was, a word out of the norm—call. Somehow or other, Al always managed to pick up on those words that hinted that here a response was necessary. "Call? I've been out in the field all morning, boss." He tossed a handful of rolled dollar bills, each rubber banded with handwritten notes on Cambria's desk. I collected four delinquent accounts from joints in the Mission, and one in Pacific Heights.

"I tracked down a fraudulent claim on the Widow and Orphan's Fund. The bank thought we had authorized a fifty buck monthly check to a widow by the name of Alice Godwin. You remember Bobby Godwin, a piano player who had no left thumb? It was a kick to watch that man play. Well, he up and died about two months ago. He fell and split his head open after drinking one too many at Barney's Place, down on the wharf. His dues were paid to date so his widow made a claim on the fund. Only, she kicked him out of the house six months prior telling him to never come back. Neighbors witnessed that. It was a common law marriage and they were not together at the time of his death. No benefits, case closed. It wouldn't look right for the union to go after the widow for the fifty bucks she already got. I saw to it that the bank made good on it, seeing that they hadn't checked into the validity of the claim the way they should have."

"And the unfortunate widow Godwin?" Cambria asked, as if he cared.

Al shrugged his shoulders. "Bobby never saved a dime, pissed it all away drinking himself into an early grave. He was a piano player, without a piano, so she didn't even have the goods to hawk to cover the funeral costs. We let her keep the fifty."

"That is what makes the union special Al; we care. If something unfortunate happens to one of our members we see that their loved ones are taken care of. It is a sad day . . . a sad day indeed I tell you, when a union member betrays the trust of a loving wife leaving her in the breach like that. Tisk . . . tisk. Make a note at the next union meeting to pass the hat and we'll see if the members can help out a little. On second thought, pass the hat, but put the money in the Widow and Orphan's Fund for some poor dear who someday may need it."

"What?' He could tell by the expression on Louis' face that the man had something to say, but was holding back.

Al had been waiting for the right moment to tell him about the Honeysuckle Rose Hotel. Cambria was always looking for a good fight and this could be one. Al was wary because sometimes Cambria liked to take a punch or two at him before making up his mind. "A couple of days ago, at the Top of the Mark, I told you about the old Alexander Hotel putting on a show without union sanction. Well, I went back there earlier this afternoon. The Hotel Alexander has changed ownership and is now called the Honeysuckle Rose Hotel, only it ain't a legit hotel. The desk guy told me that the new management is turning the place into a private boarding house for musicians, it's a pretty slick way of waltzing around everyone needing a union card. The other night there was a combo playing with a blind piano player and two Japs, one on a bass, the other playing clarinet. The old guy at the desk says 'no way', and that the lounge is closed. But, I know what I saw, and this afternoon I spotted me one of the Japs."

"Japs," Cambria said incredulously. "Two, you say? This so called boarding house, the Honeysuckle Rose, is located where? The piano player, what color is he?"

"The piano player is white and knows his way around a key board. Remember back around twenty years ago there was a hot Speakeasy down in the Tenderloin. It had a basement casino and a stage big enough for a sixteen piece orchestra."

"I do, been there a few times, always got lucky in the casino. Of course, between you and me, that was their way of adding a little sugar to their dealings with the union. That was in the Hotel Alexander. Now you say, it's called the Honeysuckle Rose?"

"That's right."

"And you can bet your ass their lounge isn't closed. They're smart; they've got the street level lounge closed to discourage curious eyes. But downstairs, in that old casino they're setting up for something big, and you can bet they don't want the union snooping around. Well, we'll see about that. Al, get a couple of the boys and we'll run over there and have a nice friendly chat."

FIFTEEN

FOUR IMPERFECT SOULS

NO ONE WANTED TO BE LEFT BEHIND, EXCEPT EARL.

Earl knew that if he did not go with Les to the Fillmore they were chancing everything to luck. Hell, they were anyway. Still, he was scared to death of venturing out into that big black unknown. His heart and his mind were in the right place, but his feet wouldn't budge.

Stella tried everything she knew—short of drugs—to get Earl out of his paralysis. Drugs would not have helped; he needed to be in top form once in the Fillmore. If he wasn't, then Les Moore became a solo act.

Finally it was Matt, who came up with the solution. In his duties cleaning the hotel, he had ventured into almost every nook and cranny. In a third floor storage room he had seen a well-worn wheelchair. He left without anyone noticing, found it, and brought it down, no one the wiser until he wheeled it off the elevator.

"Yes," Henry said when he first saw this simple solution to their dilemma. If Earl's legs were frozen in place for fear of venturing out into the unknown then they would just have to give him a lift.

Who would make the trip and who wouldn't was now the big question. Naturally, Earl would not go without Stella, so that was two. Without Les, there was no reason to make the trip. Henry must come because he wasn't white. Someone needed to accompany Les, should they not be able to find a piano, and he had become a vocal apostle for Earl's vision. Henry wanted Yukio to come, but after a short discussion it was agreed that his bass playing would only slow everyone down. Ivory wanted to come in case there was trouble.

Everyone thought the team was set when Thaddeus' question caused the makeup to come under question. "Les," Thaddeus asked, "what do you think the first impression will be when you walk into an all-black club accompanied by a Nisei, a white woman, and a blind white man in a wheelchair?"

Les played the first few bars of 'The St. Louis Blues', each note breathtaking with a titillating original bebop flare to it. The bold character of those few notes a reminder of where they were going. "At first glance no one is going to see Henry, not until he picks up his clarinet. They're going to see you, Mr. C, then Stella, and wonder why this nigger isn't pushing that chair of yours. I can't speak for the folks over there in the Fillmore. I've never been there, but back home, they'd just see the white man and his woman and smile politely till you've done had your say, and nod politely as you leave. When it comes time to have our say, we had better say it good. We got one chance to say it right. If need be, I s'pose I can do the talking, but I'm still the new boy in the room who brought white people into where they don't belong."

"I see," Mohler sighed. "Then perhaps if it were just you."

That was the one thing Earl did not want to happen. He tried to rise from his chair, but his nerves wouldn't let him untangle his legs to get a footing.

"Les, the night you first came here, you wanted to turn and run didn't you?" Stella asked.

"Yes, ma'am; I had to get off the street. I'd been told that colored folks were not allowed on the east side of Van Ness Avenue. The only thing I knew was I hadn't crossed Van Ness, so I was in the wrong place. I seen this cracker who strutted trouble, his eyes was looking first one place than another to share some grief with some unlucky soul. I was just passing through and didn't want no trouble, so I ducked in here hoping to find a dark shadow to catch my breath. I did not plan on staying'. You know I tried to leave." He glanced at Ivory who still made him feel other than welcome.

"What happens inside the Honeysuckle Rose Hotel," he pronounced the name of the hotel as if it were a sweet cool drink on a hot windless day, "is something special. Out there on the street I'd best walk quickly, keep my eyes down, and hope I'm not seen. Henry, Yukio, you all knows what I'm talking about. This place is about the music, you can taste it in the air. This place has heart and it feels right fine. Maybe this is what we all fought for in the war, the right to feel this way."

"Amen," someone said. It didn't matter who because they all were thinking it.

"What if Stub was to come with us?" Stella interrupted. "What if he was our spokesman?"

Earl squeezed Stella's hand, the squeeze asking: *What are you doing?*

Les brought his trombone up and let it speak for him. It was the Alice Russell tune 'Gabriel'.

Earl closed his eyes picking up the tune his voice hitting the exact notes that flowed from Les Moore's horn.

'Gabriel played

Gabriel played

Dancing soon became a way

"Hmmm . . . umm." Les brought his horn down, cocked his head, leaning with a smile towards Stub. 'Play Gabriel play.' Hmmm . . .umm. Stub, I'll bet that no one has ever told you that when you speak, those hard chosen words of yours, what comes out, is as sweet as any music that could come out of old Gabriel's horn. You've got more heart than any one white man ought to be allowed to have. Hmmm . . . umm, that's because you are beyond color, you are heart. Yes, Sir, you be our voice, your words will be as clear as Gabriel's horn. If the good people over there in the Fillmore can't hear that— we be talking to the wrong people."

Earl sighed.

Stella felt a little light on her feet.

"Well then, there you have it, four imperfect souls out to save the world, one song at a time," Henry said.

"Stub, are you in?" Thaddeus asked.

It was Stella who spoke next. "Four imperfect souls," she said, " a blind man, a Nisei, a black man, and a gentle white man who's words come from the heart when he can manage to find them. What better ambassadors could we have for our Rose."

"Fo … four im… imperfect souls." His eyes glistening, Stub nodded that he was.

"That we are," Les said. "That we are."

"Earl, sweetheart," Stella said, "I'm staying here." Her voice indicated that the decision was made. I'm afraid that this time I do not qualify as an imperfect soul. I'm a woman, and a white one who just might upset the applecart." She backed away from the wheelchair motioning for Stub to take her place. "Stub, you're driving."

The up button on the elevator was pushed.

The four imperfect souls rose to the challenge. They felt close, united by their faith in Earl and his majestic dream, their music, and the knowledge that they were at risk. Nobody wanted to lose their home. The Honeysuckle Rose Hotel was a better place than most of them had ever been in or might wish for.

The elevator door closed leaving Stella, Thaddeus, Matt, Yukio, and Ivory waiting in a pregnant stillness that was as deep and wide as autumn's ending.

"Four imperfect souls," Yukio said, breaking the silence.

"I wonder what that makes the rest of us?"

Stella giggled. "Whatever it is, we have some work to do." With uncertainty guiding them, it was agreed that for the time being they would button down the hotel. The devil, disguised as a union boss, promised to return. When he did they just didn't know if it would be him alone digging for more information, or a gang of thugs looking to pass on a rougher warning. San Francisco had long been a union town, with an equally long history of corruption and violence.

Now that their paranoid positions were agreed upon they quit clock watching and waited for Stub and company to return. Thaddeus Mohler would hold down the front desk, the lobby door locked. Yukio would hold down the fort out back by the alley service door. Matt would tend to the housekeeping always vigilant to the windows, the fire escapes, and the streets below for any signs of trouble.

Ivory took on a roving patrol, backing up Yukio and Thaddeus while occasionally venturing out onto the street to test the air for trouble. He would put out the word to neighboring restaurants and bars that the musician's union was looking to put the squeeze on the neighborhood. The race issue was going to be difficult and it would be helpful to know who next door 'were friends and who were foe'.

Stella went up to visit Katie, Yukio's wife. Stella had not yet taken any time to get to know her. Regardless of cultural differences they were both female and perhaps there could be that special kind of sisterhood she could not find with men.

Sixteen

The Devil Comes Knocking

THADDEUS YAWNED FROM HIS CHAIR BEHIND THE registration counter. He did not read much and reading 'Gone with the Wind' was boring and laborious. He had almost reached the point of not giving a damn. Locking down the hotel was easy, nobody wanted in—except for the union guy. The phone did not ring. There were no papers to file, or bills to forward or pay. The only guests were the so called hired help. He reminded himself to have the night bell rigged to ring up in his suite. *Can't complain too much*, he told himself, *he had been the one to hand over control of his hotel to a blind piano player with a cockamamie dream.* So here he sat.

He thought about all the characters that now inhabited the hotel. The one that intrigued him the most was Ivory Burch. He had heard some of the story about what Ivory had gone through during the war. That he could even be in the same room with the Japs didn't make sense. A man who had earned as much right to hate as he had ought to be allowed to hate the bastards. It was easy to see that Ivory carried a lot of anger and pain inside. His biggest problem was that he held it there. Thaddeus did not have to be a shrink to see that Ivory had a fragile psyche ready to blow. *Speak of the devil and he shall appear.* Thaddeus chuckled as he watched Ivory prowling the hotel's lobby, closing doors and locking them.

For the time being, no music would make its way through the hallways and corridors, nor would anyone who didn't belong. Ivory had just come out of the lounge having checked each window, front and delivery doors, for security. Here and there he tapped on the wall half expecting to find a secret passage like the ones you read about in old European castles.

Thaddeus had long forgotten the secret exit door hidden behind the bar. It hadn't been used since the old Speakeasy days, and only then as an emergency exit should the cops make a raid. More than a few of the patrons were well-healed swells—politicians, bankers and such, who did not want their pictures in the paper. The ladies being escorted were likely not their wives.

Ivory had not seen the hidden door, it was masked by some movable shelves in a small room where empty booze bottles were stored until there were enough worthwhile to roll out in barrels to the back alley. That was done through the service and delivery door, not the long forgotten exit that opened up into the rear of Walt's Tobacco and Sundries, which had a rear street entrance on the next block out of sight of anyone watching the hotel. There had never been a need for a key the door being well camouflaged. If there had been, Thaddeus wouldn't have remembered where it was anyway.

"Everything secure?" he asked as Ivory closed and locked the lounge door behind him.

"A wharf rat couldn't get in," Ivory answered. "How about letting me have a front door key? I think I'll do a little reconnaissance in the neighborhood."

"I doubt that's necessary."

Ivory picked up the business card that still lay on the counter. "You see this? It says that this guy is an officer with this so called musician's union. He'll be back all right, and soon. We haven't greased his palm, so he's planning on creasing our skulls with a nice friendly iron rod. He knows that the longer he waits the more prepared we'll be." His fingers motioned for the door key.

"Have it your way. You may be right, for all we know he could be sitting across the street having a nice hot coffee, watching us right now."

Ivory turned to look through the windows to see if he could spot someone watching back. The drapes were pulled, the only view was limited to the front doors.

Thaddeus chuckled.

Ivory turned back for the key. "You say something?"

"Me? . . . No. The door is unlocked from the inside. Just ring the night bell when you want back in. I'll be right here."

There was no coffee shop across the street, it was next to the hotel. There was a small flower shop across the street, a bakery with no table service, a small Italian grocery, and an office building whose front door listed an assortment of dentists and accountants, along with a few business's whose names gave no clue as to what they did. On the same side of the street as the hotel there was Bab's Cafe, on the opposite corner, a tobacco shop. He took a moment to check out the office building where someone could be looking down at him from any one of the windows and he wouldn't be any wiser. He made a note that when he had some back up he would recon the place to see which offices looked back across the street at the hotel.

Satisfied, he decided to take a spin around the block. In particular he wanted to check out the back alley where he suspected they were the most vulnerable.

He rubbed his hands together warming them against the January chill. A hot cup of java would do just fine. The cafe looked empty except for the gal who ran the place. He fingered his pocket for change for a cup of coffee when he noticed a black sedan pull up and park half a block away and right across from the alley. The two guys who got out looked tough and mean enough to have been Marine Military Police, the type you did not want to be confronted by. From where Ivory stood in the doorway it was doubtful they could see him. The two men glanced up and down the street, crossed, and then entered the alley. He wasn't sure, but it looked like one of them was toting a tire iron.

Frank Cambria and Al Louis sat with cigars and coffee in the back of the cafe at a table farthest from the front door and away from curious eyes and ears, especially the lady running the place. Cambria knew her type, always full of sweetness and smiles, wanting to put her nose into everyone's business.

Cambria looked at his watch. "Which of the boys are you bringing in?" He asked.

"Harry the Hammer, and Dolan" Al answered, "I asked them to take a walk through the back alley before coming here."

"Good men: men who aren't afraid to knock a few heads

together." Cambria said as he warmed his hands on the coffee cup. "What, you think they can walk straight up to the front door and be let in? I've got an idea. I want you to get ahold of Val Torrence, tell him to bring his horn, and to pack a small suitcase. I want him to check into the hotel. Say that he just got in town from San Diego. He's a sax player looking for a job and a cheap room. See if he can chat them up. In the meantime, I'm going to go in and tell them who I am, ask what the hell they think they are doing, and cite a few union rules. They are expecting someone to do just that. I wouldn't want to disappoint them. If they want to get right with me, now's the time. If they want to play games, that's their mistake."

Al went to the pay phone.

"Miss, a refill here, I'll be right back, got to put a coin in the meter." Cambria noticed a door in the back that might connect with the hotel and motioned with his eyes for Al to check it out when he got off the phone. Buttoning his coat he went out the front door and headed towards the hotel. He did not concern himself with a man with a slight limp who was walking away from the cafe.

"What do you think," Harry the Hammer said as they gauged the fire escape for accessibility.

"Too high, we'll never reach it." Dolan answered.

"Harry held his hands together. "How about I give you a boost?"

"How about I give you a knuckle sandwich!" Dolan's eyes searched the alley for anything they could use. "How about next time we bring a cane, use it like a hook?"

"Still won't work." Harry pointed to the second floor landing. "There's a safety clip right up there. You've got to release the bolt before the ladder will drop."

"What do we tell the boss?"

"Nothing, we just got here." They took one more gander at the resistant fire ladder. They did not see Ivory as he crossed the alley.

Ivory did not miss where they were looking.

The night bell rang—twice more in rapid repetition.

"Hold your horses, Ivory, I've got better things to do than be a bloody doorman." Thaddeus swore as he approached the door. "Damn, what now?" He could see that it wasn't Ivory who was impatiently punching the night button. The man wore an expensive coat, looked all business, and had union written all over him. As he approached the door the man stopped punching and held a business card up to the window: Frank Cambria, President, Musician's Union.

Thaddeus opted not to open the door. It was plain to see that there was trouble breathing on his front window pane. His daddy had told him that there are occasions in life where you sneak a little trouble through the back door, but son, never invite it through the front. He wondered where Ivory was, hoping that he had not taken a longer stroll than just around the block.

"Sorry friend, I can't read that, forgot my glasses." Thaddeus said through the closed door.

The card held in his palm, Cambria slapped it against the

glass door. "It says that you are in for a world of hurt if you don't open this god-damned door and answer a few questions. The name is Cambria, Frank Cambria, and you had better remember it well. I represent the Musician's Union and . . ."

"Sorry Mac, we're not hiring any musicians, we're a boarding house not a cabaret."

Cambria read the sign in the window that said that the Honeysuckle Rose was a residence for musicians. "Fine, I represent all the musicians. I'll take a room, pay cash, how's that?"

"Sorry, we're closed for remodeling."

Cambria was about to give the door a solid kick when he heard someone whistling *The Halls of Montezuma* right behind him. He turned to find a stocky, well-muscled man who looked like a marine recruiting poster, only no uniform. He stood with his hands on his hips, legs braced for action, with a Cheshire cat smile pasted across his face. "The name is Ivory Burch and you had better remember it well. I'm the door man and valet for the Honeysuckle Rose and if you mean to cause trouble here, you're looking at it." He gave the union boss the umpire's thumb. "You're out, you've got no more business here. The man says that we aren't open. That means we are not open."

Cambria was not one to be bullied. "Is that so?" He pulled a cigar from his coat pocket, bit the tip, and then spat it on Ivory's shoe. He reached inside his coat towards his shirt pocket for a match as the pugnacious ex-marine stripped the cigar from his lips, and broke it in half.

"Did I say the smoking lamp is lit? I did not." He

pocketed one part of the cigar, dropping the second onto the sidewalk where he shredded it with his shoe. "Is that your filthy cigar littering my nice clean entryway?" His fist smashed into the left side of the union boss's face faster than Cambria could have dodged it. Cambria was knocked to the sidewalk with that one blow.

"Pick it up," meaning the shredded cigar, Ivory ordered as he brought the toe of his shoe down on Cambria's left hand, the pressure just enough to let the man know that he was the boss and not the other way around.

Cambria slowly looked up at Ivory, his eyes glistening with rage. He looked past Ivory to the street corner to see if Al might come looking. No help this time, but he had been in tougher binds.

"I said, pick it up." Ivory slid back his shoe just enough to release the hand.

Instead of scooping up the cigar, Cambria reached inside his coat pocket fingering his Derringer. "Sonny, you don't know what trouble is?"

Ivory suspected that his hand had gone into the pocket for no good reason. "Sarge, it looks like this here fellow is a slow learner." He was about to give the mysterious pocket a jarring kick.

Sarge? Cambria glanced around to see who he was talking to.

The door to the hotel opened from the inside.

A car pulled up immediately in front of the hotel. "You gents having a problem?" A police officer asked as he slid open the car door and started to step out.

"No problem, officer," Thaddeus said as he stepped out of the hotel offering a helping hand to raise the union boss from the sidewalk. "This gentleman fell and our doorman was just helping him up."

"Is that right?" The officer asked, recognizing Cambria as he struggled to his feet.

Cambria pushed his Derringer towards the back of his pocket. He brushed himself off, then rubbing his knuckles that a moment earlier had been under Ivory's shoe. He answered. "No problem, officer, like the man said, I slipped. Who would have thought a cigar could be that slippery." He touched his swollen jaw where Ivory had punched him.

"Looks like you may have hit your head, you want a ride to the hospital?"

"No thanks, I'll be fine. I'm meeting a friend at the cafe. A cup of hot java is all I need."

The police car pulled away.

Cambria rubbed his cheek then took his hat which had come off in the scuffle from the hotel manager. He placed it securely on his head, nodding at Thaddeus with the same Cheshire cat type smile Ivory had given a few moments prior. "Have a nice day—friend—your next one might be cold and in the clay."

Ivory never took his eyes of Cambria's back as he walked to the street corner and turned into the cafe. He did not have to second guess that he was about to join up with the two thugs he had seen in the alley.

"You shouldn't have punched the guy, Ivory." Thaddeus said as they entered the hotel, locking the doors behind them.

"The guy was looking for trouble, so I got in the first lick. He got off lucky, the Sarge and me . . ." That was when Ivory remembered the fire escape. "Excuse me, I think we are about to be out flanked."

Ivory hurried to the back of the hotel where he found Yukio propped comfortably on a bar stool, his back up against the wall, the chair perched on two legs, as he paged through a November, 1947 copy of Life magazine with a saucy picture of the love goddess of America, Rita Hayworth on the cover. He looked up as Ivory skidded into the room. Ivory's ability to move on his one good leg never ceased to amaze him. "What's got you in such a lather?" Yukio asked.

A five foot section of an old iron railing leaned up against the trap door of an old coal chute. Without waiting to answer Ivory grabbed it, slamming it into the brick wall three times.

"Hay, watch it." The flying rail was coming uncomfortably close. The bar stool toppled to the floor as Yukio jumped out of the way.

The railing remained intact. Ivory grabbed the barstool next, slamming it into the wall where it shattered. He pulled free two of the broken legs handing one to Yukio. "We've got two guys checking out our back door. They're big enough to be lumber jacks and ugly enough to be union thugs. A guy by the name of Cambria just paid us a visit out front. He's the union boss and he didn't come to give us free show tickets. The Sarge and I had to get rough with him. I'm pretty sure he was armed and was going for it. A cop showed up or I would have had to deck him a second time."

Ivory was talking so fast Yukio was having a hard time taking it all in. Ivory slapped the stool leg, now a weapon, against his palm. "You ready?" The bolt to the metal delivery door was pulled and the door slid open. Ivory was in a wrestlers crouch, club in a defensive position, as he almost hopped into the alley.

Yukio dropped the magazine and followed. He wasn't looking for or prepared for a fight, nor could he allow Ivory to go it alone.

The alley was deserted.

SEVENTEEN

STRUTTING AT THE FILLMORE

STUB DROVE, WITH LES MOORE AS SHOTGUN. HENRY RODE in back with Earl. Earl's fists were clinched so tight Henry was afraid he would hurt himself and not be able to play. Earl did his best to keep his cool taking in a long slow breath before he began to sing:

'There are times when trouble's shadow

seems to hover 'round our door . . .

His voice was deep and spiritual.

Suppressed in hopes that better times

are coming bye and bye.'

Les was nervous about finally making it to the Fillmore, that mythical place that had brought him clear across the country. His eyes were moist as he listened and joined in with Earl.

Better times are coming bye and bye,

The sun will chase the shadows from the sky;

Henry did the same.

"Nah . . . nah . . . knock it o . . . off, you guys." Stubs

pleaded. "How d . . . do

. . . you expect m . . . me to drah . . . drive if I'm bawling lay . . . like a bah . . . baby at a funeral."

Henry was looking out his partially opened window. Their singing had turned a few heads on the street, most—if not all—were black.

Earl spoke. "Just trying to fortify my soul, because the rest of me is scared to death. Are we at the Fillmore yet?" His voice felt and sounded dry. "I wish to hell Stella was here. Les, you recognize anything?"

"Mr. C, I've never been here. This whole neighborhood is jumping with jazz and bebop joints everywhere I look. I don't know which one to choose. I wish I had paid better attention to the porter back on the train. He sure sounded like he knew his way round."

Driving around in circles was making it worse, not better, for Earl. He needed continuity not randomness. Everyone else's uncertainty was only pushing his angst higher. Henry worried that they might have to take Earl home before they even got started. He had never seen Earl so rattled. He was one step this side of falling back into the dragon's den. He gently reached over and tried to pry Earl's clinched fists apart. They wouldn't budge.

Les glanced into the rearview mirror and saw Henry's concern. He didn't know much about Earl's inner ghosts, but he had been told they were deep and troubling. Like him, Earl lived and breathed music, so he figured it was music that was needed now, something uplifting not somber.

Les never considered himself much of a crooner, he was a

horn man. He wasn't about to try to play his trombone in a car already filled with four grown men. "Stub, he said, I just remembered a little tune my old man sang back when I was a boy. It always cracked us kids up:

'Well, if you want to see a brother made happy,

I'll tell you what to do,

Trip over to the neighbor's yard,

there take down a chicken or two,

Why you slip around a dark night,

when the chickens cannot see,

G'wine see that the bulldog's tied up,

then peek up to the tree,

For you take a pole just to knock 'em off,

then slap him like a goat,

Well if he hollers loudly,

want shove 'em up under your coat,

"Okay, now here comes the chorus. You all listen well because you're coming in the second round."

'Bake that chicken, Lord put on lots of smiles,

Oh, Lord, how I'd like to have just a piece of that

chicken pie . . .'

Henry thought he felt Earl's hands loosen just a bit.

'Well the pullets that flop their wings and crow,

When the brother passes by,

171

Seems to say that they can't be caught, and there ain't

no use for to try . . ."

Stub had a good memory for words, because words came hard fought for him he cherished the good ones. He joined Les for a second round of the chorus. Stub's stutter was better when he sang, but this song was a story told through music and his stutter was as clear as a chicken clucking.

That brought a chuckle from Earl, which brought a sigh of relief from Henry, who then rolled down the window, brought out his clarinet, adding a bit of good natured sound to 'Bake That Chicken Pie'.

Les could see in the mirror a little color come back to Earl's face. He was still white, but not as pale. Slowly, as Earl relaxed, he joined in. First softly, a timidity unusual for the showman, then his voice gathered matching the horn.

They drove around the block twice more. There were three or four jazz joints on each side of the streets. When they had laughed their fool heads off and could sing no more Earl said, "Thank you Mr. Moore, I needed that." A chuckle still echoed in his voice. "Keep the music going, for God's sakes, keep the music flowing and we will get through this day."

Henry began to play *Oh Lady Be Good.*

And it was good.

Stub didn't need to be asked. He pulled over into the nearest parking spot. All eyes were on them. They did not need to go into a jazz club to get some attention. They were making their own sound right there. Henry opened his door and stepped out onto the street. The car behind honked. The driver, deciding that there was no hurry settled in to watch the show.

A crowd gathered as Les stepped out onto the sidewalk and raised his trombone. He gave Henry a nod. And the clarinet then faded out on a long high note which quickly transitioned as Les opened up with 'Begin the Beguine'. This place was about music, every Bob, Leroy, and Harry carried an instrument. Traffic was stopped, no one honked, some folks stepping outside their cars, each wanting to see. Everyone knew someone who played, and there were a lot of good players, this was something special, the moment when some new real talent moved in. Les mesmerized them. It was his moment, while Henry added a touch of his own magic. It was Les's trombone that melted into the wind, bringing his music to the air that touched each and every one.

Earl sat in the back, his head moving to the music, everything from his shoulders down seemingly locked tight. It was a start, Stub thought as he leaned into the car to help him out. "Mr. C, don't you . . . you do th . . . this to me. I'm not abow . . . about to try to drah . . . drag you kicking and scream . . . screaming out of there. We are heh . . .here, so let's get . . . going." Keeping a tight grip on Earl's biceps, Stub coached him out of the car. "I got the whe . . . wheel cha . . . chair right here. You sit, I'll dra . . .drive."

This was the moment Earl did not want to face, stepping out into that great dark unknown. Stub kept hold telling him to just listen to the music. He did. The music was spontaneous and phenomenal. The more he listened the less intimidating whatever was out there in his black swampland became. His fingers tapped away at invisible ivories as Stub moved him slowly forward. He ached to be part of the music—he had no piano—that was what Stub was promising him—just a few more steps, a few more steps away.

God let there be a piano for Mr. C, Stub thought. He knew that if he could get Earl to a piano, any piano, the music was going to explode from him like a Yellowstone geyser, only it wasn't going to dry out for some time to come. When his paranoia of the dark got ahold of him it drug him so far down into the dark that he feared Stella thought he would never be able to find his way out. Then he would catch hold of one note of music which would multiply and rise like a multitude of exotic birds swarming towards the heavens. He would ride these notes, leaving his dark dragon behind. When he reached the surface his music would be glorious. This short trip from the hotel to the Fillmore had nearly paralyzed him, when the music came, it would not be Les Moore whose music reigned, it would be Earl whose voice would be thunderous and soul moving.

The next tune was for the ladies: *Good Morning Heartache.* The crowd grew as people left other neighborhood jazz clubs to see and hear what was going on outside The Alley Cat. Stub was the first to see it, Henry and Les were too focused on their music to see that some of the faces coming out of the jazz clubs were white. Jazz and bebop were changing the narrow-mindedness of prejudice. These people did not care what color another person was because they saw the same exotic birds that Earl did, and they were every color in the rainbow. Here it was all about the music.

Stub told Earl what he was seeing as he slowly navigated him through the crowd. When Stub whispered, his stutter almost disappeared, which worked if you could hear him. There was nothing wrong with Earl's hearing.

The nearest club was called *The Alley Cat.* At the door Stub asked if they had a piano Earl could play,. He indicated that the clarinet and the trombone players were with them.

The answer was yes.

Stub blew out a shrill whistle waving for Les and Henry to bring their music inside. "Just follow the music." Stub kept whispering to Earl. Only now the music was following them as Les rolled into 'Cherokee' with a few extra dance steps to get the crowd moving.

The Alley Cat was a small smoke filled bebop joint like most of the others in the neighborhood. There were two doors, the one they had come through, and a door that led into a small space tucked away behind some chicken wire—where the neighborhood kids could come and listen. It could seat about forty around small compact tables. There was no room for a dance floor. There was no stage, just a clear area focused around an upright piano centered against the back wall. The overhead lights were dim, small candles flickered on the tables, adding their own waxy smoke to the atmosphere. A small, rose quartz glass chandelier hung above the piano adding a touch of out of place class. The walls were covered with red velvet drapes. There was no need for a microphone, it was a cozy space where the musicians could be intimate with the audience, just the way Earl liked it. He smiled as Stub described it to the smallest detail.

A dark ivory, barrel chested black man, late forties, mostly bald, with a never ending smile beneath a thin Charlie Chaplin mustache, held the piano bench. He had stopped playing with all the attention on the street performers headed his way. He didn't mind, he was the owner of the Alley cat, and something new was always welcome. "Loyal Williams Jones," he said greeting them, "most folks call me Bud.

"Welcome to The Alley Cat. I take it one of you is looking to borrow my piano."

Earl smiled back, "and I'd be pleased to loan you mine back at my place."

"Your place?"

"The Honeysuckle Rose Hotel." Earl answered looking for the opportunity for a little show and tell.

The black pianist didn't take the bait. "I know there are some good piano-men who are blind—you are, I take it . . ."

"Blind, ohhh yeah" Earl said with a deep knowing chuckle. He tapped the hand-rail on his wheelchair. "The chair is a loaner, easier to move through crowds." Earl guessed where Loyal Williams was, rolled forward on his own, and extended his hand.

"I've heard one or two on the radio, blind musicians I mean, though most of them are not as bright and shiny as you. His laugh was gravel in a large base drum. "That makes no difference here. Here we're all gray just as long as you play."

"I think we all have something in common. When we play, we're talking about heart and soul." Earl, hungry for the piano, grew tired of the small talk. "This here is my driver, Stub Wilcox." Stub stepped forward, unable to get around Earl's chair he nodded a respectful greeting. "Plea . . . pleased ta me . . . meet you."

Loyal William Jones couldn't help but respond. "Don't this beat all. We got ourselves a blind white brute, a Japanese clarinetist, a black man who sounds like he's hell on wheels on the trombone, and another white man with funny talk. Don't tell me that you are the crooner?"

176

"No, Sir. I ca . . . can't sing a no . . . note." Stub replied. "That's Mr. C's jah . . . job."

"Mr. C?" Loyal Williams asked.

About damn time, Earl Thought. "Earl Crier."

Les Moore and Henry were half way through the bar with a crowd of admirers. "Well Mr. C, Earl, I'd best get out of your way. It looks like you and your friends are about to shake this place up a little. Here's the piano, have at it. It looks like Jessie, my partner, is going to need some help behind the bar."

Stub guided Earl to the piano bench, then tucked the wheelchair against the wall nearby. Les Moore set himself up just to the right of the piano with Henry two steps away, and one step behind. Trombone players needed some free room to work the horn. Their horns faded to a moment of silence while they collected themselves, allowing for the crowd to fill the bar to capacity, with more still in the street.

Earl tested the piano keys, then reached around to see if there was a mic. None found, he brought his hands back to the ivories, playing a little back up music as he introduced The Honeysuckle Rose Quartet.

EIGHTEEN

THE VENDETTA

HARRY AND DOLAN ENTERED THE CAFE EXPECTING TO SEE the boss. The honor of being called before Cambria was usually a mixed blessing. You did not know if you were being called before the almighty to plead for mercy, or to do his bidding for which he would bestow small favors. Being on Cambria's good side was a good thing and the reason to show up in the first place. Being on Cambria's bad side was something you wanted to avoid at all costs, and not showing up would be a big mistake. This time they knew that Cambria was pissed at some assholes at the Honeysuckle Rose Hotel. That was their bad luck and the payday for Harry and Dolan could be good.

The cafe was empty except for two waitresses working the place. Wrong place? Cambria was unforgiving on being stood-up. The menu sitting on the nearby coffee counter said it was *Bab's Place.* "Miss," Dolan hissed at the nearest waitress, "we was supposed to meet a guy about this tall,"— he held a hand up to indicate Cambria's approximate height—"forty something, on the porky side with . . ."

Harry the Hammer gave Dolan an elbow. Cambria was standing just inside the doorway. He was breathing hard and beet red angry. "Oh, crap," Harry sighed through tight lips.

Dolan gave Harry the '*I'll second that*' look as he realized that Cambria had been there long enough to overhear him being described as being porky—fat.

Al came out of the men's room. "Hey boss, I couldn't reach Val Torrence, his wife said the bum skipped town with some floozy he met at a dance hall—his whereabouts unknown." The look on Cambria's face was enough to stop a rabid dog in his tracks. He looked at Harry and Dolan who both looked like they had bitten into something rancid.

Beulah had seen this type of trouble before. She picked up the phone, afraid that this was going to turn into some kind of a gangster hit.

"Hold it lady, they're with me," Al said, holding the palms of his hands out in appeasement to the lady who was about to call the cops, and to his boss who looked like someone she ought to be calling the cops on. "Over there, guys." Al pointed towards the booth in the back of the cafe. "Boss, are you okay?"

"Do I look okay?" Cambria took a long breath and marched to the booth Harry and Dolan had been ordered to. Yes, he had heard Dolan's insult, and he would deal with that later. Right now he had more important fish to fry—deep fry.

No, boss, you look like shit, Al thought, but he knew better than to answer. He could not remember the last times he had seen his boss this angry. *Just shut up, you'll find out soon enough what—who—has lit a fire under the boss's ass. Don't give him a chance to take a bite out of yours.* He followed Cambria to the rear booth.

Beulah still held the phone, undecided if the cops were needed or not.

Ivory Burch was not a happy soldier. The enemy had just done a recon of the place. He had done his best to lock the place down but a place this big had its vulnerabilities. It was growing dark, he was working with an old man who had probably never raised a fist in self-defense in his life, and two Nisei he didn't trust. He had spent four of the most miserable years of his life as a prisoner of the slant-eyed sons-of-bitches. Now, he was supposed to forgive, forget, and soldier on with them covering his backside. He thought about Earl, Stub, Henry, and the new guy, Les Moore, the craziest crew he had ever served with.

Where was Stella? She would know what to do? Wait a minute, Stella was a smart gal, he owed her a lot, but he did not want to alarm her. It was his job as a marine to protect women folk. Only he wasn't a marine anymore, he was a one-legged, civilian, nut case barely hanging onto the edge. *Bull, once a marine, always a marine.* "Okay, Sarge, it's you and me, we've been up against worse. In China we were ordered to throw down our guns and surrender, not this time . . . not this time."

Cambria ordered a beer, which the waitress was reluctant to serve. Al, and his two minions, sat quietly and waited for Cambria to either calm down or explode. Cambria had taken the seat facing the door, forcing the other three to scrunch into the booth together leaving no elbow room for free movement. Silent and brooding, Cambria stared alternately at

180

the front door and Beulah until he finished his beer.

After about ten minutes he raised his hand with one finger pointed up ordering another beer. Once delivered, he waited until the waitress was outside of listening distance, took a sip, then slowly raised his eyebrows. "No one, no one disrespects Francis Cambria and gets away with it. No one. If a cop hadn't of come by I would have put a bullet through the son-of-a-bitch's head. Just like that."

The three men would have jumped out of their seats at the sharp snap of Cambria's fingers had they been able to move. None had an idea of what he was talking about. The good news, if there was any, was that Cambria seemed to have forgotten about the fat comment.

Al knew that when Cambria used his given birth name—Francis—a vendetta was now in place and it did not matter who got hurt, or how many, until the insult to Francis Albert Cambria had been paid for. It was old school, but that was how Cambria worked. Cambria did not care much for beer, that he was drinking a second one was ominous. Al cleared his throat, trying to time his question, not to interrupt. "Boss?"

"What?"

Al spoke without making eye contact. "What do you want us to do?"

Cambria took another sip of beer leaving one hand on his chin as he pondered the question. "What to do, that is the crux of the matter isn't it. I know what I'd like to do, but I don't care much for the food at San Quentin."

He remained silent for a long hard minute. "You said that

181

Val Torrence skipped town. All right, get ahold of Beauty, and tell him to get his ugly puss down here, sooner rather than later. Cambria glanced across the cafe at Beulah, then the front door. Satisfied that no one was eavesdropping he asked one more question of Al. "Tony Genaro, I heard he got out of prison. Last October, I hear. He still in town? It doesn't matter; wherever he is I want to see him, so you put the word out that I've got a job for him."

Al Lewis squeezed himself out of the booth. He had two phone calls to make. He still didn't know what had happened to the boss, and he wasn't about to ask. Tony Genaro was an arsonist, which caused Al to wonder again about the food at San Quentin.

NINETEEN

HOMESICK

STELLA HAD FORGOTTEN WHAT IT WAS LIKE TO BE AROUND children. She married Earl late, too late to have or to think about raising a kid of their own. Earl had an inner child that was both spontaneous and unrelenting. He had an innocence she hadn't found in any other man. Plenty of women had babies at her age, but not that many started at her age. Still, the question nagged her as a woman, had she sacrificed something that in its very essence made her a woman.

Baby Jack was all energy, all boy. She marveled at his mother's calmness in herding the little ball of curious energy.

There hadn't been much girl talk. Katie saw Stella as an employer, and a temporary one at that. She understood that her husband Yukio and Henry were like brothers. Their war experience had bound them strongly together, blood and honor a power bond. She on the other hand wanted nothing more than to return to a traditional Japanese neighborhood, family, with traditional values. Her internment had left an indelible scar that she felt deeply, though, someone like Stella, could never see it.

Katie had spent the war at Camp Topaz. Some 11,000 stunned and bewildered people were confined in the Topaz

Internment Camp in the center of Utah. She remembered the barbed wire fence and the guard towers where guns were aimed down into the camp. 'Welcome to Topaz: Jewel of the Desert,' a banner had read. Topaz was built on 20,000 acres of barren desert often plagued with mosquitoes and temperatures that soared above 105 degrees in summer and below zero in winter. The internment camp was comprised of 42 blocks. Thirty-six of those blocks used for housing were comprised of 12 barracks framed in pine and covered with tarpaper. Each barrack had cots and mattresses, a coal-burning stove, an electric light, no insulation, and no running water. Housing in the barracks was cramped and restrictive, communal, crowded, and noisy. Privacy in the barracks was nearly impossible.

Yukio, a friend of her brother Ichiro had escaped the camp by volunteering to serve in the 442nd all Nisei Division. Ichiro's squad had been on a scouting mission when their unit encountered some buildings encircled by barbed wire, near the small Bavarian town of Lager Lechfeld. Ichiro was sent back to Battalion HQ to report that they had come upon something important. A sniper made sure he never delivered that message. Later that day Yukio and Henry were among the first G.I.s to enter and liberate part of the Dachau Concentration Camp.

As the war wound down, and the interns at Camp Topaz were resettled. Yukio came to tell her parents of her brother's death. Katie and Yukio were soon married. It was her father's wish. It was also his wish that she give up her Japanese name

Kazumi and take the name Katie. In the privacy of their own home Yukio honored his wife, Kazumi, to all others she was known as Katie.

Stella tried, but could not cross that breach that Katie held onto, never allowing someone who was not of her heritage to share her heart. So, Stella wished her well as she closed the door to their room. The hotel that had echoed with so much music since the day they first arrived sounded ominously quiet. She bit her lip hoping that all was going well for her Earl. There had been no girl talk and her emotional basket was now fuller than it had been when she first had sought Katie out.

Having cleaned what needed to be cleaned, Matt returned to their shared apartment to find his brother's wife in tears. When asked, Katie responded as her parents had back at Topaz, in the spirit of shikataganai, or "It can't be helped". It had become her normalcy.

TWENTY

LADY YOU ARE BETTER THAN GOOD

LOYAL WILLIAM JONES WASN'T NEEDED BEHIND THE BAR, AT least not yet. Folks were too enamored with the music to be sidetracked ordering drinks. He had never seen the place this jammed. Folks continued to push their way through the front door. Few were drinking, most edging forward, or danced in place as Earl finished their introduction.

The crowd quieted as Les Moore raised his horn and began to play *String of Pearls.* "Will you listen to that?" Loyal said to Jessie his business partner and bartender," if one was to close his eyes you just might think that was Bobby Hackett playing.

"Nobody played it like Bobby," Jessie said, but this boy has an edge to him. He's young, given some time and the right musicians to work with he's going someplace. I can tell you this, no one in this town can hold a candle to him."

The Honeysuckle Rose Quartet played for forty short minutes. Earl sang and moved the ivories the best he had ever played. Henry had his moments, his clarinet sweet and pure, but it was Les Moore who owned the house. That is the way Earl wanted it, and it had happened just that way. His fingers tightening, his voice growing dry and tired, he intended to wind it down with his heart song – *Stella by Starlight.*

Henry and Les faded out on the last stanza to allow Earl his final solo when an attractive woman, light brown, with an hour-glassed figure, shrouded in a metaphoric glow, who looked strikingly like the newly popular Eartha Kit, sauntered through the crowd. The applause that had begun for Earl, Les, and Henry abruptly died when she plunged into *Day In, Day Out,* a rollicking jazz-infused arrangement of a Bloom-Mercer standard that had risen to the top of the charts in 1946. Immediately she had the place hooked. Surprised by her appearance the band backed her up as if she was one of their own. Her notes were insistent, they rushed and leaped, toying with the beat, moving behind it, shadowing it. She heard each note Earl played, matching her voice to perfection. The horns swung a high-speed brassy subtext. The pace was breakneck in their rush to get the thing going, the quartet and the singer nearly outrunning themselves. That they had never performed together didn't seem possible. Her voice and Les' trombone were a jazz moment few would forget.

"Oh, my . . . my . . . my, and that ladies and gentlemen is how it is done," Earl said as he brought the piano notes down, lower and slower, as the crowd roared for more.

The young lady wanted to oblige. Her bow was a graceful dance, her smile the moon in the sky. She looked at Earl urging him to give her just one more song. She hadn't realized until that moment that he was blind.

She turn to Les.

Les was too tired to blow another note. His heart had skipped a beat when she first sang. He smiled encouragingly, but he seriously needed a break.

Earl couldn't quiet the crowd.

Loyal William Jones came to their aid, raising his arms up and down. "People . . . people, I've got something to say. This has been the sweetest night we have had since The Alley Cat first opened her doors. You are going to have a story to tell when asked where you where this night." He walked over and put a welcoming hand on Earl's shoulder. "The Honeysuckle Quartet—how sweet you are. I'm told that they have never played together before a live audience."

"Not quite true," Earl added as he flushed with the attention. "Henry and I go back a ways. Ladies and gentlemen, on the clarinet Mr. Henry Akita. On the trombone, Mr. Les Moore, a new arrival to the San Francisco music scene, and God blessed us all the first moment he picked up his horn."

It took another few minutes for the applause to quiet.

"Earl, you didn't tell me about this sweet thing," Loyal continued.

"That's because I've never laid eyes on her before in my life," Earl jested. "Hmmm. Lady you're better than good." Earl turned on the piano bench in the direction he thought her to be. "What is your name?"

"Imogene," she answered with a sexy lilt that melted the room, "Imogene Wick. My daddy calls me his little songbird."

Loyal had to quiet the crowd one more time.

Squeezing down on Earl's shoulder, he begged, "How about it fellas, will you give these good folks one more chance to hear this little songbird sing?"

This was a tough one, the boys were tired, just this side of letting their music slide downhill. One always finished on a high note, never on a slippery slope.

They played one, then two more songs and no matter what the rhythm of the song, her body moved as if being guided, as if the notes were caressing her. Her voice left no doubt who owned the night.

She hadn't meant to steal the moment from Les Moore. Like Les, she was new in town, her first day looking for a gig in the Fillmore. Les and Henry's street performance had drawn her in.

When the music was done the air went out of the room.

Loyal William Jones made a point of asking Earl and The Honeysuckle Rose Quartet to come back again, that their doors were always open to them and their newly discovered songbird.

Earl puffed out his chest, he couldn't have been prouder. He had faced down his dragon, and come to this place afraid that their odd mixture would be met by hostility from a black community struggling to rise against a living bigotry that made every day hard and unjust in this golden city by the bay. Inside he knew that he had played better than he had ever played before and was so sorry that Stella had not been here to share the moment. He wasn't sure if he had Les Moore for much longer. The day had been paradoxical at best, then it had turned back full circle. He had tried to give him this moment, all tied up in a bow. Instead, he had taken a good second place to Miss Imogene Wick, who prior to a few moments ago he had never met. Now it was assumed that their show bill would display *'The Honeysuckle Rose Quartet' presents Miss Imogene Wick, San Francisco's Song Bird.* He didn't even know if she would be interested.

Earl rose from the piano seat. "Thank you Mr. Jones, Bud. We'd love to come back. But first we'd like to invite you all to our place." He picked the next Thursday night, careful not to eat into The Alley Cat's weekend traffic.

He gave the address, and then his voice dropped an octave. "I know that for many in this room the Honeysuckle Rose Hotel is east of Van Ness Avenue where people of color have not been, and are not welcome. The Honeysuckle Rose Hotel is a private residency hotel for musicians whether black, white, or any color in the rainbow, just as long as they live and breathe music, as we all do here. It doesn't matter if you're looking for your first gig or you've got the raw talent of Mr. Les Moore here. We have a large performance hall downstairs that can sit better than a hundred, maybe a hundred and fifty, if a few don't mind standing. For now our rooms are as cheap as we can make them without insulting ourselves. Because," he paused, played a four note flourish on the piano, "because, we want to prove a point. There is something wrong when Duke Ellington can play at the *Top of the Mark* or any other top hat stage east of Van Ness Avenue, but he can only get a room here in the Fillmore. Don't get me wrong, I'm sure you have nice rooms here."

"None fittin' for the Duke," someone said in the crowd.

"For years the unions in this town have made it hard for a colored man to get a fair waged job. Downtown, you can't get a job clearing tables or washing dishes."

An angry murmur swept through the room.

"Dishwashers don't earn much, but since the shipyards

closed, and the G.I.s have come home, any job is hard to find. The San Francisco Musician's Union wants to close the Honeysuckle Rose down because we are not union contracted. And our musicians aren't all white." He held one hand up as if he were inspecting it. "I never could figure that out."

Voices of support were raised promising not just a show but a rally next Thursday night.

Loyal William Jones said that he could drop by the next day to check things out. He already respected Earl for his music, this added frosting to the cake, but more importantly, he wanted to do what he could to prevent a race riot. He understood the power of the unions and didn't trust one of them, especially the musician's union.

Stub brought up Earl's wheelchair, while Henry and Les wiped the sweat from their brows and packed up their instruments.

"Earl?"

It was the song bird. Earl turned in his chair hoping against hope that she wasn't saying goodbye.

"I was looking for a boarding room when I heard these gentlemen playing out on the street. I hope you don't mind that I crashed your show. I just can't stop singing, especially when the music is good." She took a breath. "I need a room, and I heard that the Honeysuckle Rose is the best place in town for a girl like me."

"A girl, like you?" Earl asked.

"That's right. A girl a long ways from home whose looking for a singing career, if you'll have me?"

Damned if it's not raining honey . . . Earl thought.

With all the talk about trouble coming to the Honeysuckle Rose, Les hadn't been sure if he was going to stay on. He liked the feel of the Fillmore, there were people of his own kind, community, music; then again, Miss Imogene Wicks was the most all around gorgeous woman he had seen this side of Paris.

"Stub, do we have room in the car for one little song bird?'

Earl asked.

Imogene giggled at Stub's answer; she had never heard a stutter before.

"Now, don't that beat all," Loyal Williams Jones said to himself as he sat down at his own piano. "Now what the hell am I going to play that anyone will listen to after all that?" He waved to a couple of musicians he knew in the crowd. "Come on up boys, I'm going to need some help here."

TWENTY-ONE

MICHAEL BEAUTY O'DEA

MICHAEL O'DEA PARTIALLY OPENED THE DOOR TO THE CAFE, not sure if he was in the right place.

"Beauty, over here," Cambria called from the far side of the cafe. O'Dea was not a handsome man. He was barely five feet four, had large ears, and a long stretched out leprechaun like face that ended with a sharp lantern jaw. He had small pox as a boy which left his face scarred, making some places hard to shave. He was mostly bald except for an auburn patch that he greased and combed into a ludicrous quiff. Homely might be the kindest description of Michael O'Dea. When he had first shown up at the union hall the secretary taking down his information to get him his union card had just said, "Now aren't you the beauty." From that day forward few called him Mike or Michael, it was Beauty, as unkind a comment as it was meant to be.

He made more as a union thug than he did as a musician, only thing is he wasn't a thug. He wasn't big enough or strong enough to bring another man down to his knees. The union thugs usually traveled in a pack. As long as he was with them he was left alone, otherwise he was fair game. When the thugs were hitting and kicking someone, Beauty just had to look like he was getting in a few licks. It wasn't in his nature to hurt someone.

Cambria liked Beauty. He was an easy guy to manipulate. At first he had thought the guy to be a coward, so beaten down that he had no balls. After a while he learned that under the right circumstances Beauty would step over the line where other guys wouldn't. It wasn't Beauty's balls that mattered, it was that he seemed to have no conscience, a man after Cambria's own making—which showed what a poor judge of character he was. And for what Cambria had planned for the assholes at the so called Honeysuckle Rose Hotel, Beauty was just the man for the job.

With Beauty working alongside Tony Genaro, The Honeysuckle Rose was already toast. What's another tragic fire in a city that had suffered so many others?

Ivory and Yukio had gone up to the second floor and replaced the bolt that dropped the fire escape ladder with a padlock. They taped the key to the underside of a rail. The last four feet of exposed ladder that dropped down to the alley they smeared with grease they got from the elevator. If there was an emergency one could go down, but it wasn't likely that anyone was going to find a way up.

Thaddeus was more than worried about what had just happened between the union boss and Ivory Burch. His gut told him that Ivory had just made a bad situation far worse. Unions in San Francisco had a history of violence and intimidation. That Pandora's box, having just been opened gave him grave concerns for the safety of the hotel and everyone in it.

"Quiet night," Stella said as she stepped off the elevator.

"Quiet, yes, but that is not the word I might have chosen," Thaddeus answered.

"Oh, what word would you use instead?"

Before Thaddeus could answer the night bell rang, softly, a single non-urgent ring, followed a moment later by a short whisper of a bell not quite there. "I'll get it" Stella said.

Without concern for who might be on the other side, Stella unlocked and opened the door. "Hello, and welcome to the Honeysuckle Hotel. How can I help you?"

Outside, stood two women wearing raincoats and hats, though it was a cold clear night. They appeared to be in their mid-twenties, each with a suitcase in tow. One had an instrument case which appeared to be too large for her petite figure to handle easily. The other carried only her suitcase. The one who lacked the extra burden of an oversized musical instrument responded. "Hi, we read on the sign in your window that this is a private residence for musicians, we just got into town. The big hotels, where we would like to stay, are too expensive. Most of the others we've passed are frankly a little scary. We're musicians. Do you rent by the night, week, or only by the month?"

"Let's just say that we are flexible," Stella said with a bright, motherly smile. "You said that you are musicians?" She had to ask, the large instrument case not to be missed. Things being the way they are, they couldn't be too careful. She felt a little foolish, if not paranoid, but she asked.

"Oh yes, I play the piano, and Rosemary plays the cello. Rose is to try out for the San Francisco Symphony a week from tomorrow. I'm here to help keep her nerves from turning into jelly."

Stella eyed the cello case. "Oh, how delightful, I love the cello. Please come in. You said that you play the piano?" The question was loaded with, 'Who are you' and 'Please explain' to the point of being nosy.

"I'm sorry, I'm Mollie, Mollie Gabrielson, and this is Rosemary Sadowski." Mollie was a fast talker, a little breathy, a little high pitched, with a mid-western accent that only made her that more adorable. "I haven't been around a lot, I mean night clubs and that sort of thing. I've been doing mostly studio work, background music for movies, a few records, mostly classical, nothing really important, at least not yet."

The girls took a room for two weeks, at least for a start. They paid cash upfront for a room on the third floor, two twins, with their own bath. It was a bargain at twice the price. Thaddeus was ecstatic. Their first two paying customers were women musicians with classical backgrounds.

Matt understood Katie's heartbreak. He did not like the Honeysuckle Rose and its sense of isolation. The free room was the only positive thing, but if one rarely left the hotel your world shrunk down to a very small place. The promise of a small wage and tips from waiting in the bar had not materialized. He had tried his best to honor his older brother's wishes. But now, he had to speak up.

No sooner had Stella left her, then Katie had called her mother where her family now lived in Minnesota. Her father had come on the phone. At first, he was angry that she was not honoring her husband by making this call without his permission. Finally, a father's love ruled over tradition, he felt his daughter's pain, and he and his wife had not yet seen their grandson. He gave his permission for his daughter to come home, with the knowledge that Yukio and Matt had no choice but to follow. There would be an honorable place for both men on the farm where the family now lived. The money needed for their return would be forwarded to the nearest Western Union office.

Matt had come on the line telling Katie's father about the problems with the union. Matt was told to tell Yukio that they were all to leave the Honeysuckle Rose Hotel that night. They were to go to the Hokubei Hotel. The hotel provided some shelter for returning Nisei families, who still thought of San Francisco as their home.

Stella took Mollie and Rosemary up to their room.

Thaddeus hummed his favorite tune as he recounted the cash the girls had just paid. Perhaps everything is going to work out just fine, he told himself. This union stuff will fade away with no harm done.

The night bell rang again.

The bell was shrill and unexpected; however, instead of frightening him, he approached the door with an hotelier's welcoming esprit.

"It says here that you cater to musicians?" The man said as soon as he opened the door. The man's facial features startled Thaddeus and he started to close the door.

"Please sir, I've tried four other places and been told that there are no rooms. I've been on the road for four days and am bone weary." He held out a ten dollar bill to show that he had more than enough for the night. He held up his saxophone with his other hand. "If you'd like I can play you something. I don't have any other way to prove that I'm a musician except this here horn; no union card if that be what you're wanting. I just need a room for two or three days so I can rest, after that I need to get home to Lincoln, Nebraska, where my sainted mother is on death's door."

Everything about the man, the way he stood, the way he whined, his look, told Thaddeus not to trust him. He glanced back into the hotel to see if Ivory was around. He was alone and it was his decision to make. The chances that the union might send in a stooge were pretty big. If asked to bet two bits that this guy was a stooge he would bet just that. Still, the ten bucks floating just under his nose tempted him to open the castle gates. An empty hotel was an easier target for union shenanigans than a hotel full of witnesses. They had two paying guests, not exactly a full house. Maybe lady luck was sending them one or two at a time.

"I can see that you are cold hearted bastard and I won't be wanting your room after all." The man almost spat, as he turned to leave.

Thaddeus snapped the ten dollar bill from the man's hand before he had finished his insult. "Come in. I meant no insult in keeping the door barred, We've had some trouble in the neighborhood—nothing for you to be concerned about—but as the manager of this hotel I have to be careful." Thaddeus keep his pace three steps ahead of the man as he guided him towards registration. *The guy is too ugly to be a stooge,* Thaddeus thought as he charged him full rate on the room.

He had given the two women a room on the third floor, so he gave this ugly duckling a room on the second, with the bath down the hall. "Mr. O'Dea, you are in room# 209, just take the elevator down the hall up to the second floor. Your room will be to the right. There is no coffee or room service, the cafe next door opens at seven thirty in the morning."

Michael O'Dea nodded, then took himself to the elevator without another word exchanged between them. Beauty was used to people's stares. This guy's condescending attitude had gotten under his skin. He didn't know what Frank Cambria had in mind for the place; whatever it was they deserved it. The empty mail slots behind the counter which also stored the room keys showed the hotel to be mostly empty. Beauty thought that he should wait twenty minutes or so before he did a quiet look-see on each floor. Cambria especially wanted to know what was in the basement.

TWENTY- TWO

A BIG WOW . . .

FEELING A LITTLE MELANCHOLY, STELLA POURED HERSELF A brandy while she prepared herself a much needed bubble bath. The brandy was a new drink that Thaddeus had introduced to her. It did indeed warm her from the inside out on a cold San Francisco night. She had not undressed yet, the room still chilled, the tub's steam having not taken over yet.

"Damn it." That was another thing that was new: she had more of a tendency to swear at the little disappointments than she did when they were back at Stella's Starlight Lounge and their little apartment above. "Damn it," she was out of bubble bath. A hot tub without bubbles was about as much fun as flat champagne. It just didn't tickle you in the right places and get you where you wanted to go.

She reached to turn the water off when she heard a car pull noisily up in front of the hotel. She went to the steamy window and had to open it to see out, the brisk night air sending a sudden chill to her cheeks and all the way to her toes. It was her car and she had gotten there in time to see the doors fly open.

Henry was the first out of the front passenger seat. He looked up at her as if he expected her to be there and gave her a big thumbs-up. Stubs popped out of the car giving a quick wave as he hurried to help Earl out of the car. She had expected him to retrieve the wheelchair from the trunk, to her dismay he didn't. Earl planned on walking on his own two feet the rest of the way home—knowing that made her feel almost giddy.

Tall and lean, Les Moore stepped out of the car with his trombone ready. The streetlight added a soft shine to his dark ebony features. Everything reminded her of one of those great Hollywood screen moments. Les was about to let the whole neighborhood know that they had been to Rome and they had come back victorious. Stepping around the car he brought up his horn and began to play a rambunctious version of 'When The Saints Go Marching In.'

Stella clapped her hands together with unabashed joy.

She had prepared herself for Earl to return home dejected with his dreams and aspirations as broken down as this old hotel. It was hard for Earl to admit that they had bitten off more than they could chew. Now this squabble with the union threatened to bring it all down.

After leaving Katie's room it had occurred to her that like, Yukio's young wife, she and Earl were in the wrong place—perhaps with Earl's handicap their old place, small as it was, was just the right size. Her woman's heart had wanted to take in Henry, Stub, and Ivory, each broken in their own way. Her motherly instinct wanting to take care of her grown up children that had never been hers in the first place. It made her heart ache to go back on her word with these men, but her first responsibility was to the man she loved. While she had started the bath water she had been seriously thinking about telling Earl that enough is enough and they were going home to Stella's Starlight Lounge and their little nest where they had been safe and away from harm. If they didn't go now they might not ever get the chance again. Their old home was for sale, and if given the asking price they would have no choice but to let it go. The look on the men's faces told her that packing up their luggage and going home was not going to be a subject for pillow talk tonight. She missed her home and did not know if this big empty hotel could ever become one.

Oh my gosh, the bath water. She raced to the tub before the steaming water spilled over the side. She stopped the flow, but had run the water too hot, and for the time being was unable to pull the drain plug. Her jaunt back to the tub pulled her away from the window just as an adorable young negro woman got out of the car. She missed seeing her take Earl's elbow, guiding him to the front door, where Thaddeus stood clapping to the music.

Yes, sir, Thaddeus thought, *paying customers and from the sound of things Earl and company did all right over in the Fillmore. Yes, Sir everything is going to be all right.* When he first set eyes on Imogene his hands missed as he momentarily forgot how to clap. He had never thought one way or another about colored women being attractive, but this one was knock-out gorgeous.

A few of the neighbors and folks passing by gathered up and down the block to watch the small but spontaneous celebration. Many clapped along with Thaddeus—except for the four men who had stepped out of the cafe to see where the non-union sanctioned music was coming from.

Mollie threw open their window as the first notes floated up from Les' horn. "Look, Rose, it's some sort of celebration. Let's go down."

"Oh let's," Rosemary answered gleefully. "Let's jazz it up a little, this is going to be fun." She was growing weary of somber, each note in its proper place, classical music. She loved all music. Studio work had been dry and un-inspirational. She was crazy about jazz. If she had it all to do over again she would have gone against her mother and father's wishes and not gone into classical. At heart, she was a Benny Goodman kind of gal.

Mollie felt much the same way, they were both becoming bummed on Brahms.

The guys were proud as peacocks strutting their stuff. They had all hoped, but no one had dared to think how well their trip to the Fillmore might go. They had expected slippery ice, as thirsty men they got water. They hadn't walked on it, they had danced. And so they danced Mardi Gras style behind Les as they made a full circle back out onto the street, circled the car, before leaving their street stage for the warmth and welcoming embrace of the Honeysuckle Rose Hotel.

Earl had been tired when they had called it a night and packed it in at The Alley Cat. Forty minutes of intense music making, ala Les Moore, had left his fingers feeling twenty years older than when he had first sat down at the piano. It didn't dawn on him that the stress he had put on himself had added to it.

Running from the dragon takes a lot out of you.

Now, he felt rejuvenated. "Oh yeah!" Hell, he had just danced—danced—holding onto the waist of a beautiful young woman as they had gotten out of the car and danced that damned dragon back into his lair. Now that was something. "Stella," he called out as they entered the hotel hoping that she had seen . . . He took his hands off Imogene's waist; maybe that's not such a good idea.

It was late enough for Stub to leave the car where it was until morning.

Thaddeus checked the street in both directions before securing the hotel's entryway. *Maybe this will help fill a few more tables soon as we get the place open again* he thought as he pulled the front doors closed behind him—but not before he caught sight of the union boss, watching with three other men he had not seen before, standing just outside the cafe.

Following the jubilant music, Yukio and Ivory came down from upstairs where they had been working to secure all three fire escapes.

Matt had gone downstairs where he hoped to find his brother in the laundry room. The telephone call he and Katie had shared with her parents had been daunting. He was in no mood for music. For the moment there was no joy in his heart, his thoughts mired in the difficulty he faced in telling Yukio that his family would be leaving with or without him.

The only thing missing was Stella's shoes as she left the tub steaming and hurried the down button on the elevator. She was going to have to do something about this damn elevator, she thought impatiently, at times it seemed to run infuriatingly slow.

It stopped on the third floor. "What's all the excitement?" Mollie beamed as she and Rosemary boarded.

Stella was too caught up in wondering how well things had gone in the Fillmore to give them much of an answer. She had a dozen questions fluttering around her head, none willing to land where an answer might be found. "Let's go find out."

The elevator stopped again on the second floor. His was a face that could leave on first impression a woman unnerved and a little afraid, which it did with with all three women.

Like the hotel, Beauty had expected the elevator to be empty. Startled, he took a step back, the elevator's door closed stopping his exit. He did not want to be seen, his face too unforgettable. "Ah, Ladies, going down?"

His presence stopped all conversation.

The hideous man appearing so suddenly in a big old hotel like this frightened Rosemary and Mollie to the point that they had barely taken a breath as the elevator descended down to the lobby. When the door slid open at the lobby they hurried off forgetting why they had come down. They had been nervous when they first arrived in San Francisco, this was the first time they were scared.

Scared, that was exactly the way Stella felt when Elroy Hawks the maniacal intern back at the Veteran's Hospital had first met her. She had known that Elroy was evil, had stood up to him, and almost paid with her life. The man in the elevator had given her a deep chill. What was he doing here? How did he get in and what does he want? She should call the police. Why, because a man was ugly enough to give her the cold shivers? Ivory—she needed to find Ivory right away. Without making eye contact, barely uttering an audible "good evening" as she pressed by the man, she stepped off the elevator." The elevator door slid shut with the man safely on the other side. Stella let go of a low deep breath as she felt the elevator take the danger away.

The lobby was full of music, joy and celebration. Henry brought out his clarinet as Earl started filling in the vocals. She spotted Ivory and waved at him. He did not see her. She was distracted when she saw Imogene at Earl's side which caused her to forget briefly why she had just waved at Ivory. It did not occur to her that the elevator had just taken their intruder downstairs where hotel guests had no business going.

Imogene joined Earl in song as their music exploded around them.

'Come and join me in my journey,

Cause it's time that we begin;

And we'll be there for that judgment,

When the saints go marching in . . .'

"Oh, my." Stella said, "Earl what have you done now?" This she meant in a positive way. The young colored woman was gorgeous, and Stella wasn't sure if she had ever heard someone sing as beautifully as she did. Her voice next to Earl's accompanied by the trombone and clarinet brought out an agreed upon, 'Wow!' from Stella, Rosemary, and Mollie as they were all stopped in their tracks by the sound that had just lifted Earl's Honeysuckle Rose Quartet from good to a big WOW, with all capital letters.

TWENTY-THREE

LONESOME FOR A MUSICIAN'S CARESS

STELLA'S GROTTO. THE SIGN WAS SURROUNDED BY MUSICAL notes. The notes seemed to swim along the wall as if guiding him to the left. Beauty followed the notes as the elevator floor slid closed behind him. The doors to a grand ballroom were open. The lights were on, the tables were set as if they were expected to be filled at any moment. There were two bars on each side of the room, fully stocked and ready to go. Everything centered on two pianos backed by a stage which was set for a sixteen piece orchestra, most of the instruments in place.

So this is what's got Cambria so hot under the collar, Beauty thought as he let out a low whistle. He hadn't expected to find anything like this. He had to admire what they had done, with the right promotion this could easily become one of the hottest places in town. San Francisco had been jumping during the war and just before. Ever since the war ended money was tight, few had the time or money to swing and dance all night. The right place, with the right sound, could light this city up again. He scratched his head thinking: *Cambria wants to shut the place down. What a waste.*

There were three saxophones resting up against chairs on the stage. The tenor sax whispered to him that it was lonesome for a musician's caress. He had heard the sound of his own steps and was aware of the room's great acoustics. He glanced one more time around the room for prying eyes, then approached the stage with cautious steps. He picked up the saxophone, admiring it, fondling it, wanting to make music with it. This was not the time. He expected to hear the electric hiss of the elevator at any moment, the hotel's security having been told that he had come down here. Wherever he went either security or the cops were on his case, he just had that look. He was used to being thrown out of joints for no other reason than he made people uncomfortable.

The elevator had not made a sound, never-the-less, there were loud clicking steps coming from the hallway that extended beyond the elevator where there were other rooms he had yet to explore. He would be hard pressed to explain why he was down here, a saxophone not his own in hand, in a room obviously closed, and only a few minutes from when he had begged to be given a room.

There was a swinging service door just to the left of the nearest bar. He guessed that it led to a kitchen which meant there was most likely another exit. The saxophone wouldn't let him go as he made for the service door before whoever was coming could ask any unwanted questions.

Matt found the laundry room empty. There was bedding and table linen to be folded. That was his brother's job, and it hadn't been done. He waited for his brother while he folded the linen stacking them carefully on designated shelves knowing that Earl and Stella were going to have trouble finding good help. He would at least leave them with his job—Yukio's job—done.

He heard the elevator open and close at the other end of the corridor. Instead of calling out Yukio's name he decided that he would just go and see who it was.

In the lobby the celebration continued. Earl moved the celebration down to the Grotto, the risk that the union might come poking around too strong to take any chances. When his fingers weren't on the ivories he always felt a bit tongue tied. He knew there would be lots of questions. Tonight he had more to say than there were questions, much to be answered in song.

Henry followed the pied piper ready for anything.

Les wanted to show off, especially to Miss Imogene.

Imogene, ready to explode in song, could hardly contain herself.

Excitedly, Stub tried to tell Stella of their evening, his words all but lost in his enthusiasm.

Stella felt all of their joy, adding her own infectious laughter. Her smile and sparkling eyes told Rosemary and Mollie they were welcome.

Thaddeus wanted to follow the party, but couldn't leave the registration desk.

Yukio caught up with Henry as the elevator opened.

For the moment, the stranger on the elevator was all but forgotten.

Beauty quietly looked for another way out of the basement

kitchen.

Ivory stayed behind. This gave Thaddeus a way out of desk duty. "Ivory, would you mind taking over here for a while. I doubt we'll have any more registrations tonight, but until I get the night bell rewired up to my room, someone's got to be here for at least another hour."

"No problem, you go ahead and join the others, I'll stand watch here. The place is about as secure as I can make it until daylight tomorrow. "Say," Ivory continued, "isn't there some kind of an apartment on the other side of that door behind you?"

"There is, but it hasn't been used for some time. It was for the night clerk when we had one. There is a bed, everything the rooms upstairs have, a bath, even a small refrigerator," Thaddeus explained.

"Well, hells bells, don't bother to wire the night bell all the way upstairs. Leave it right here. I'll move my kit down here where me and the Sarge can do some good. Give me two minutes to go up and get my kit and I'll relieve you of duty."

Ivory's military jargon drove Thaddeus nuts, but he had to admit having Ivory down here as the full time night clerk took a lot of stress and boredom off his shoulders.

Ivory returned a few minutes later with his marine duffel bag. It looked as if he had never unpacked. Thaddeus gave Ivory instructions as to the do's and don'ts of registering a guest, and explicit orders that if there were any problems, regardless of the hour, to give him a call. Ready for some music, Thaddeus joined everyone in the Grotto.

TWENTY-FOUR

PLANS OF EVIL MEN

AL LOUIS RETURNED TO THE TABLE AFTER MAKING ONE MORE phone call. "I just got word that Tony Genaro is in the slammer in San Diego. Arson? Don't ask. This will be his third bust for arson. With his record he'll be doing hard time until he's too old to strike a match."

"Lucky for the Honeysuckle Rose," Cambria said as he tapped his fingers on the table top. "Let's call it a night while I rethink our options."

Harry the Hammer and Dolan shifted in their seats anxious to get up. Al motioned for them to hold still a moment, the boss wasn't done.

Cambria continued. "The way I see it we should take the pressure off for a few days. Let's let Beauty do his thing. Once we know who is running the show, what they're planning, and the layout of the hotel, we'll make our move. In the meantime I'm going to get ahold of a few of the other union bosses. At the right time we'll put the squeeze on them until they choke on it. If they've got any union housekeepers, waiters, bartenders, they're going to walk. No food or booze deliveries will be made, and nothing is to go from this cafe to anyone over there." He eyed Beulah, who had been keeping a stern eye on him all evening.

Cambria started to rise, he was tired and the beer alongside a slice of rutabaga pie had disagreed with him. Evidence of that had been unpleasant for the other men who could neither complain nor excuse themselves for fresh air. "Starting tomorrow," Cambria continued, "I want someone in this cafe from the moment they open until they close. Don't start nothing yet, I'll tell you when. In the meantime I want eyes and ears right here. When Beauty has what I need he'll come here looking for a cup of coffee. You pick up that phone and call me. Now get out of here and get some sleep. Harry you've got first watch tomorrow morning."

TWENTY-FIVE

An Opportunity not to be Wasted

BEAUTY WAS TRAPPED. THE SERVICE ELEVATOR TO THE kitchen was locked off on an upper floor. There had to be a stairwell that led up to the lobby lounge but he hadn't found it. The kitchen was loaded with counters, sinks, storage units, and lots of hanging pots and pans ready to clang with his slightest movement. It was damn dark and he couldn't turn on a light least he draw attention to himself. The one set of footsteps he heard had turned into a crowd. God, he hoped they weren't hungry.

With no other options he slid to the floor next to a rolling service table, cuddled the saxophone into his lap to wait it out. He wished he knew what time it was, but due to the lack of a regular gig he had pawned his watch last spring and had never found enough excess cash to buy it back.

Stella barely recognized her Earl from the beaten down man in a wheelchair he had been just a few hours prior. Now look at him, he still had a little dance left in his step as he led everyone from the elevator to his palace throne, his piano and center-piece in the grotto.

Earl played the first few bars of *Chattanooga Choo Choo*. Les' trombone slid sweetly into the forth note. Henry brought his clarinet up as Imogene brought the lyrics to life. Glenn Miller himself couldn't have been prouder if he had been right there with them.

Stella almost fell over backwards at what she was seeing.

She did not know who this charming young colored girl was, or where she came from, but her voice and Les' trombone were symbiotic and world class. The next sound took everyone by surprise. The rich rhythmic boom of a tenor bass brought it all together. It wasn't Yukio, he wasn't that good. Without being invited Rosemary had climbed on stage, picked up the old mahogany colored bass, and brought her cello playing skills and love of jazz to the party. You could tell by the way she held her notes that her classical training brought a special gift as she fingered the bass. The bass needed a little tuning, but that didn't stop her from sticking note to note, with some improvisations. This time it was Henry who struggled to keep up with the rest.

Yukio stepped back ashamed. He had nothing to offer against the rich sound that Rosemary had just brought to Stella's Grotto.

Mollie's feet danced as she stood next to Stella. There was a second piano, however her classical and studio skills did not fit here. She couldn't adapt, nor did she have the spontaneity that these musicians had. She was partially sad because she was being left out while her heart sang with joy as she watched Rosemary play.

Beauty sat up in his dark hideaway. He turned the sax, fingering the valves playing silent notes, while realizing in moments that in all his life he had never played with musicians like this. He ached to join them, if nothing else to watch and learn from some masters. It felt like the sax wanted to be played more than he did.

With a raised hand and a flourish Earl brought the Chattanooga home. "How sweet was that" He turned towards where the sound of the bass had come from. "Yukio, you surprise me—why have you been holding back?"

Stella saw Yukio bow slightly as he stepped towards the back near where his brother Matt waited. "Earl, sweetheart, our mystery bass player is a new guest. Rosemary, I'm thrilled to introduce you to my husband Earl."

Rose did a short curtsy as she plucked a few creative notes.

"Hi, Earl, I hope you didn't mind me jumping in. I just couldn't help myself."

Earl laughed.

"And who, Mr. Crier," Stella said with a slightly scolding tap—tap of her foot, "is this lovely songbird?"

"Imogene Wick. Imogene, before I get myself in trouble I'd best introduce you to the Missus, the lovely Stella Tate Crier, my wife, manager, and god-send.

"Sweetheart, we were about to pack it in at The Alley Cat, a great BeBop club we wowed in the Fillmore, when at the last moment Imogene decided that she wanted to try out."

"I'm going to guess that she did just fine" Stella said as she approached her husband with a warm hug. "And?"

"And what?" Earl quipped as he playfully played the first stanza of Three Blind Mice.

Thaddeus got off the elevator just in time to hear the story.

Earl dearly loved to show off, he was not a braggart—well maybe a little—but their evening was worthy of good-natured bragging. It took the next half an hour for Stub—with long interruptions of laughter—and Henry, to regale the room with the triumphs of the evening. As far as Earl was concerned the icing on the cake was their announcement of their forth-coming performance here at the Honeysuckle Rose this coming Thursday."

The applause no sooner ended than Earl asked: "Miss Rosemary, if you're planning on hanging around would you care to join us in rehearsal and sit in next Thursday night?

"Would I? You bet."

Henry, who had seen the hurt look on Yukio's face, quietly excused himself and headed towards the rear laundry room where he guessed Yukio and Matt had gone.

It was Thaddeus who threw a little cold water on the enthusiastic fire that was warming the room. "How many people can we expect next Thursday? How many of them might be colored, and how many white. I know you said that it was a mixed crowd at the Bebop place you were at, but we all know that this is a white neighborhood. I'm not saying it is right, lord knows I've had to do some powerful soul searching myself these last few weeks, but how are you going to get seventy—eighty—a hundred colored folks into this hotel with the Klu Klux Klan waiting for the call." Thaddeus shuffled his feet uncomfortably. "Earl, I don't want to suggest that you've bitten off more than you can chew here, but we've got to be realistic. Please don't take any offense Les, Miss Imogene, if Earl wants to make Stella's Grotto into a colored's club he is making a big mistake. Stella, I'm sorry."

"You done?" Earl asked with an angry edge to his voice.

"No," Thaddeus answered. "While you were gone we've had some visitors here at the hotel. It was the president of the San Francisco Musician's Union, and a couple of his hired thugs. They mean business and they play rough. I wouldn't open the door to him and things started to get ugly. When push came to shove Ivory knocked the union boss to the ground. If a couple of cops hadn't of come around Ivory might have bought a bullet. Now you want to add race to a fire that is already licking at our foundation, you are too late that match has already been struck."

Upstairs, Ivory bristled at the suggestion that he couldn't take care of himself. Stella saw that and for a moment she could almost see the Sarge telling him to never back down. "Oh dear." She hadn't heard about this, and if it was as bad as Thaddeus said, the thought came to her again that: *Maybe it is time to go home.*

"I see," Earl said softly. He then pounded out the first few notes of Dixie. "A fellow by the name of Loyal William Jones will be by tomorrow. He is the owner of The Alley Cat, a gifted musician, and as colored as they come. Mr. Jones understands the dilemma our invitation lends itself to. He's coming by to help us figure out how we all can have a good time without creating a third world war. So let's hold off any final decision making until we have a chance to hear what Mr. Jones has to say. That being said," Earl continued, "there are some here who have the right to vote, to say their peace on this matter. Les, what say you?"

"I could have stayed at the Fillmore and been just fine. I

didn't—still could—but I won't. The music we're making is too special, and I think that what Mr. C is trying to do is an opportunity not to be wasted, so here I be."

"Imogene, you don't need this kind of trouble. Stub here will take you back to the Fillmore anytime you say. Loyal William Jones would be more than happy to see that you are taken care of."

"Earl, you all are giving me the chance I've been waiting for. I'll take my chances right here with you." She gave Les a wink that was happily returned.

"Rosemary, pardon me for asking," Earl asked. "What color are you?"

Rosemary smiled, picked up the bow that was partner to the bass. She nodded towards Mollie who quickly stepped up to her side. "Does it matter?" Rosemary said as she positioned the bow and began to play a tear raising rendition of 'We're Coming Brother Abraham'— which Mollie sang.

'We are coming, Father Abraham, 300,000 more,

From Mississippi's winding stream and from New England's shore.

We leave our plows and workshops, our wives and children dear,

With hearts too full for utterance, with but a silent tear.

We dare not look behind us but steadfastly before.

We are coming, Father Abraham, 300,000 more!'

No one else in the room knew the song—its' message of struggle and sacrifice clear and haunting. "The verse," Mollie said, "was written in response to President Lincoln's call in

July 1862, after a series of disheartening Union defeats, for 300,000 Union volunteers to enlist for three years. The song was first performed for President Lincoln at Ford's Theater in Washington, D.C. A chorus, led by the President's flag waving son, Tad, sang "We Are Coming, Father Abraham."

Rosemary had performed it on cello before as part of a full orchestra. It sounded just fine to everyone in the room as she played it solo on bass. "What color I am isn't important," was all she had said as the room grew quiet and listened.

Beauty listened and heard it all to.

TWENTY-SIX

THE DECISION WAS NOT HIS

YUKIO'S EYES HARDENED, HIS LIPS QUIVERED SLIGHTLY AS HE first listened to his younger brother. Without exchanging more words, he went upstairs to confront Katie—his wife.

She loved her husband and had never challenged him—not until this moment. At first, moving into the hotel had been full of surprise and promise, which evaporated quickly. She had felt isolated and taken advantage of. She had been left alone with baby Jake and the hotel's housekeeping to fill her hours. She had not once stepped foot outside of the hotel. She was a stranger trapped in a strange land and her husband had not seen or felt her sorrow as they grew apart.

Yukio entered their small apartment.

At first she could not look him in his eyes, but she could not say what she had to say if she did not. Finally her small fair chin rose until she looked up at him from the chair in which she sat.

Her eyes met his. "My husband, you may stay if that is what you must do. I cannot. If I stay here I will surely wilt as a sunflower does come the shorter colder days of fall." Her breath was a soft wet sigh. "Your brother Matt, Jake and I, will all be leaving tomorrow. If you do not come you will break my heart, but your son will live and grow where the earth is green and full of promise, where the sky is blue, where the stars and the moon will humble him. He will grow up knowing his people are of Japanese blood living in a distant land where they have been promised much, and given little."

Yukio had felt his own heart slipping away from this place for some days now—something he had dared not speak about to anyone; something that he had not dared question within himself. Now his heart was heavy, a few moments prior he had been humiliated by a woman who played the bass far better than he ever would. Mr. Crier had sounded disappointed that it had not been him who had made the instrument sing. The disappointment was greater within his own heart. At first his pride had been humbled because his music was not good enough, now he felt the bitter angst of exclusion. It had been the wrong decision to follow Henry to this place. Now he was given the choice of losing his wife, child, and his honor, or breaking the promise he had made to Henry, or both.

The door to their apartment had been left open. Matt stood just outside, anxious for his brother's decision. If Yukio stayed, then Matt would care for his wife and child until their son had grown to be a man. Katie would not be his wife, but with the obligation it meant that Matt would probably never marry.

Yukio stood silent for a long heart wrenching moment. Finally he said, "My sunflower, when a precious flower is moved into the wrong type of soil which lacks something vital then it will wilt as you have said. This must not happen. Please pack our things. Now I must tell Henry that we are to leave this place."

Matt stepped aside then turned to follow his brother as Yukio went to find Henry. "No little brother, this is something I must do alone."

Henry had followed Yukio and Matt upstairs and had quietly waited by the elevator. He hadn't heard it all, but he had heard enough and his heart ached for Yukio because of the decision he had just made. He had quit medical school and returned to Stella's Starlight Lounge because his father had disowned him. He was desperately lonely for family and thought that Stella and Earl were about as close as he would ever find. The chaos and confusion that he had brought into their lives when he had asked to be taken in had uprooted everyone's lives. What Earl was trying to do with the Honeysuckle Rose Hotel was both risky and great. He was fortunate to have known Earl, for few men with his vision and greatness come along in one's life time.

Yukio was Nisei, a bond Henry could never share with Earl and Stella. He and Yukio shared much and were sometimes closer than Yukio was with his brother Matt. It was not his choice; the choice had been made for him. Henry stored his tears for another time as he steeled himself for what was to come. The music that drifted up the elevator shaft divided his emotions as he watched Yukio approach. He stepped out from the elevator and bowed to his Yukio; their bond forged in the bitter battles of war. "I have heard," he said, not yet rising from his bow. "And I am sad that you must go. I understand."

Yukio returned and held the bow. Though both were second or third generation American there were honorable Japanese traditions they would forever hold in place. "Please forgive me," Yukio asked.

"There is nothing to forgive. This place is not your home, what will happen is not your fight. You fought yours in Europe as your family waited cold and shivering in the camps, as was mine. Mr. C's struggle is the terror of his own blindness, music keeps him from giving into madness. These new people bring to him a gift of healing music that neither of us can give to him. If you will have me, I will return with you to your family's farmland and be of help wherever I can." The music drifting up through the elevator shaft made him instantly regret the words he had just spoken.

Yukio deepened his bow, then straightened, asking Henry to do the same. "You know that you are welcome."

TWENTY-SEVEN

LONELY MUSIC LATE INTO THE NIGHT

IT HAD BEEN A LONG INCREDIBLE DAY.

Rosemary, Mollie and Imogene could have played and sang all night. Henry had disappeared several hours earlier. Exhausted, Thaddeus called it a night when his argument regarding the hotel's future intertwined with a mostly colored audience got him nowhere. Finally, exhaustion closed the grotto down when Earl's exaggerated yawn told Les Moore it was alright to call it a night.

Ivory Burch had the front desk covered, it was late, everyone but Ivory followed Earl upstairs for a good night's rest.

Stella still had questions as they got into bed. Most would have to wait until morning because Earl was ready to start 'letting the sheep into the field.'

"I'm worried about Ivory," she said. "He's come so far since the Veteran's Hospital. However, he has a violent rage locked up within him and I'm afraid that to prove himself still a man he's going to do something crazy and someone is going to get hurt. He may look fit, but I don't think he has the stamina to go down that road again and come back."

"I've been thinking the same," Earl answered back with one last yawn. She reached over and gave Earl a warm lingering kiss. She suddenly sat straight up. "Oh my gosh, I forgot to tell Ivory that there was a strange man in the hotel. He was very frightening and . . ." Her tired mind shifted to another thought. "Thaddeus told me. The poor guy is as ugly as a bad Halloween mask," Thaddeus said. "He is a saxophone player. He paid full fair, and will be moving on in a couple of days. *Sax player, he said, I wonder how long he might be willing to stay; if he is any good that is?*

"Night."

Earl didn't answer, he was too busy counting sheep.

It was too late to tell Stella and Earl his decision. Henry didn't know how to say good-bye; perhaps by morning he would be able to find the words.

Beauty waited in the darkened kitchen until all was quiet, and then for what he thought was another forty minutes, just to be safe. Finally when he was certain that everyone in the hotel was quietly bedded down, he stood, found a light in a refrigerated storage room. Closing himself inside he played his newly acquired saxophone tenderly as if he were caressing a lover. His choice was *When the Angels Sing.* The music came from his heart, and it felt good. The people he had heard just on the other side of the kitchen doors lived and breathed music—the way he yearned to—but had never been allowed— always the loner and that reality was part of his musical character. This night had troubled him to his soul as he wrestled with the evil deed he had been sent here to do.

No sense taking risks I don't have to, he thought as he pushed open the kitchen doors. The ballroom they called Stella's Grotto was as dark as the kitchen had been. He hesitated for a short second as he passed the orchestra's stage. He kept the saxophone, telling himself that he would sneak down his old one and replace it in the morning.

The stairwell lit, he quietly retreated to his room. He had a full report and then some to give boss Cambria, enough to get a bonus if Cambria was in a generous mood. He choked on that thought as he remembered a story he had heard at the orphanage. It came from Dante's Inferno. *Still journeying toward the center of the Ninth Circle of Hell, Dante become aware of a great shape in the distance, hidden by the fog. Right under his feet, however, he notices sinners completely covered in ice, sometimes several feet deep, contorted into various positions. These souls constitute the most evil of all sinners—the Traitors to their Benefactors. Their part of Hell, the Fourth Ring of the Ninth Circle, is called Judecca. Was he walking in Judah's ancient footprints? NO, he almost screamed. Cambria is not a benefactor, he is not paying me out of kindness, love, or caring anything for my wellbeing. He will pay me a token to help him plot against these people who have done me no harm. People who I have come to admire because of the beauty they bring to the world.* These thoughts troubled Beauty as few thoughts had before.

When he reached his room he set the saxophone down on the bed next to where he would sleep, took off his shoes and socks, and laid down. Sleep did not find him, nor he it. His thoughts fell back to the Grotto, the people and their music.

With his looks he doubted that they would ever accept him as part of their musical family. His conscience bothered him. He had almost forgotten what that felt like.

The hotel was as quiet as an Egyptian tomb. Exhausted and bleary-eyed Ivory did one last security check of the premises. All doors were locked, the fire escape windows on all floors secure. From the outside it did not appear that any of the ladders had been tampered with. Having gone through the hotel floor by floor he took the elevator down from the fifth floor. *Strange,* he thought, *everyone had turned in for the night.* The elevator stopped at the lobby level, where he got off. He almost reached his room behind the registration desk when he thought he was hearing a saxophone. No one here plays one that I know of. He turned back to the elevator and pressed the down button.

The stairwell door closed behind Beauty as the elevator descended.

Stella's Grotto was dark and oddly quiet. There was something not quite right about the place when there wasn't any music. Excusing the thought that he had heard a saxophone in his tired state, Ivory called it a night.

TWENTY—EIGHT

HARD DEPARTURE

As usual Earl slept only a few hours, then, careful not to wake Stella, he dressed and took the elevator down to the Grotto where he planned on playing some serious thinking music. Two thoughts were on the top of his list of concerns— Stella's worry about Ivory, and how to beat the union boss at his own game. For the moment he didn't fret about the race issue that was brewing around the Honeysuckle Rose. The show next Thursday was too far away. He also wanted to hear Loyal William's take on it.

Around six in the morning he went up to the lobby where he knew there was a phone. There was one downstairs, however, he did not know where it was located which made it useless for him. He found the zero and dialed the operator. "Hello, operator I'd like to place a call to a Sam Newman, he lives here in San Francisco." There were three he was told, he narrowed it down to the Sam Newman that lived in the Sunset District remembering that Sam had said something about that. Earl had heard that Sam had retired.

Officer Sam Newman, San Francisco Police Department, had been the first officer on scene after a racist gang had nearly beaten Henry and Gibby to death back at Adam's Place. He had arrived in time to hear the two shots Earl had fired. The first had killed Louis Stark, the leader of the gang of thugs. The second shot Earl took out a second thug that had gotten within striking distance of Earl himself. The newspaper made quite a big deal about how a blind man had shot to death two armed felons.

Earl had heard that Sam had retired.

"Hello Sam?"

Sam was groggy having been woken abruptly by the shrill ring of his phone.

"Sam this is Earl Crier."

"Who? Oh, wait a moment . . . sure, sure . . . I remember you. You're the blind pianist who took down those two armed thugs a couple of years back." Sam looked at the alarm clock, which wasn't set, no need to when you're retired. "Do you know what time it is? Never mind, what can I do for you Mr. Crier? First, you ought to know that I'm retired now and no longer carry a badge and a gun."

"You *are* retired, that is exactly what I wanted to hear," Earl said, and then explained the reason for his call and how the retired police officer might fit into the grand scheme of things.

Sam agreed to meet Earl at the Honeysuckle Rose within the hour. Sam would then escort Earl around the corner to the cafe where Earl could spell out his plan over coffee and scrambled eggs.

Earl let out a dry chuckle on that one. It would be the second time in twenty-four hours that he would have ventured out into the dragon's lair. He had not been to the cafe yet for fear of that damned dragon.

The second part of his plan he couldn't put into place without Stella's help. He would call himself a fool a million times over for even thinking of it, but what he was about to ask Stella to do, if she could, was to bring Brooks Weingarden back home. *Maybe hell just froze over*, he thought. *I swore that I would never be in the same room with that son-of-a-bitch until it did. Damn, if I don't feel a cold daft.*

He had never liked Brooks, the truth being that neither of the two blind men could stand the sight of each other. If Brooks would buy into what Earl had in mind the union boss had just lost the war before it even started—that and Sam Newman's help.

He carefully dialed the three numbers of their room to wake Stella. "Sorry to wake you love, but something earth shaking is about to happen that I thought you ought to know about. No, the hotel is not on fire, and no one has died that I know of. We've got company coming within the hour, so get dressed and come on down, and I'll paint a smile on your goddess face."

Stella had actually risen and dressed about twenty minutes prior to Earl's call. She was worried about almost everything, hard to get a good night's sleep with that much on your mind. When Earl got up to play some serious thinking music she knew that it wouldn't be long before he dropped a mountain of *what ifs* and *change* in her lap. Change was inevitable, Earl had a tendency to hurry things along. *God bless you lover man*, with that thought she was on her way down.

"Earth shaking news?" Henry asked as Earl hung up the phone.

230

"Henry, what are you doing up at this hour? Earl asked. Sam Newman had told him the time.

"I've been doing some heavy thinking and couldn't sleep," Henry answered, his heart heavy as he struggled to find the words. Finally he said: "I'll bet you a dollar to a donut that my news is more earth shaking than yours."

"You just lost a dollar son, we're going to ask Brooks to live here and be part of the party."

Henry sucked in a breath on that one. He knew how much Earl disliked Brooks. He thought that Earl would rather try to take a bite out of his dragon's tail than say a kind word to Brooks. Still it had been Brooks that had brought Stella and Earl back together again.

"Perhaps I should wait until Stella gets here," Henry said.

Earl could tell by Henry's voice that whatever news he had was grave. "Might as well spit it out, Henry. I've got the feeling that I'm the one who is about to owe you that dollar. Why don't you go ahead and get whatever is weighing on you off your chest. Stella is going to have enough on her plate as it is."

"Yukio and his family are leaving this afternoon to join their family in Minnesota. There is no changing their minds. I'm sorry Earl, but I'm going with them."

The air just went out of Earl's balloon of hope and aspiration. When Henry had come back there had been no room at the inn. His return had kicked off the first pebble rolling down the proverbial hill that became the inescapable landslide that began moving The Honeysuckle Rose towards whatever future was racing at them at a speed greater than the

231

avalanche behind it. Earl was just beginning to understand that the roller coaster ride they had all been on since the day Henry had stepped back into their lives was responsible for his inexplicable decision to face down his dragon. The invitation to the colored community to tear down the racial wall that was Van Ness Avenue, as difficult and impossible as it might be, would not have happened if Henry had not come back to Stella's Starlight Lounge and announced that he had left medical school and wanted to come home. Now he is telling us that he is leaving again, for how long? Forever?

One thing that confused Earl was that Henry had been with them at Adam's place—a sanctuary offered through the generosity of Gibby's heart—which when it gave out—had cast Earl, Stella, and Brooks, into places where it was unlikely they would ever see each other again. Now everything was coming about full circle, and damned if it wasn't dizzying.

"I can't tell you anything more than I'm sorry," Henry said, "but this is something I must do. I don't have the courage to say good-bye to Stella. Would you . . . ?"

"Not on your life," Earl answered, "because she is standing right behind you." He had heard the elevator door and knew by heart the sound of Stella's footsteps.

Henry turned. "Stella?"

Tears glistened on her checks.

"You heard?" Henry said with a remorseful catch to his voice.

"I don't understand . . . after everything . . . how can you?" Her emotions kept her from finishing what she was trying to say.

The look on her face almost brought tears to Henry's eyes; however, he held them carefully in check. Since he had graduated from high school, life had presented one rocky road after another, some of which he had to travel with bare feet - sometimes in bitter cold snow, or blistering hot sands. And each time, he'd move forward, he knew that the road ahead would not be easy. The last time he had cried had been when they had liberated the Nazis death camp. His tears had been soul wrenching bitter tears. He had promised himself that he would never cry again.

The decision to leave had been made. Now, as he looked into Stella's eyes he felt lost. Yes, he had a brother's bond with Yukio, and had given his word; but to betray Stella's love? These were two powerful bonds pulling his heart in opposite directions. To betray either left him with no honor.

Stella understood. "You don't need to say anything more right now. It must have been a very difficult decision. The best place to be in the world is in the arms of someone who will not only hold you when you are at your best, but will pick you up and hug you tight at your weakest moment. You came back to us because you had nowhere else to go and we welcomed you with open arms. You have a bond with Yukio that lives deep within your soul. I think I can understand why Yukio, especially Katie, would want to leave. Earl and I wish them well, with no hard feelings."

"Henry, you are torn between us. Someone who is worthy of your love will never put you in a situation where you feel that you must sacrifice your honor, your integrity, or your self-worth to be with them. In our hearts you will always be with us. You are family and will always be welcomed back without question or reservation."

Tears finally flowed from Henry's eyes as he returned Stella's heart-felt hug.

For once Earl was glad for his dark glasses which hid his own tears. Rarely short of words, he struggled for any worthy enough to follow what Stella had just expressed.

The night bell rang.

Henry recognized former police officer Sam Newman. With difficulty he edged away from Stella's hug. "I think I'll go and pack now. It looks like you and Earl have company."

Stella had never met Sam Newman and had no idea that he had been a police officer, or why he was here at this hour of the morning. She had also arrived a second too late to hear Earl's announcement to Henry that he wanted Brooks to come back. Her learning of Henry's leaving had caused a river of emotions—now she braced herself for a tidal wave of unpredictability.

Henry bowed. "Mr. C, thank you for everything. You build that bridge, a bridge wide enough for everyone, welcoming, and more inspiring then the mighty Golden Gate. Strangers will be drawn to you not by the lonely moan of a fog horn, but by the music you give to all of us." He then turned and walked silently back to the elevator. This time his tears flowed freely.

TWENTY-NINE

ROLLING THE DICE

STELLA HAD MADE IT AS EASY FOR HENRY TO SAY GOOD-BYE as she could—that did not make it any easier on her heart. So much was happening, at such a fast pace, it left her reeling. She was just about at the point of emotionally unraveling; that would have to wait for a more convent time. Right now, she needed to unlock and open the front door and let in Earl's next chapter of chaos and confusion, whatever that might be. She just had to keep telling herself that everything will be all right, and keep telling herself that until she believed it; just a little.

Earl followed the sound of her steps. "Sam, thanks for coming." He thought Sam had come in and extended his hand in greeting too soon to be met. Sam still stood outside the door.

Earl pulled back his hand. He wasn't about to go out the door until he was good and ready. He was never ready, but that was beside the point. "Sam, this is my lovely bride, Stella. Stella, please meet Sam Newman, formally of the San Francisco Police Department." Before his feet became mired in cement Earl knew that he either had to get moving or freeze in place. The first step was always the hardest. "I know you both have a passel of questions." He found Stella's arm, and hooked it around his so she could guide him. "First let's go next door where we can talk over coffee and flapjacks." It wasn't that easy to pull his feet out of the emotional cement he had been pouring around them—the second and third steps weren't any easier—he could feel that dragon lusting for him as each step seemed to draw it nearer.

"You sure you want to do this?" Stella asked.

Earl patted her arm affectionately. "I'm sure, once I get used to the route, I'll be fine. Ask me again sometime in 1962."

Harry the Hammer rapped forcefully on the door to Bab's Cafe a couple of minutes before they normally opened. Eva Marie, the morning girl, hadn't been on duty when Cambria and company had occupied the table in the back the evening before. If she had, she probably would not have opened the door. She regretted doing so the moment she let him in.

Harry was an intimidating man, towering in both bulk and weight as he stalked through the door taking the same table in the back of the cafe where Cambria had held court a few hours prior. "Coffee, black," he growled when she brought him a menu. This was the type of guy whose bite promised to be worse than his bark. She had been in a couple of bad relationships and knew the warning signs. After his first bark she kept a respectful distance, that and his ham-hock sized hands looked like they could break the table in two with little effort.

Stella, Earl, and Sam Newman took the first booth at the

front of the cafe. Sam noted the man in the back of the cafe as soon as they came in. A good cop, retired or not, can always smell trouble. The menu stuck in front of the guy's face blocked any further identification. Sam took the seat facing the door. The man in the back's reflection could seen in the window. He appeared to be waiting for someone as he nervously looked at the wall clock time and time again. Earl was in some sort of trouble, and that trouble just might be connected to the restless ogre sitting behind them.

"Flapjacks, bacon, scrambled eggs—wet—and coffee all around," Earl ordered. Earl had the habit of ordering for everyone the rare times they ever went out. He also talked non-stop when he was out of his comfort zone, which was anywhere away from home and his piano. Earl said: "Why waste time studying a menu, which I can't see anyway. Just tell me what the chef likes to cook and we'll start there. If it is dinner, and I can't ask the chef, I'll order the blue plate special."

Stella didn't get a change to eat out much since she and Earl married. She was familiar with the cafe's menu because she had ordered food to go more often than she liked. Their suite only had a very small, almost useless kitchen. She had never won any awards for her own cooking, and preferred not to cook. She liked a little variety in life, but drew the line on the blue plate special, especially if it was Beaulah's meat loaf. Most blue plate meat loaves were inedible; Beaulah's meat loaf stayed true to the reputation. Earl liked it? But then again, he didn't have to look at it.

Eager to break the ice Sam regaled Stella with the story of Earl's heroic stand against the thugs that had nearly cost Henry and Gibby their lives. Earl had found a gun and shot two of the four thugs dead, a remarkable feat that the newspapers had run front page highlighting his courage, heroism, ands possible Sainthood.

Beauty did not like himself much this morning, not that his self-esteem had ever been much above muddy water. When he had been asked to check into the Honeysuckle Rose Hotel and report back to boss Cambria with whatever dirt he could dig up he thought it might be an easy way to make a buck. At the time he barely had that much in his pocket. Cambria had given him twenty dollars in advance to cover the room for a couple of days with enough left over to eat a real meal.

He hadn't slept well, the voices and music that had emanated from the Grotto haunted him. He felt bad about what he was about to do, deciding he would short change Cambria the information, then get the hell out of town, and as far away as possible. Once pissed off Cambria was as unforgiving as a Sicilian vendetta.

Cambria had a long reach and how far would be far enough was becoming a troublesome question.

But, it didn't feel right ratting out the Honeysuckle Rose. While he hadn't met anyone, except for a quick howdy in the elevator to the pretty blond lady, he had felt their heart and passions in their music. If he had it to do it all over again, he should have just walked right out there and asked if he could sit in. So, here he was about to be the worst sap he had ever been—and he had played that role more often than he liked to admit.

Entering the cafe he saw Harry the Hammer holding down

a booth at the rear of the cafe. A pay phone hung on the wall right behind him. Harry nodded. Beauty nodded back. He would feed Harry a touch of truth buried in a pack of lies, hope that he bought it and passed it on to Cambria.

Sam couldn't help but notice when Beauty came in, his was not a face you soon forgot. Sam caught the mirrored reflection of Harry in the window sheen. This time he recognized the face. Over the years he had arrested Harry three or four times, nothing that stuck long enough to give him any hard time. Harry was trouble, and now that Sam was a civilian he knew to keep a respectful distance. This new guy, with the ugly dog's face, he did not know, but if he was here to meet with Harry, Sam would put him on the watch list.

Beauty saw Stella, and thought he recognized Sam. Instead of going to Harry, Beauty gave him a nod which said to hold off, then took a seat at the counter and ordered a coffee.

Sam continued the story, all the while keeping an eye on the two union boys sitting as if they didn't know each other, when he bloody well knew they did.

As Sam finished his story about Earl's heroic deeds steaming platters of food were served. Earl got down to business. "Sam, on the phone you cautioned me about playing any games with the unions, in particular the musician's union."

"And I still do. Frank Cambria, the musician union's boss is no one to mess around with. When it comes to the unions in this town Cambria is the boss of bosses. If he's not Mafia, I'd be surprised. Over the years I've known of five people who have tangled with him and been shot to death—always self-defense—never an indictment. There's no guessing how many more have been hurt or worse by his thugs." He took a bit of food, never taking his eyes of the two men who shared the cafe with them. "That being said, I like your idea and think it might work. Might. It's about time someone took Cambria down a notch or two."

"Earl?" It always seemed to Stella that she was playing catch-up when Earl got an idea in his head and acted on it. She was still trying to register Henry's leaving when he announced that they were having breakfast out with a retired cop—and the cop seems to think that Earl wants to take on the Mafia. "Earl?"

"Sweetheart", Earl said almost too loudly, "I want to make the place a popular hangout for retired cops. That is why our friend Sam is here. I want to open up the Lobby Lounge from as early in the morning as we can until as late as we can into the night. Coffee and donuts are on the house to all cops, if they're not retired so much the better. From three in the afternoon until close they can buy beer and cocktails at a discount. We'll put together a small bar menu, and either do it ourselves or get it from Bab's."

Eating and talking at the same time does not come easy for a blind man. The talking, yes—the eating takes more concentration, and the pile of napkins Stella kept at hand.

"Stella, I can read your mind. You're thinking that I'm well out of my league here taking on the union," Earl said. "The union already has us marked. Fine, so be it. If these union jokers want to bust into The Honeysuckle Rose they'll be in for a big surprise. We've got the marines guarding our front door." He chuckled. "The marines meaning a one legged marine and his deceased sergeant," he said to Sam. Legally, Sam and the rest of the retired cops can't do much. "That is exactly what I want, because these union bastards know that all it will take is one phone call to the nearest police precinct that a cop is in trouble, retired or not, and half the police force will be here."

"And?" She liked what she was hearing, it was brash, surprisingly well thought out, and two steps in front of whatever the union might have in mind. It would also take Ivory off the hook in trying to protect them singlehandedly. After a moment and a couple of bites of scrambled eggs she threw out the next curve ball. "What about picket lines?"

"Let them have at it," Earl replied. "The more they want to threaten and intimidate, the better the press. The Honeysuckle Rose is a private residence for musicians and the lounge is open for any of our guests to rehearse anytime they like. Sam and his pals get free entertainment. No union rule is broken because no one is getting paid. The fact that some of our guest musicians are colored will get some attention. The San Francisco Musician's Union is a closed shop when it comes to the coloreds. Anyone who is a registered guest here has the same right as any other musician, regardless of color, to rehearse in our lounge. The press is going to get wind of this, and ten to one someone is going to want to raise a stink. That is exactly what this guy Cambria wants, the press on his side. Only our chief resident musician will be wearing a mask and gloves—no one will be able to tell if he's black, white, or green."

Earl had to laugh aloud as he reached for and found Stella's hand "That my love, is where you come in. It's time to mend some fences. Do you think the one and only Brooks Weingarden would be willing to put bad feeling aside and become part of our Honeysuckle Rose family?" He paused for a moment, forked some egg, but not eating it as he continued. "Let's call that our sympathy play, which should get the press to come down on the union while giving us some favorable attention."

"You've got to be kidding me? Earl, have you already spoken with Brooks . . . and he agreed?" She couldn't believe it. "This can't be happening, can it?" She looked at Sam for confirmation.

Sam had not yet heard this part of the plan, and it was the first time he had even heard Brook's name. Putting musician's right there in the front windows of the hotel for all to see was inviting the union for a fight. The more he thought about it, the more he thought it might work. He even knew of a couple of retired beat cops who played a modest piano—nothing like Earl, but enough to have some fun. *Who was this Brooks character, and what bad feelings?*

Earl squeezed Stella's hand. "That my love is where I need your magic. "Go see Brooks and bring him home. We'll work it out."

Stella sipped her coffee, having now lost her appetite, and pondered what Earl had just laid down for her. Earl and Brooks never have and never will like each other—and neither will ever be whole until they can figure out how to get rid of their mutual spite. *Earl wants Brooks to headline the lobby lounge. Okay . . . if Earl will keep his act down in the Grotto. If the two of them are rarely in the same room and never have to share a piano. Maybe. She smiled a woman's smile, then said,*

"One more free hotel room, Thaddeus will love that one. All in all it just might work. Now, how do I sell Brooks?"

The next question she asked Sam. "Are you in? We can't pay a dime. We need you. It also sounds like there could be some trouble."

"Stella, the life of a retired cop is one big snooze. Some guys take on a security job so they can sleep somewhere besides their own couch. Yeah, I'm in, and I can think of a half dozen other guys who can be here by this afternoon." He eyed Harry the Hammer's reflection in the window. If looks were lethal Harry was throwing some dangerous eye daggers at the guy sitting at the counter.

"I think I know of a couple of young ladies—Rosemary and Mollie who will help out Brooks. What about your Miss Imogene?" Stella asked.

"She needs some good rehearsal time with Les and me," Earl answered.

"I don't want the union gents to see any provocative color just yet."

"Earl, this had better work." Stella gave him a smile he could feel as if it were the sun rising to warm a new spring day."

"If it doesn't, we lose everything, and I'm stuck with Brooks. He shook his head with intended humor and exasperation.

Sam still didn't know who Brooks was.

Stella just gave Sam a wink saying: "Sam, there is no way I can tell you about Brooks and do him justice. You will see soon enough." *That is if he will buy in?* She thought, then what?

Beauty—Michael O'Dea—dropped some change on the counter for the coffee and a tip. He did not look back at Harry who was staring at him with hard eyes. Instead, he stopped at the table, hat in hand, ignored both Sam and Earl the best he could. His business was with the lady.

Sam hadn't thought that the union man could overhear anything that was being said—then again Sam had his own hearing problems.

Michael O'Dea had overheard everything. "Miss, excuse me, we met briefly on the elevator yesterday. I'm staying at the hotel for a couple of days." He turned towards Sam. "You're an ex-cop, right? And I'm an ex-union creep, as of today. Frank Cambria, the union boss sent me in to find out everything I could that he could use to shut the Hotel Honeysuckle Rose down. I can't do it." He was still talking to Sam. "You see that guy at the back of the cafe. He's goes by the name Harry the Hammer, he's a union henchman, and mean as the day is long.

"I know him," Sam said.

Crap, now Harry knows I'm talking to a cop. Michael thought as he realized that there was no turning back now.

"Sit down, friend." Earl said. "I'm Earl Crier, Stella and I own the Honeysuckle Rose. I didn't catch your name?"

Sam Newman made room for one more.

"Michael O'Dea," Beauty said, "most folks just call me Beauty."

When Sam made room for Beauty, Harry got a good view

of Sam's face. Beauty was ratting them out to a cop. His fist slammed down hard enough on the table to knock over his coffee. Everyone in the cafe, including Sam, turned at the sound of sudden violence. Harry's hard eyes went lethal as he pointed a finger at Beauty. A moment later he was dropping a dime into the pay phone.

Sam motioned for the waitress's attention. "Miss, is the owner in?"

"Not for another hour," she answered, her eyes still fearfully of Harry.

"You have a right to be scared of that guy, Miss, he's bad trouble. Has he been in here before, with anyone else?"

"Beulah, she's the owner, left me a note that there were four guys here last night that took up that same table for most of the night. They looked and sounded like trouble so she told me that if they came back this morning to call the cops. I guess that's one of them, huh?"

Sam showed her his police badge. He wasn't supposed to carry it, but a lot of retired cops did. It was better than the one you could get out of a box of crackerjacks. "When Beulah comes in will you have her give me a ring, or better yet, drop over to the hotel, so we can have a chat. Those men she was concerned about are with a union that has a history of graft, violence and extortion. Word is that they are planning to do some harm to Stella and Earl here. If they make this cafe their front office there is no telling what might happen—nothing good, that's for sure."

THIRTY

ROYALLY PISSED—OFF

IT WAS TOO EARLY IN THE MORNING TO WAKE FRANK CAMBRIA. He did not drink much in public believing that one does not show one's weakness to a potential enemy. His weakness was gin and he needed to sleep off the half bottle he had consumed in the privacy of his own home as he fretted over the Honeysuckle god-damned hotel. He shouldn't have drunk the damed beer earlier, it unsettled his stomach.

Harry dropped a dime in the pay phone.

Al was used to getting the dirty call at all the wrong hours. He was the only one allowed to wake Cambria, and only then when smoke had turned to fire. He had read somewhere that on D-Day as the Allies were landing at Normandy the Generals could not move up the Panzer tanks without Hitler's direct order. No one dared wake Der Fuhrer; the rest is history. Al knew the news was bad before he picked up the phone. Good news could always wait. He got all the calls with bad news regardless of the hour because bad news was often on a slippery slope headed towards worse.

"Tell me it's good news just once. Just give me a second, Okay." Al mumbled into the phone. The silence was as dark as a rat's burrow. Al set the phone down for a moment, rubbed his eyes, looked at his watch, took a drink of water, and picked up the phone again. "Wrong number, right?"

"Al it's Harry, I've got news the boss ain't going to like."

"On a scale of one through five, five being the worst, how bad is it?"

"Seven, could be an eight."

"Crap!" Don't tell me on the phone. Are you at the Cafe? I'll be there in a few minutes."

Harry told him anyway.

Al poured a shot of whiskey in black coffee before he called Cambria. The boss would not take it well when he heard that Beauty had turned traitor. Worse, that the scum-bag traitor had ratted them out to a cop. Neither Cambria nor Lewis knew that Sam Newman was retired.

"Put the word out that I've got two hundred and fifty, no make that three hundred bucks, for the guy who brings me Beauty's pecker in a match box." Frank Cambria slammed the phone down, yanked the cord from the fall, then threw it through his open bedroom window. His temper volatile, he kept a supply of extra phones beneath his bed.

THIRTY-ONE

Help Wanted

Back at the hotel . . .

Beauty did not know much—that he had been checked into the hotel under false pretenses said it all. The big red flag that was raised was the name Tony Gennaro. Sam knew the name, he was a known arsonist, and thought it best to not tell Earl or Stella until he was certain that Gennaro had been hired to do the job. He did tell them that the discovery of Beauty meant that the threat from the union was no false promise, they are planning on something big—and soon.

A telephone call made to an arson investigator with the San Francisco Fire Department told Sam the good news—Tony Gennaro was in jail in San Diego. The bad news was that if Cambria intended for the hotel to burn they hadn't a clue as to who he might have contracted the job out to. If the Hotel Honeysuckle Rose were a navy ship at sea it just went to General Quarters.

Sam made some calls, recruiting four retired officers he trusted and had known for years. All agreed to report for duty as soon as they could get there. He also called Gavin Hoyt, a private detective he had run into professionally a time or two. Hoyt gave him an uneasy feeling. He was an enigma. He was a long time Cambria watch dog. He had also witnessed two, if not three, shootings by Cambria and acted as a witness that they had all been in self-defense. Sam had checked with the District Attorney's office and been told that they had contracted Hoyt on numerous occasions to come up with something the Grand Jury could use. Hoyt had come up empty-handed. Sam decided that if anyone could second guess Cambria it might be Detective Hoyt. He still felt uneasy, but for now Hoyt was the only leg up they had.

After a phone call from Sam, Detective Hoyt made two calls: one to his office, the other he made from a phone booth, then made a bee-line for the Honeysuckle Rose Hotel.

Stella woke Ivory. His role as chief of security had just become critical. He would become their main liaison with the cops. Ivory had a tendency to over-react. But he had been a marine, once a marine, always a marine—loyal as a home grown pit bull and would lay his life on the line to protect them.

She was grateful that Sam had stuck around, making his calls from the hotel. If something happened before they could bring in all the resources they were reaching out for they would be stretched out pretty thin. She also promised herself that as soon as she got back from convincing Brooks to leave his safe and cushy job and leap into this hornet's nest she was going to stay glued to her Earl.

Stella's next conversation was with Thaddeus. Legally he was still the General Manager of the hotel; as such he was on the top of the 'need to know' list. Thaddeus tried not to interfere with Earl. Earl did not know a thing about hoteling. The result of this mismatched management team could sometimes be humorous, and she often thought of them as a kindred to the Keystone Cops. Unlike most everyone else in the hotel Thaddeus was not an early riser. When he finally answered the phone her words were short and spoken from a dry, cotton mouth. "Thaddeus," she said, "our conflict with the union has reached critical. Are you awake?"

She could almost could hear his nod.

"Thaddeus, go to the bathroom and splash some water on your face. Take a quick cold shower, then meet Earl in the Grotto. Did you hear what I first said when you answered the phone?"

He thought about it and honestly had to say that he didn't.

"Thaddeus," she repeated, "our conflict with the union has reached a crisis point. The police have been brought in." That was a small fudge of the truth. "Now, take that cold shower and get down to the Grotto as soon as you can."

Michael O'Dea had gone to his room to get his saxophone, as well as the one he had stolen.

Earl chuckled at Michael's meek confession, then allowed him to place his old sax on the bandstand, keeping the better one, under the terms that first he had better be as good as he said he was, and second, everything that he had been telling them had better be the truth; and nothing but the truth.

Stella was surprised to find Les Moore awake.

Like her, everything had been coming at him for the last twenty-four hours faster than he could absorb it. More than once in the early morning hours he had wanted to pack his bag, cut and run. However, Earl's revolutionary vision worked as a powerful magnet. The music, well that spoke for itself. For the moment he did not understand his true motivation in staying; overtime he thought of Imogene he smiled.

After listening to Stella, and agreeing to meet at the Grotto, he called Bab's Cafe and ordered a large coffee, country fried chicken with grits, to go. No grits, he had to settle on fried potatoes.

She next called Rosemary and Mollie's room asking them if they would meet her in the lobby lounge. She did the same with Imogene. These girls were all new, it wasn't their fight, and she wanted to give them an option to leave while they still had a chance. What Earl had to say downstairs was scary, not that she wasn't already scared herself, she just hadn't had time to feel scared. Once she knew the girls were onboard she would send them down to the Grotto.

The calls made, Stella took a moment to calm her nerves and to light a cigarette. Her pack was almost empty. She had two left, by this time in the morning she normally would have gone through twice that many. This morning there just hadn't been time. She did not feel safe leaving the hotel in search of a new pack. She would hold onto her last two until she really needed one. The most difficult challenge still lay ahead; Brooks.

"Stella," Ivory asked, "I can't find Henry or Yukio. I knocked on their doors and got no answer, not even Yukio's wife."

Stella swallowed hard, wished she had taken that cigarette. "Yukio's family is homesick. They've gone to be with their family in Minnesota. Henry went with them."

"Jesus, that's great timing. Who's going to do the house keeping?" Ivory said. This was more a statement of fact rather than a question. Then it hit him. "Henry gone? Will he be coming back?" Here he wanted an answer. Ivory didn't mind the rest of the Nisei leaving. Their Japanese faces blended too closely with the faces in his nightmares. Henry's leaving caught him by surprise. The first time he and Henry had met Ivory had been thrashing in his bed caught in a horrific nightmare that returned him to one of his bleakest days as a POW. Henry had shaken him out of his nightmare. When he came back to the real world the first words he heard were '*It's only a dream son. It's only a dream.*' Henry's Nisei face had been only a few inches from his. Their friendship had been hard in coming, that there had been no goodbye created a painful emptiness.

"Come on Sarge," Ivory said as he shook off thoughts of his own loss, the words from the Marines Hymn called him to action.

'If the Army and the Navy

Ever look on Heaven's scenes,

They will find the streets are guarded

By United States Marines.'

"Come on Sarge, it looks like the squad is short one man and we are going to have to hold the CP—Command Post— on our own." Ivory went into his room behind the reservation desk, returning a moment later with a baseball bat. "Time to make the rounds."

Stella did not answer the question about Henry. How could she? "Ivory, soon as you've checked all the windows and doors, go down to the Grotto and . . . on second thought go down now, everything else can wait. Earl has some important news."

"Wait up there marine, I'll go down with you." Sam introduced himself. "Stella has told me that you are the head of security around here. I think we need to talk."

The unusual activity on the elevator woke Stub. Not one to linger in bed, he met Les going down. After Les got off at the lobby level, Stub continued on to the Grotto.

Stella dialed the phone one more time. "Hello operator, give me the Mark Hopkins Hotel, their front desk please." She couldn't remember which alias Brooks was using. He had taken the name of some Hollywood big shot, who had died in a car accident in order to trick the Mark Hopkins into a room with some perks. He had no money and made a deal playing the piano in their happy hour lounge in exchange for a room. The alias he had taken was too well known so, he told them he wanted to protect his privacy, and ran with a second alias, or was it a third. Stella could not remember, but thought it might be Otto something or other."

The hotel's desk clerk knew exactly who she wanted—Oscar Katz—and connected her to his room.

"Brooks, its Stella. How are you my dear?"

Brooks did not sound like the old Brooks she had known. That Brooks had been a whiny, debilitated alcoholic, as well as a pompous ass, who was constantly a thorn in Earl's hind side. Brooks had been born to wealth, had better looks than talent, and had spent the war as an army officer assigned to the USO. His piano playing was just a little better than his singing which wasn't that great. A Nazi VII rocket struck a favorite pub he frequented in London, taking his sight as well as most of his face. The damage to his face was so severe that he would wear a mask for the rest of his life.

Earl and Brooks had not gotten along since the first moment they met, their conflict becoming both bitter and personal. It was their mutual hatred for each other that had helped both of them accept their mutual challenges in being blind.

When Adam's Place closed Earl and Brooks had each gone their own way with no love lost. Brooks landed a job as a resident pianist at the Mark Hopkins in exchange for room and meals—which was not a bad deal since everything he presented about himself was based on lies.

Brooks, surprised and delighted by her call, listened to Stella, readily accepted her offer to pack his bags and join them at The Honeysuckle Rose—Earl Crier be damned. Brooks hadn't quite put it that way, but she could read the reflections within his voice the same as she could Earl. These two would never become bosom buddies, however, she knew that with some men, arguments ad nauseam can become an inviolate bond. Brooks had agreed too easily and she suspected that his past relationship with Earl was not going to be soon forgotten or forgiven. That was not something she could deal with over the telephone. They agreed that she would pick him up in little more than an hour. For now, what was important was that he was coming home.

For Brooks, moving back in with Earl, was not an option he could ignore. He was blind, disfigured, of modest talent at the piano, and short changed vocally. His only gift was that he could whistle—now that the scar tissue had tightened his whistling days were mostly over. What he hadn't told Stella was that he had just been fired.

When Brooks had left Adam's Place he had stepped out into the street and was nearly struck by a car. That had been his good luck. The driver, Saul Feldman, had strong guilt feeling having almost run over a blind man. Brooks had told him that he was Oscar Brandt, a famous pianist, who in truth had been killed in an automobile accident. Feldman had been a studio musician and was delighted to see that Brandt was alive. His fully bandaged face, and loss of sight, came at great surprise. Feldman had taken him to the Mark Hopkins and introduced him to the hotel's food and beverage manager. That was how Brooks got the job. After Feldman left, Brooks had told his new boss that he wanted anonymity as the former Oscar Brandt because of his disfigurement. His play bill was changed to Oscar Katz.

Better than a year had passed and Saul Feldman returned bringing with him another studio musician who had actually known Brandt. Only now Brandt was Katz, and Katz was Brooks, a down and out blind pianist no one had ever heard of. In exchange for his mediocre piano playing, he had bought himself a comfortable year where he regained some self-confidence, a little dignity, a room, three square meals, and just enough booze to keep his hands from shaking, and suicide a little farther from his thoughts. However, now discovering his fraud, the hotel had little tolerance for Brook's deceit, and was fired immediately.

If he had not been blind and disfigured Brooks would have been given only a few hours to vacate the premises. Brook's pay had been room and board, so his eviction came with his pockets empty.

Thank you Stella, I'll try to behave.

Earl was a man who found it easy to forgive other men's transgressions. Life is not perfect, and who is he to judge others—except for Brooks Weingarden, the miserable son-of-a bitch, his very presence being unforgivable.

Everyone was abuzz with empty rumors as they waited for Earl to tell them why they had all been summoned. There was a stranger in their midst that could not be ignored. First thing first, Earl put Michael O'Dea to the test by asking him to prove his heart through his music.

Beauty chose 'Cherokee,' his favorite Charlie Parker tune.

Earl understood why, when he had finished. "That was beautiful Michael. You sound as if you are one with your horn. Is that why some folks call you Beauty?"

Michael could not remember the last time he had been asked to explain his regrettable nickname.

"Your mother named you Michael, and in her heart I'm sure she saw your beauty. Unfortunately, that word has become warped. Michael is your given name. Welcome to our family, Michael," Earl said warmly.

Even though Earl could not see him, Michael had to turn away. Never had he heard such kind words. His mother had abandoned him at an orphanage with a note attached saying that his deformity was a punishment for her sins. He aged out of the orphanage, too ugly to adopt. The Good Sisters of Charity had found him an easy target frequently punishing him for his mother's sins and sins of his own makings. His saxophone become his best friend, his impassioned loneliness coming alive, hauntingly, when he played.

"I will caution you Michael, that I will share with them how you came to us. It is only fair. There will be some who will be skeptical and may view you with distrusting eyes. Your music may win their hearts, otherwise it will be up to you to earn their trust."

Les Moore hurried downstairs, passing Stella who was on the phone. He waved as he left the hotel to pick up his breakfast. He reminded himself to ask Mr. Mohler about getting the service door open between the hotel and the cafe.

Inside Les sat at the counter and sipped on coffee as they finished cooking his breakfast. Over the years he had experienced the cold feeling of having eyes drilled through his back by white men who didn't like a nigger sitting where he wasn't wanted. A black man could not sit at a white man's cafe counter, drink from the same fountain, or use the white man's toilet. The cracker seated at the rear of the cafe was drilling nails of hated right in his direction. Earl's talk about equal rights had fired him up. At the moment he had a good mind to turn right around and give the ignorant cracker a good piece of his mind.

The waitress saw what he was thinking and quickly changed his mind. "You're the new trombone player staying next door?"

He nodded that he was. "Yes, Miss, I play the trombone."

Her voice became almost a whisper. She directed Les's

attention towards the rear of the cafe with her eyes. "Earl and Stella were just in here with a cop. Don't mess with that guy, he's a henchman for the union that wants to shut the Honeysuckle Rose down. Something happened while Earl and Stella were here that really pissed him off. Believe me, if I ever saw a guy looking for a fight, that's him. Did you see the size of the arms on him?"

The morning cook rang a bell that told her that Les' order was ready to go. She got his brown bagged breakfast, charged it to the hotel as she had been told to, saying "Sugar, you've got to be careful."

Harry the Hammer rose from his table. He had seen the expression on the nigger's face in the mirror. Rumor was that there was a tall nigger staying at the hotel. He was sure the nigger had given him a belligerent look, and he had decided it was time to teach the bastard a lesson.

Eva Marie, didn't have anything against colored folk. Still, it was best if they kept to their own kind. Few ever came into the cafe, that's because they we're not allowed in the neighborhood. It wasn't a law or anything like that, it had just been that way for as long as she could remember. She had been told by Stub, who was a regular, that this one was a very talented musician, that he would most likely be famous someday. Despite him being black, she found him on the handsome side. "You had better go, and be quick about it," she cautioned as she directed his eyes to the mirror where he could see the sadistic beast coming for him."

"Can you unlock the service door between the cafe and the hotel?" He asked urgently.

"There's a key for the hotel's side, and a button just inside the kitchen to open it from in here. You push that and the door will pop right open."

The breakfast cook dinged a little bell a second time telling Eva that his breakfast was ready.

Eva quickly deliver it to him.

"I'd be obliged if you would push that button for me in about one minute." Les rose from his seat at the counter just as Harry the Hammer reached him. The enraged bully was not going to wait until Les got outside to start trouble. Les ducked as the man lunged, his clinched fist connected to an arm as large as Les' thigh. Tall and lean, Les ducked low, sidestepping the huge fist, as he spun towards the service door, but not before he threw the remains of his hot coffee into his assailant's face. Holding onto his brown bag as if it were a football he sprinted towards the back service door.

Harry the Hammer roared, momentarily blinded.

Eva Marie punched the button as the morning cook, cleaver in hand, came out to see what the trouble was.

The door popped open. Les slammed it shut a second after he had passed safely through.

The sudden opening of the service door, with Les Moore doing an abbreviated hundred yard dash, startled Stella. "What the hell?"

"That was not the word I had in mind," Les said as he checked to make sure the door was securely locked behind him. Harry hammered on the door a moment later. "When you and Earl were just over there did you see the guerrilla that was seated in the back. Well, that cracker just about took my head off for no reason . . ."

"That guerrilla is a henchman for the Union." Stella replied.

"So I am told."

"There most likely will be more like him before this day is over." She thought she could almost see his face go darker. "Don't worry, we're bringing in the cavalry. Earl will explain everything downstairs."

Les took the stairs down to the Grotto.

Stella lit one of her cigarettes as she walked over and tested the front door. It was locked, but a guerrilla like she had seen next door could bust it down easyily. Now she was sorry that she had sent Ivory downstairs.

Rosemary and Mollie met Imogene on the elevator. Rosemary brought her cello as Stella had suggested. Imogene followed the sound of the music down to the Grotto while Rosemary and Mollie kept their meeting with Stella.

Now that the girls were here Stella didn't feel quite so vulnerable. She did not soft-step the reality of their situation as she began to explain it to them. "Ladies, a few things have changed since yesterday. If you decide to pack your bags and check out there will be no hard feelings. Earl is explaining everything downstairs, but first I wanted to have a little girl to girl talk."

By the time Les got down to the Grotto he had lost most of his appetite. Knocking heads with that gorilla could have meant no appetite ever again. Entering the Grotto the first thing he saw was Michael. "Say, now who is this?" He hadn't paid much any attention to the music as he had come down the stairs, his thoughts still caught up in the events back at the cafe. *Tenor sax, long and mellow with definite heart. Where did Earl come up with him?* His heart did a triple flip-flop because just as he entered the room Imogene, backed by Earl and this new saxophonist, began to sing the sexiest, sensual rendition of *Good Morning Heartache* he had ever heard.

'*Good morning, heartache, here we go again*

Good morning, heartache, you're the one who knew me when . . .'

His horn lay on top of the piano, but for the moment he was too mesmerized to join in. He was a grown man, had seen more of the world than anyone in his family—hell more than any of the colored folks back in his home town. He had never had what one might call a steady girlfriend. Some of the girls he had dated back home were too churchy for his taste, others just wanted to get married and start popping out babies, making more mouths to feed in the southern poverty they had been born into. He wasn't a virgin, having known a woman or four in France—but Miss Imogene Wick, she made him flush all over.

After the incident in the cafe he had been tempted to walk away from The Honeysuckle Rose; not anymore. He would stay the course and make sweet music with this magnificent little songbird. He picked up his trombone and added some of his heart to their music.

"Thank you, Les?" Earl said as the song finished. Earl had heard him come down the stairs. Just after that the elevator door opened, admitting someone else. Who else we got here?"

"Ivory Burch, reporting."

"Now I see what you are talking about." Sam Newman

said. Stepping off the elevator he was instantly transfixed on Imogene and surprised as all get out that Beauty could handle the saxophone as well as he did. Now he took in the size and scope of the Grotto. The lounge upstairs was nice and cozy. The Grotto, on the other hand, had the potential to upstage any of the ballrooms in the best hotels in the city.

"Earl," Sam said, "I don't think we're going to have a problem recruiting enough retired cops to do the job. I've got four on their way here now. The problem is that with the swell music you just played it will be hard to get anyone to leave." Sam took measure of the tall colored man, the cop in him weary.

Les had learned over the years to never trust a cop. His breakfast all but forgotten, he brought his trombone back up as he gave Imogene a shy wink. "Nice sax." There wasn't much else he could say when he got a good look at Michael. "Earl, where did you come up with him?"

"Good talent just keeps knocking on our door. Michael O'Dea, meet Les Moore, and this lovely young lady is Miss Imogene Wick. Sam why don't you and Ivory take a seat and get acquainted. Just as soon as everyone gets here I'll make the introductions and explain why trouble is blowing our way and what we are going to do about. Les, you ready to jump in?" Earl asked as he tickled the first few notes to give everyone the key. "Imogene, you know Moonlight Serenade? Michael?"

The song was second nature to all.

Earl finished with a final flourish on the piano. "Now that is what I'm talking about, the sweet talent that keeps sweetening the Honeysuckle Rose."

Henry, Matt, Yukio, wife and child, met Thaddeus in the elevator. He guessed by their luggage that they were jumping ship. He smiled down at their little boy. "Right now this is no place for a kid. I don't hold any hard feelings for leaving while the leaving is still good. Henry, you take care. I'm going to miss your clarinet." The elevator dropped them off on the first floor. Thaddeus continued on down to the Grotto.

The music swelling up the elevator shaft had almost brought tears to Henry's eyes as they turned from the elevator towards the rear service entrance. A quiet exit, no more emotional exchanges.

Stella did not tell Mollie and Rosemary much more than she needed to—that was Earl's job. She was having a hard enough time figuring it all out for herself. She had given the girls a choice: if they stayed she needed to know that they would be willing to put in some long hours playing in the lobby lounge for the next few days or even weeks. She told them about the retired cops, the risk, and that she could only pay them with gratitude.

They readily agreed.

She gave them free room and board for the duration, which she didn't have to. Rosemary and Molly were on board for all the right reasons.

They were about to join everyone else in the Grotto when the front door bell rang. A man in a long raincoat, with dark shadows beneath his eyes held up a badge to the window

263

identifying himself as Gavin Hoyt, Private Detective. Upon opening the door she was told that Sam Newman had invited him and that he had a long time interest in the criminal activities of the musician's union, and in particular Frank Cambria.

Everyone joined Earl in the grotto.

Hopefully, first impressions are always the best. Detective Hoyt was impressed with what he heard and saw. He met with Sam and Ivory discussing tactics while Earl gave everyone a chance to bond together with their music. At the finish of a fourth tune Earl ran a long slide of fingers from one end of the keyboard to the other. "Okay, ladies and gents let's get down to business. Some of you know each other, some don't, so I'll ask each of you to introduce yourself and how you came to be here at The Honeysuckle Rose. I'll start, and Michael, you come in last, because there are a few things I want to say when you're done."

"Me, I'm Earl Crier, and Stella, who you have all met, is my wife. We own this joint, along with Thaddeus Mohler. Thaddeus show your hand. Stella and me, we used to have a sweet little piano bar out on the avenues—Stella's Starlight Lounge.

Then one day, Henry Akita, a longtime friend and gifted musician, came back to us asking for a job and a roof over his head. We had the job, but no spare room. Well, Stub and Ivory both needed a place, so we took it on ourselves to move to larger digs. And here we sit, ain't she grand."

Earl let out a long sigh. "This morning, Henry and his extended family elected to leave us. Yukio and his wife have a two year old son. With this union trouble coming at us, let's just say it's not the best place to raise a small child. Henry, I don't know whether to thank you or kick you in the ass, if it hadn't of been for you we wouldn't be here."

Stella looked around the room. "Sweetheart, when I look across the room at all of our new friends, and old, the word is thank-you."

Each in turn introduced themselves. Gavin Hoyt said his piece just before Michael. Hoyt's experience in dealing with Cambria and his connections within the District Attorney's office came as a welcome bonus.

THIRTY-TWO

HE WASN'T BLUFFING

NO ONE PUSHES FRANK CAMBRIA AROUND. CAMBRIA DOESN'T waste his time pushing back. His response is always an avalanche of retribution that leaves few standing. Over the years he had let very few crawl away like whimpering dogs to lick their wounds. Most he beat to the ground, leaving little room for them to rise again. Now his wrath is aimed directly at The Honeysuckle Rose Hotel, its owners and employees were all going to be made to pay a steep price. He had been humiliated by their so called head of security, and betrayed by Beauty. That was enough, word might get out that he's getting soft, and there is nothing soft about Frank Cambria.

He had made a few discrete inquires which gave him a penny to ponder. Cambria didn't want a penny, he wanted the whole damn dollar. A guy by the name of Thaddeus Mohler owned the Hotel Alexander. Call it the Honeysuckle Rose if you want, but it was still listed in the city tax records and business permits as the Alexander. There was no official documentation—as of yet—recognizing a change of ownership. Cambria made a note to call the department supervisor in the permit office to see if there was a way to pull the hotel's license.

The Alexander had once had a popular speakeasy, and from their own records, they had always played it straight with the union—but that had been some time ago. Thaddeus Mohler was a dandy who had almost run the hotel he had inherited into the ground. He was not a man to take chances, if he had been more of a risk taker, he might have been able to keep the hotel from falling as close to financial ruin as it had. Someone else was running the show and he couldn't put a finger on who. Beauty's treason had left him in the frustrating dark. Why? It didn't matter, because in the end Beauty had signed his own death warrant.

Cambria could order a picket line to be set up stopping all business at the hotel. He was about to put the squeeze on all of their suppliers and creditors who would start demanding immediate payments on any bills, putting a halt on all deliveries. He made another note to see if they were behind on their water and electric bills. Nobody wants to stay in a hotel where the toilets won't flush, and the lights are out. Give it a couple of weeks and the place would be out of business—case closed. He smiled smugly. *That would be too easy.* Cambria had been humiliated by their gimpy head of security. That scumbag, and Beauty, were on the top of his hit list. In this game of poker he had all the aces and the wild cards. He wasn't bluffing, and no one is allowed to drop out of the game.

He had decided that the picket line would go up today, the bill collectors would start making their calls as soon as he made his, and before the dump could go out of business it would be his pleasure to watch it burn to the ground. A short, but productive, phone call he had received a few minutes prior had set all that into motion. The man with the torch had been on his payroll for along time, was in too deep to ever dream of doing what Beauty had done. He was getting to much dough, a deep plant nobody would figure out. No one knew his identity except for Cambria.

THIRTY-THREE

THE HOT SEAT

EARL KNEW THAT HE WAS ABOUT TO PUT MICHAEL O'DEA on the hot seat. Michael had two choices, sink or swim, with no other options. It was only fair, he had come into their midst with deceit, as a spy, and for what it is worth still might be one.

Beauty had asked for sanctuary if he confessed his sins. He promised to fight alongside them in their battle against the union for the privilege of sharing their music. Their music had moved his soul, or so he said. If he did not get that sanctuary, Earl suspected that his life expectancy wouldn't allow him to get much beyond the hotel's doors. He made a tough decision, and now he had to lay it on the line, because he was asking those who were about to judge him for both forgiveness and acceptance. When his name was called, Michael did not step up as Earl had expected him to.

Beauty did not like to be in the spot light and that spotlight was about to shine down on him hot and heavy. He desperately needed to be accepted by these people, strangers all, except the cop. Between his looks and his deeds he wasn't going to get much sympathy.

"Michael, if you are not standing, then do so." Earl said as he tapped out a repetitive D—major. The single note grated on everyone's nerves as they waited in silence for Michael to speak. They had no idea what he had done, nor why he was on the hot seat. Everything that had been said this morning sounded urgent and dire regarding their deteriorating situation with the union. Those that didn't know guessed that this curious trial had to do with that. Now they were growing impatient. Earl spoke again, the tone in his voice clear that he was not going to call on Michael a third time. "You have all heard Michael on the saxophone. He is a gifted musician who has come to our door and I welcomed him. Michael, you and I have talked about this. If you are to be allowed to stay it must be by a unanimous vote of everyone in this room. My vote is yes. Detective Hoyt, Sam, you each have a vote here because whichever way the vote goes it will have a significant impact regarding our battle with the union. Okay Michael, here's your chance—you won't get another offer."

Michael O'Dea had an overwhelming burden weighing him down as he stood, straight as he could. He slowly looked around the room, taking in each face, allowing each in turn to see his. He held his sax as if he intended to play rather than say anything. *Well, here goes nothing.* He opened his mouth to speak. "I'm not much for talking," he said apologetically. The truth is I don't have much to say that would be of much interest to anyone once you know the truth. This here saxophone is how I speak with most folks. She says what I can't, so if you don't mind I'll mix words with a few notes . . . otherwise, I might as well leave now."

He looked at Thaddeus. "When I checked in to the hotel I lied, not about being a musician, but my intent. I ain't got no sainted mother near death's door waiting for me. I was dumped at an orphanage because of I was born an ugly bastard, so ugly my own mother would not have me. I checked into the hotel as a spy for the union, with orders to find out whatever I could that would open up the doors of this place so the union could bring you down. I didn't know nothing about you except for the few dollars I was paid to do this evil thing. Why the union boss has made you his personal target I don't know, nor do I know anything about what they are planning. Whatever it is, it ain't good."

Everyone's reaction, except for Sam, Stella, and Earl, was exactly what Michael thought it would be. When deceived, and threatened, most folks would rather run you out of town on a rail than bake you a cake. As he listened to the angry murmurs being exchanged he brought up his sax and played a sweetly sad original piece that expressed his sorrow.

As he finished Earl tapped that same D-major key a couple of times to get everyone's attention. "Go on, you're doing fine."

"Last night I was casing the joint and found myself down here. While you were playing I hid in the kitchen. Whatever good there may be left in me screamed at me to come out in the open. I never wanted to play so much in my poor, miserable life. But I couldn't, I had my orders, and that was to report back to boss Cambria what I had found out so he could do you all harm."

Ivory nearly blew a gasket. Fortunately he was sitting with Sam and Gavin Hoyt who restrained him.

"This morning I went to the cafe next door where I was supposed to meet with a guy who goes by the name Harry the Hammer. When I saw that SOB I knew I couldn't betray you folks, though all I know about you is your music. So, I turned my back on Harry and introduced myself to Stella, Earl, and the cop they were sitting with. When Harry saw that I was also talking to a cop, I had just signed my own death sentence."

The room held a deep silence as everyone registered what he had just said.

"All my life folks have thought me to be ugly. There's truth in that, I'm no beauty, which is why I've been saddled with the nickname, Beauty."

A tear came to Mollie's eye.

"Earl, it's been so long since I've been called Michael I almost forgot it's my name. I thank you for that." He played more of the melodic tune he had played earlier, then finished. "I'm asking your forgiveness for coming here the way I did.

I hope my actions show you where my heart is. I'd like nothing more than to stay. I'll stand beside you against the union. I ask for nothing more than your forgiveness and to play alongside some of the best musicians I've ever done heard." This time Michael didn't play. With tears in his eyes he searched the faces around him as if his life depended on it.

"That includes Michael volunteering to help with the music upstairs in the lounge." Earl said. "That takes some courage, the union thugs most likely will take that personally."

Les, who had an ear for music remembered much of the tune Michael had played. He voted by picking up his trombone and playing it. Rosemary added her own interpretation of Michael's heart rendering piece.

"I . . . I say yah . . yes." Stub voted.

Stella voted yes, then motioned to Stub that it was time for them to pick up Brooks. She heard all yes votes as they left and expected that when they returned Michael O'Dea would have been added to her problematic family.

One by one everyone voted yes, accept for Ivory who remained silent. "Ivory," asked Earl, "I said that Michael's fate depends on a unanimous vote if he is to be allowed to stay. A non-vote is the same as a no."

Mollie bit her knuckles as they waited for Ivory to have his say.

Ivory remained silent.

"Mr. Ivory," Michael said, trying not to sound as if he were begging. But he was. "I'm told that you are head of security around here. And that you were once a proud United States Marine who has served his country well, who won't take crap from no one. I'm guessing that if you vote for me to stay you'll be watching my every move, like a cat watches a canary bird, for some time to come. If I go out that door they'll shoot me down sure as night follows day. If I betray your trust you have my permission to shoot me down the same."

"Whew," responded Imogene, her eyes doing the begging that Michael had fought so hard to avoid.

"Mr. C," Ivory said loud and clear so there was no mistaking his words. "I'm going to come off sounding like one hard-assed SOB; so be it. You gave us the right to vote our conscience and I'm going to do just that. When I was in the corps, in China, and in the Jap prison camps, not one marine turned traitor, each man preferring death to dishonor. The boss man of the San Francisco Musician's Union paid O'Dea here a few lousy bucks to lie his way into the Honeysuckle Rose, spy on us, and report back with enough dirt to do us grievous harm. If a marine had gone over to the Japs, for whatever reason, and then came back saying: I was wrong fellas, will you forgive me, and take me back. I promise not to do it again. No sir, once that line is crossed a traitor is a traitor and can never be trusted again.

My vote is no." He paused for a moment giving O'Dea a long hard look then said his answer directly to him, "No."

Imogene, Mollie and Rosemary, all let out a surprise gasp with the words—*No, you can't do this*—buried within.

Otherwise there was stone cold silence.

The sentence was harsh, as Michael O'Dea stood convicted and unforgiven before them. He had no words left to say, he had gotten himself into this mess, and had a hard time forgiving himself. All he had wanted was some acceptance and to play some music without being looked down upon. After a moment he took the saxophone and laid it on the piano in front of Earl. He knew what faced him once he walked out of the hotel. There would be no sanctuary. Cambria was not the forgiving kind.

The door to the stairway closed slowly behind him.

As the door caught with a barely audible click, Ivory spoke breaking the graveside silence. "I'm sorry, I . . ."

"You voted your conscience. That is all I asked from each of you." Earl said. "I disagree, and I can't say that I'm not just a bit surprised. However, the vote had to be unanimous. Many of us in the room have had lives we wished we could turn the time clock back on. We can't change our miseries past, and neither can Michael O'Dea. Enough said, now let's bring our hearts and energies back to this union thing—foul weather is coming our way."

Ivory led the way upstairs, unlocking the lounge, and turning on all the lights. This included the lounge's front doors to the street. Mollie and Rosemary would start the music and keep it going for the next couple of hours as the rest of Earl's plan came together.

Thaddeus took up the front counter duty.

Sam Newman and Hoyt each took a seat opposite from each other in the lounge near the front door.

Earl stayed downstairs with Les and Imogene. It was important to not let the union spies, wherever they were, see the color of their skins, at least not yet. The Michael O'Dea vote had been a sad affair. Earl cleared his mind, with Imogene and Les working together they would be making some mighty fine music. Now he needed to wrap his thoughts around Brooks, bringing him here was not only risky, it would mean swallowing a lot of his own pride.

Ivory was not comfortable with their limited manpower and held his post in the lounge impatiently waiting for the additional retired cops to arrive.

No one looked at or spoke to Beauty who sat in the lobby a few feet from the front door, afraid to face his executioners.

THIRTY-FOUR

SECONDS TO SPARE

AFTER THE INCIDENT AT THE CAFE IT WAS DEEMED UNSAFE for anyone to leave the hotel alone.

Stub had gone with Stella to pick up Brooks. Stub had never met Brooks. What he knew came from numerous stories that had made Brooks an irascible legend at best. Earl enjoyed telling stories about Brooks, it gave him an opportunity to bad mouth the man one more time—which he relished. This he would do only when Stella was not present, for one thing she would not allow, was bringing down Brooks any further then he had taken himself. Which brought one question to Stub: *If Earl detested the man that much why bring him back into all this, didn't they have enough trouble already?*

Stub drove while Stella shared what she could as they drove to the Mark Hopkins Hotel. "Back at the veteran's hospital," she told him, "Earl and Brooks were roommates. They disliked each other from the first moment of their meeting. They were like two blind jackasses trying to pin the tail on each other's ass, each with a sharp barb vying in the dark to see who could be king of their pitch black mountain. Henry and I decided to distract their perpetual testosterone wars by bringing in someone they could set their sights on—no pun intended—

who needed more serious help. So we moved Ivory in with them. Ivory was brought in as what they called a wait and see patient. A wait and see patient is a patient who the doctors couldn't do much more for unless the patient regains the will to live. That was Ivory, he was very ill physically, mentally, and spiritually. The doctors did not give him long to live. Ivory's deteriorating situation distracted Earl and Brooks from each other as they fixed their energies on helping a seriously broken man.

They pissed Ivory off so bad that he began to rally enough strength to try to escape their exasperating banter. Then Earl hit him with a double shot of his magic—his music and his heart—which had helped more than one broken soldier find life worth living again.

She did not have enough time to tell Stub the rest of the story. That these two men have never liked each other, and never would, was self- evident. She hoped that somehow their mutual hatred for each other would create a bond that would bring them together as if they were combative brothers. She just hoped that before this was all over their friction didn't start a fire and burn down the hotel, saving the union the trouble.

On the telephone, she had not told Brooks all of how he fit into Earl's plan to save the hotel. Surprisingly, he hadn't asked for the rest of Earl's plan, which bothered her. No doubt Brooks was hiding something from her because so far he had shown little concern about reuniting with the bitter bastard he had never been able to best. Neither did she plan on trying to explain any more of Earl's plan to Brooks, that she would leave to Earl. She didn't quite get it herself.

Their arrival at the Mark Hopkins saved her from trying to explain anything further to Stub. Brooks was waiting outside the front doors of the Mark Hopkins as promised. Considering everything he had heard, Stub was surprised at the dashing figure the once wretched figure Brooks had become. He was all decked out in a black tux with a ruffled white shirt, a tall shiny top hat that sat on a white silk cloth that draped gently over his head coming to rest on his shoulders. Sewn into the white silk was a black sash placed where his eyes should have been. Stub thought that it reminded him somewhat of a raccoon, in a mysterious oddly sensual way.

Henry had once told Stub that a Nazis VII rocket had hit a London pub Brooks frequented blowing away much of his face leaving him blind and his face horribly mutilated. There was no amount of surgery that could ever mend that much damage. Stella had made a cloth mask to replace the hideous bandages that had wrapped his entire head. The silk mask gave him a unique sense of mystery. There were no holes for his mouth or nose, it rustled when he breathed. He could feed himself by lowering his head allowing room for a fork or spoon.

"Well, I'll be damned," Stub said as he and Stella got out of the car to greet him.

"Stella is that you?" Brooks asked with obvious delight.

THIRTY-FIVE

THE BATTLE BEGINS

FRANK CAMBRIA ORDERED AL LOUIS TO TAKE CHARGE OF setting up the picket line. He wanted it done fast, with no misunderstanding as to their intention. The Honeysuckle Rose Hotel was to be picketed twenty-four hours a day by union men who would use force if needed to stop anyone from crossing their line. Cambria did not care about bad press—maximum pressure was to be leveraged short of storming the place. Pickets were to cover both of the front doors as well as the alley, delivery and service doors. If a hotel guest or an employee were to leave they would not be allowed to return. No deliveries of any kind. Eight men in front, four in the back, and an equal number waiting nearby to alternate crews every two hours, or to help break a few skulls if needed. The cafe was to serve as their on-site union headquarters. He would pay the cafe more than their worth to keep the coffee pouring late into the night and into the early morning, and to mind their own business. If they did not like it he would see to it they met the same fate as the god-damned hotel.

Harry the Hammer told Al about the service door between the cafe and the hotel. Al told Cambria. Cambria told Beulah the cafe was now off limits to the hotel, not one crumb was to be served. The service door was to remain closed as tight as if it had been nailed shut. If she gave them any problems she was to get the same treatment as the hotel. For the moment it was convenient to use the cafe, but Cambria knew that she was siding with the hotel and in time they would have to shut it down just the same.

Ivory did not know it at the time but his confrontation with Cambria had opened a Pandora's box. Cambria was now putting all other union business on hold while he concentrated on bringing down the Honeysuckle Rose Hotel and everyone within it.

Al, along with four experienced picketers arrived to set up the picket line. At the same time Martin Mintzer a retired cop from the 5th Precinct entered the lounge.

"Marty, glad you could make it, we appreciate the help." Sam said shaking Marty's hand. "As you can see things are getting interesting real fast."

"I got tired of reading dime novels and gardening," Marty answered. "It appears that I'm not a minute too late. How serious is this union beef?"

Sam followed Marty's gaze as a blue Ford pick-up truck pulled up in front of the hotel's front doors dropping off four more picketers with strong arm signs. While a bit heavy these picket signs can easily be reversed and used as clubs when needed. A moment later a second pick up pulled up delivering six more pickets, of which four joined the picket line forming in front of the hotel, the remaining two headed towards the alley. *Four guys is all you need to picket something like this*, Sam thought. *They're making this a bigger deal than it ought to be.* He stepped back into the lounge. "Ivory, we've got company, and plenty of it."

Ivory shook hands with Marty, his eyes drifting quickly out to the street. The Japanese had surrounded Shanghai for months before they made their move. It looked like the union was not planning on wasting any time.

"Are you armed?" Ivory asked the newest member of his security detail.

Marty winked saying," I'm not supposed to be, but an old guy like me can't be too careful."

Ivory had soldiered with plenty of grizzled marines who looked older than their years. They were tough men not to be challenged. Sam and Marty were retired cops. Retired. They were old men past their prime. While he was appreciative of all the help he could get, the Sarge kept telling him that these two old geezers would need more protecting than they could return when things got hot. It wasn't hot yet, but things were heating up.

"Okay, ladies let's start the music, something lively that will let them know we are not asleep in here." Ivory walked to the open lounge doors and stepped out onto the sidewalk to catch the picketers' attention. When he had it, he smiled, and returned their snarls with an extended middle finger.

Back inside the expression on his face showed his concern. "Where are the damned marines when you need 'em? Sam, we don't have enough men to hold the line. If they decide to take the hotel they'll have it, and there is not much we can do about it. They can have this place ablaze long before the cops can get here. Anybody armed here besides Marty?"

Detective Hoyt patted his coat indicating that he was. That made two, not that it made much of a difference.

Marty gave everyone a knowing smile. "I wouldn't worry too much; the union will only go so far. We've got three other officers coming, all good men. Word will get out and we'll have plenty of support before dark."

Shit I couldn't be in all the places I need to be. Ivory cursed his own misfortune. "I'd better check the back, we've got nobody covering the back doors and who knows what damage that traitor O'Dea has already done." Ivory got his baseball bat from behind the reservation desk. Marty joined him, wanting to check out the hotel's layout.

Michael O'Dea sat still by the front door in the lobby. If he had any chance for escape he had waited too long. An overwhelmed ex-marine was about to throw him out onto the street. Two steps out the door the picketers would have him. They'd beat him half to death, throw him in the back of a pick-up, then finish the job without any witnesses. He was a dead man, too ugly for either heaven or hell. Ivory, armed with a baseball bat, and a tough looking older guy he hadn't seen before, walked in Michael's direction. Ivory waved the bat threateningly. "I'll be back in about fifteen minutes, if you are not gone by then, I'll throw you out the door myself."

"What's the beef?" Marty asked, taking a second good look at O'Dea. "Whew, he's one ugly son-of-a-gun. He looks harmless enough, shaking there like an old coon dog about to be put down."

Ivory began to tell Marty about Beauty's treachery as they headed to check the rear service doors.

Thaddeus shook his head as he overheard Ivory's remarks. Michael O'Dea was a sad story from beginning to end and Thaddeus did not want to watch as they drug him away kicking and screaming. Ivory should have given him a chance. He thought about taking it on his own shoulders to hide Michael upstairs in one of the rooms until things cooled off a bit. On the other hand if Ivory was right this pitiful scared little man could do some damage that might do them all some harm. On another day, under different circumstances Thaddeus might have extended his hand—but with the union picketers beginning to yell and make trouble just outside the front doors he couldn't risk it.

Stub slowed the car down as he turned the corner and approached the Hotel. Stella saw what he saw. The sidewalk in front of the cafe and the hotel was blocked by eight strong picketers who looked more like waterfront stevedores than representatives of a musician's union. Maybe they were from the waterfront, the unions did lend each other their resources when one union had a strike or a picket issue.

"Don't stop, go around the block," urged Stella, "they might not be covering the alley yet." As they passed the hotel a third pick-up truck pulled up directly in front of the lounge doors. Five men got out, each armed with rubber truncheons. The pick-up stayed, grey smoke from a cigar drifting from the driver's window.

Sam, who sat just inside the lounge's front doors, guessed these were the union's goon squad. These boys did not wait for trouble they started it. Their job description is to create havoc; to bash as many of the opposition as necessary to get them to kowtow to the union's will. Their message was simple—we win and you lose— and the next time that we come back we won't be as friendly. Sam knew that when these

283

guys came to the party they were not going to wait hours or days to show you what they had in mind. With Ivory and Marty elsewhere in the hotel he and Detective Hoyt were no match. He tanked God that Hoyt had a gun, but would he use it?

Ivory was the one in charge, but he wasn't present, so Sam made the decision. "Okay, Earl wants to draw the union to us. It looks like that goal is accomplished, too damn soon. We need enough time for Earl to bring the rest of the plan together and for us to get some more help. Okay, listen up, for now we need to back down and make ourselves as small of a target as we can. You ladies get downstairs, use the stairs behind the bar and lock the door behind you. When you see Earl tell him to stay put, that the union's goon squad is about to knock on our front door. Secure the Grotto tight against intruders and lock off the elevator. Detective, lock the lounge doors and barricade them with a couple of tables, pull all the curtains." Sam ordered. "If there is going to be a fight let's keep it out of here, the booze is flammable. If they bust it up and strike a match it's all over. I'll meet you in the lobby. If they are going to make their move let it be there."

Mollie and Rosemary wasted no time leaving. Rosemary was a little slower because she would not leave her cello behind.

Detective Hoyt locked the door and quickly scrambled together a makeshift barricade of tables blocking the street door to the lounge.

Sam zeroed in on the reception desk taking the phone practically out of Thaddeus's hands. He eyed Thaddeus one more time. Thaddeus was a semi-retired gentleman who most likely had never raised a hand in anger in his life. One look told Sam that Thaddeus would not be able to take care of himself with the brutes they were about to face. "Thaddeus, we've got big trouble, get downstairs and lock the stairwell doors behind you. I'm calling the active duty police, I just hope they can get here in time." He dialed the phone while yelling at the top of his voice. "Ivory, Marty, where the hell are you?"

There was no answer. There was no plan for constant communication.

After checking the back doors Ivory and Marty took the elevator up to the fifth floor. A security key allowed the elevator to take them up to the roof.

As soon as Mollie and Rosemary reached the Grotto, Mollie ran the elevator down to the third floor and pushed the master control button in the basement which locked it off from being recalled to any of the other floors.

Unknown to them Ivory and Marty were now stuck on the roof. The elevator was shut off and the emergency stairwell leading down was locked from the inside. Ivory ran to the front street side and looked down. There was an army of trouble down there ready to move. He immediately ran back to the elevator finding it non-responsive. Marty tried the door to the stairs.

"Ahhh shit, Sarge, what are we going to do?"

Marty looked puzzled. *Sarge?* "We can take the fire escape."

"We can, if we want to get down to the street level real fast. I thought it smart to grease the rails and steps up here, the middle landing, and the section nearest the street. I used elevator grease and its slick as hell."

"Is there a fire hose up here?" Marty asked. "Maybe we can power wash the grease off."

"I don't know." Ivory rushed back to the front of the building and looked down at the union goons. "We had better find out quick."

Stub had driven around the block three times. There were picketers in the alley. They were effectively locked out unless they wanted to confront the pickets which would be a stupid thing to do. They parked just around the corner where there was a phone booth.

Stella tried to call the hotel but the line was busy. After two or three tries she got back into the car. "Now what?" She was beginning to lose her nerve, and she had Brooks and Stub to look after. Stub was slow in healing from his gun shoot wounds, she doubted that he could take a beating and survive. She also knew that he would try to defend her. She could call the police, but they wouldn't come until a crime was being committed, by then it would be too late. They couldn't just sit there, Earl was inside and she had to be by his side.

Earl loved playing with Les and with each passing moment he was becoming more and more enchanted by Imogene. *Oh God, that gal can sing.* What his group needed now was a good drummer. If there were problems outside the Grotto they seemed as far away as trouble ought to be.

Imogene owned the lyrics as she sang 'Blueberry Hill'.

Michael O'Dea's tenor saxophone and a little bass is exactly what Imogene needs here, Earl thought. His heart felt a little twinge as he regretted Michael's sad fate. *Okay, no sax, how about bringing in a bit of cello in here. It might bring something a little different that will cause folks to sit up and take notice.* Working with talent like this made it easy to forget the storm brewing not far away.

"Okay, Stub said. "It loh . . . looks like their main bah . . . body is focused on the lounge. I say we drive straight to the lobby dah . . . doors. If I pull up onto the sah . . . sidewalk the car will block most of them, but . . . but not more than a few seconds. If we go in with the horn blar . . . blar . . . blaring we should be able to get Thaddeus's attention."

The idea scared Stella to death, but no one had come up with anything better. Stub was doing his best, and one thing she was grateful for was Brooks, he hadn't complained one iota. In fact, he was unusually calm.

"I'm game," Brooks said.

"Okay," Stub said as sweat broke out on his forehead. "Stella, you get in the backseat with Broh . . . Brooks. Everyone get out on the driver's side of the car. Leave the cah . . . car doors open, that's two more ob . . . obstacles before these guys can get at us. You get Brooks inside. I'm coming in as our last la . . . line . . . line of defense."

They sat in the car afraid to make the next move.

"If you wait any longer we will chicken out for all the right reasons." Brooks said.

Stub moved the stick into gear.

Sam knew the desk sergeant who answered the phone. The police had their own union, and the police union did not like to put its officers up against another union unless it had no other choice. Sam was a retired cop who was still a dues paying member. The sergeant promised he would have five patrol cars there as soon as possible.

The desk sergeant knew that some of the cops would be reluctant to go up against the goon squad. The goons also knew that the cops did not want a confrontation. If Cambria was paying enough money they would go up against the police just as long as they outnumbered them. There were no patrol cars in the immediate area—soon might be too late.

Sam hung up the phone as Hoyt closed off the lounge from the inside.

"I've done all I can do," Hoyt said. "Doors are barricaded, lights off, and the blackout curtains have been drawn. If they decide to break through the windows there's not much to be done." Hoyt didn't sound as threatened as Sam felt.

"Okay,' Sam ran through their options. "You stay in the lounge just on the other side of the doors. You are the one who is armed, if they try to smash through the windows fire off a shot that might stop them for the moment. We've got cops on the way. What I can't tell you in how long."

"Great." The detective gave a quirky smile as he closed the doors behind him. "Where the hell are Marty and Ivory?" Hoyt moved into the shadows and waited until he was sure that Sam was not going to change his mind and follow. He quietly moved towards a hallway located behind the bar. Once there he took a small flashlight out of his coat pocket and looked around for something he had seen on one of the hotel's Thaddeus had shown him.

The doors to the hotel were locked from the inside. Sam could see through the window that most of the picketers and the goon squad were gathered in front of the lounge. They were after human targets, not mere bar bashing—it wouldn't be long before they realized their prey was in the hotel, not the lounge. He looked around for a weapon, finding only a broom, he leaned it up against the counter for leverage and broke off the wooden handle. "Hey Beauty, take this, you might as well go down fighting." The broom handle clattered on the floor near where Michael sat. He did not reach for it.

The loud blare of a car horn and the screech of brakes resounded through the lobby as a car almost plowed through the front door.

The car doors flew open.

Stella got out of the back of the car helping someone Sam couldn't quite make out. What happened next took place in seconds, not minutes.

The car's sudden arrival pivoted the union goons into immediate action. They had been looking for an easy target and it didn't matter that one of the people trying to bust through their lines was a woman. Hidden partially by the car no one saw that Brooks was blind. Like hunting dogs following the scent of blood, they moved towards the car with a malicious roar. These men thrived on violence, it was their calling card as was their intent.

Beauty did not have time to think. He saw that Stella was

in trouble. He also knew how vicious these goons could be. With no thought to his own safety he grabbed the broom handle, threw open the doors to the hotel and flung himself out as a human shield to protect this wonderful woman who had treated him as a human being. She and Earl had given him his name back and if he died here he would go out as Michael O'Dea and not as the pitiful Beauty.

For a brief moment, he was startled by a well-dressed man whose head was entirely covered by a silk hood. He was floundering, confused as to what direction he needed to go. Stella and the guy everyone called Stub were losing precious seconds in trying to get this guy pointed towards the door.

Sam held the door open.

The goons reached the car.

One, a big swarthy man with long dark red hair and a full beard, jumped up on the hood. Sam knew the man as a lumper down at the fisherman's market. He had a list of assault and battery charges as long as the picket sign he wielded, the sign reversed so the handle could be used as a club. He raised it towards Stella, his club coming down was a powerful sweeping motion.

Michael was a fraction of a second faster. His broken broom stick struck the man in the knee causing his aim to be off just enough for Stella to escape being hit by inches. The goon's second swing hit Michael in the shoulder. Michael heard a crack, felt a sharp pain, a numbness slide down his arm like an electric shock. The crack had come from the picket sign's sturdy handle—not sturdy enough—it was the handle that had cracked not the shoulder. Michael was going to have one hell of a bruise but his arm was still operational.

He switched his grip to his other hand swinging the broom stick painfully into the goon's groin causing him to fall backwards from the hood of the car with a shriek from pain. Michael's forward lunge put him off balance causing him to fall to one knee, his weapon rolling beneath the car.

Another goon rounded the rear of the car, the open door hindering his reach as Sam reached out and caught Stella's hand pulling her inside the hotel. She in turn pulled Brooks. Stub stopped just long enough to help Michael to his feet.

Two of he goons coming around the rear of the car had truncheons and were just short of being able to bring one down on the back of Stub's head. "Hey, it's Beauty," one called out, "that SOB is mine. He raised the truncheon and . . .

A powerful and well aimed stream of water blasted the closest of their assailants back while others tried to climb over the car. From the roof of the hotel Ivory and Marty held them at bay with a powerful stream from a fire hose. The hose had barely reached the edge of the roof limiting their aim.

Sam slammed and locked the front door as Stub and Michael sprinted inside. There were a dozen angry men outside, the door would not hold them back for long even with the firehose spraying straight down on them. There was nothing left to do but roll a lobby couch up in front of the door. They hadn't enough furniture or time to build a barricade. The stairs were locked off as was the elevator. The goons could bust in at will and they would be trapped in the lobby.

The door shook, bowing slightly as the men on the outside kicked and slammed their body weight against it to bring it down.

BLAM!

The pounding on the door fell abruptly silent.

BLAM! Detective Hoyt, who had shoved his way through his own barricade now stood outside the lounge door with his pistol pointed towards the sky. He brought it down aiming it at the group of men trying to force their way into the hotel.

The men backed off, took measure of Hoyt, spread out and started to move towards him. "You might get one or two of us, but you are dead meat, pal." One threatened boldly!

Holding his crotch, unsteady on his feet, the lumper with the red beard, rose and stumbled towards Hoyt. The blood lust evident in his eyes told Hoyt that his next shoot wasn't going to be into the air. He could not let this raging bull reach him. He cocked the gun ready to fire.

"That's enough." Cambria roared, hoping to be heard against the mayhem. He had arrived at the cafe just in time to watch his picketers and the goon squad rush the hotel, letting Beauty get away in the process; that Beauty had the guts to take a stand against them only angered Cambria more. A police siren wailed from a couple of blocks away. A second siren wailed from a different direction. He was surprised to see that it was Detective Hoyt who was holding a gun on his boys. He looked up at the fire hose that was still raining down blocking the entrance to the hotel. Cambria needed to defuse the situation for the moment.

Two more of the retired police officers who had volunteered came skidding down the street on foot. Breathing heavily, both were too old and out of shape to make a run like that, they now stood next to Hoyt. While retired, they were each licensed to carry a gun - both now pointed their weapons at the union goons.

"I said, that's enough." Cambria roared again, this time loud enough to be heard by all.

Ivory shut the fire hose off, keeping it at the ready.

The three guns remained pointed at the union men who were now frozen in place. Red beard, still hobbled by an injured crotch dropped to one knee, sick to his stomach.

"You men, get Paddy to his feet, get in that damn pick-up truck and go get some dry clothes. Coffee is on me at the cafe after you are dry and tempers have simmered some." The reserve team of union picketers who had been in the cafe now stood behind Cambria. Al Louis pushed his way through prodding and pushing the soaked union thugs into the back of the pick-up. The overloaded truck pulled away with angry looks and promises for revenge.

With no more union men left in the cafe Beulah closed and locked the door, reversing the open sign to closed. She would be damned if she was going to stick around to be caught in the middle of this thing.

The reserve picketers took up position across the street from the hotel.

Frank Cambria uttered a low dry chuckle as he tipped his hat. "Well played Detective, well played. You have a good day, you hear. We'll chat again in the near future."

THIRTY-SIX

A Changed Vote

THE POLICE ARRIVED TO A RELATIVELY CALM SCENE.

Detective Hoyt whispered to the two new volunteer cops that it would be helpful if they stood just inside the lounge with the doors open. He then walked over to the nearest police officer, offered them coffee inside the lounge, where they would get enough information to fill out their reports. He walked past Frank Cambria, and the remaining picketer sentries, as if they were invisible, to the front door of the hotel—knocked—and was let in.

Cambria, questioned by the police, said little, when pushed, he simply stated that any further conversation would be with the union's attorneys.

A bored reporter from a local radio station dropped by looking for a story. He was brushed off by Al Louis, who like Cambria said little the reporter could use.

A deep collective sigh greeted Detective Hoyt's return. Everyone was scared. No one was hurt accept Beauty. No one was fooling themselves that this had been a very close call.

Sam shook hands with Hoyt, delivering a meaningful thank-you. Then Sam ended the victory celebration with a reality check. "Well, I guess it is now all, or nothing. We've crossed that line with the union. As long as the police are here we're fine, but as soon as they leave—as soon as we let our guard down—make just one mistake—they'll move in a lot faster than we can get the cops here."

Brooks sat on the couch next to Michael. For obvious reasons Brooks could not see Beauty, nor Beauty Brooks, because of his silken hood. Having not been introduced, and still stunned by his violent reception, Brooks chose to say nothing until he found out what the hell was going on. His dominant question: *Where the hell is Earl?*

Michael's shoulder ached, he had taken a pretty good whack. It did not feel like anything was broken, but it was going to be pretty damned sore and stiff for some time to come. Time, that was something he didn't have much of. He was about to be thrown out of the hotel right into the hands of his executioners. The tears in his eyes were not so much from the pain, as the realization that he had just done a very foolish thing. But, what did that matter, in a short matter of time he would be dead anyway. He also did not speak. What more was there to say. He had pleaded for his life, lost, and was about to pay the price for being a foolish man. His brief journey outside had confirmed that he hadn't a chance in hell when he stepped outside a second time. He might get a police escort, but to where? Cambria would likely pay a tidy sum to the cop who turned him over to his thugs.

First thing, first, Stella called down to the Grotto. A few moments later she heard the hum of the elevator. Everyone else were on their way up.

The elevator now unlocked, Ivory and Marty would be

coming down. She then guided Brooks over to the piano in the lounge, and got him settled in. "I know, I've got a lot of explaining," she told Brooks. "Just give me a couple of minutes to get everything sorted out. In the meantime please play. This is now your piano, Earl has his downstairs. You have an audience, mostly police, and hopefully there will be more of them soon. We are offering free coffee and music to keep them entertained. We have some new musicians. I'll introduce you to as soon as we can find some time. There is a lot going on right now." Stella said. In the meantime, play something, and whistle if you want. But, Brooks, sweetheart, please try to remember that you are a poet, and we both know poets can't sing."

Brooks chuckled quietly to himself. There had been a time, when he was told that he was a poet that could not sing, it was meant as an insult. Now he secretly wore the mantle of a poet as a badge of honor. He had always known that he was not much of a singer. His voice was good, he just couldn't stay on key. His piano playing was only good for a noisy tavern where the drunks did the off-key singing to his mediocre playing. He had once been able to whistle—pretty damn good to—now the scar tissue around his disfigured face had tightened leaving him without the ability to whistle with any charm.

It hadn't taken long for him to realize that no one listened to him when he tried his best to perform at the Mark Hopkins. Sadly, the only thing entertaining was his mask, and the mystery behind it. After a few months, he had hit a new low, and was tempted to drink himself to death, or step off the hotel's roof, which would have only validated Earl's opinion of him: 'Brooks you are nothing but a no talent bum'. He never took that next last step, because it would have made Earl right. Then one day he decided that the charade had to come to an end. He stopped singing, limited his piano playing, and never whistled again. It was when he accidentally began to recite poetry, backed just enough with his piano, that people stopped what they were doing, and listened. He got applause, and gained some self respect.

Brooks Weingarten disappeared into his former world of lies and self loathing. He became instead Oscar Katz, someone he had come to like and respect. Now, as he sat at the piano in the Honeysuckle Rose Hotel it was not Brooks who was about to be reunited with Earl Crier, it was Oscar Katz, who did not need to sing because he had become a gifted artist in his own right. He wanted to tell Stella that Brooks was gone, that she had brought Oscar Katz back to perform at Earl's side.

Stella paused. Brooks smiled, seeming unexpectedly calm. She had thought that he would be as tense as a pending stroke as he was about to come face to face again with Earl. He wasn't.

Thaddeus was the first one off the elevator. Everyone except for Sam and Ivory moved into the lounge. With flashing police lights just outside the front windows he followed the sound of Stella's voice. "Stella, what the hell happened?" He asked as soon as he entered the lounge.

"Wait until everyone gets here," she admonished. She didn't mean to sound rude, but she was still shook up, and hadn't had a chance to get herself together yet. "I'm sorry, first things first, Thaddeus meet Brooks."

Needless to say, Thaddeus's expression in seeing a masked pianist, in a tux, sitting at the piano with his fingers getting set to play, said it all. *First Beauty, now this masked . . .*

Stella gave Thaddeus an almost motherly look. "Later . . ."

Brooks turned in the direction of Thaddeus's voice. "Pleased to meet you Thaddeus, the name is Oscar, Oscar Katz." He laughter pleasantly then said, "Stella, later . . ."

Brooks . . . Oscar, almost made her cry as he started to play *Stella By Starlight*, he did not play well, but his heart was in the right place.

"Oscar?" Confused, Stella put the Oscar issue aside for the moment. She continued, "We've got six policemen outside who we have promised coffee and donuts. Please put on some coffee, and call the bakery across the street; they do bake donuts, don't they?"

"They do, but not at this hour, their closed." Thaddeus shrugged his shoulders. "The baker comes in around four. Sorry."

Stub, escorted by Detective Hoyt, went to park Stella's car.

Earl, who always liked to make an entrance, heard the piano and knew instantly that it was Brooks. Tapping his cane on the floor, he entered the lounge as HE addressed Imogene, Rosemary and Molly, who had guided him up from the Grotto. "Ladies, the idiot on the keyboard is Brooks Weingarden, the Third. That there have been three of them, only proves that God has a sense of humor. Stella where are you?"

"Earl, behave." Stella admonished.

"Never," He responded with a laugh. Like everyone else he wanted to know what had happened. "Well?"

Brooks lifted his fingers from the piano keys to respond to Earl. "Well?"

"Now that is the jackass we have all come to revile," Earl said "I wish I could say it was good to see you again."

"Wish I could say the same." Brooks played the piano lightly, then slowly began to speak, his voice rich with authority, wisdom, and warmth, rendering the lyrics into a poem fitting the moment:

'My story is much to sad to be told

There was a time when practically everything left me totally cold

The only exception I know is the case

When Earl Crier sings . . .

When your music takes me to a marvelous place.

There was a time when I drank

Now mere alcohol doesn't thrill me at all

So tell me why should it be true?

That Earl, I get a Kick Out of you

I think Sinatra would to.

I get a kick every time I hear your playing and singing

Because there is no one else like you around

I get a kick though it's clear for everyone to see,

You obviously do not adore me.[1]

---

[1] Adapted from 'I Get A Kick Out Of You' by Frank Sinatra

Earl cleared his throat. "Welcome home." He said, the word welcome hard to admit. There had been a lot of bad words exchanged between them, but now he had to admit that he had missed Brooks. Bringing him here had been the right thing to do. "Brooks, this is not easy for me to say, but I get a kick out of you to."

"Brooks? " Oscar asked. "Anyone here with that name? I thought not. Oscar Katz raise your hand." He did, "Stella, Earl, gather round and I'll explain."

Two minutes later Ivory and Marty stepped out of the elevator.

Seeing Ivory, Michael O'Dea nearly pissed himself. Ivory's last words to him had been, that if he was still there when he got back, he would throw him out the door himself.

"Oscar it is." Earl said, now lets shake hands. The transition from Brooks to Oscar had been utterly confusing, but it made sense. Earl and Brooks would never be able to share the same space. Earl intensely disliked Brooks, nothing would change that unless Brooks changed. Earl certainly wasn't about to. No one liked Brooks, not even Brooks, so as he found those little things that he came to like about himself he became a different person. If he remained Brooks, people might not be willing to see the changes, so he left Brooks behind. Tears welled up in Stella's eyes as she welcomed Oscar into her heart.

There would be a moment for tears, but this wasn't it. Stella knew that if they did not act fast the tears would be for the loss of The Honeysuckle Rose and perhaps each other. "Is everyone here," Stella called out?

Are they always like this?" Thaddeus asked—meaning Earl and Oscar.

"Always has a past and a future, the past is gone," Stella responded. She looked around the room. Stub and Detective Hoyt were absent, otherwise everyone was present, plus three police officers, who had just come in off the street. The other three officers remained outside to keep an eye on Cambria's crew.

She miscounted. Michael O'Dea was still out in the lobby. She looked at Ivory, her eyes asking what he was going to do.

Ivory walked across the lounge to the lobby doorway.

Michael cringed.

"Mr. Michael O'Dea, you my friend, at your own peril saved Stella, Brooks, and Stub from harm. That makes you okay in my book. Earl, if it is not too late, I would like to change my vote to yes."

Earl laughed. "Well done, Ivory, that makes it unanimous. Mr. O'Dea, I think you had best come in here. You have a shoulder that needs looking after. And please bring your saxophone with you—if you think you can play with that shoulder, we have some music to make."

Stub and Detective Hoyt got back just in time to see Ivory and Michael shaking hands. "This is one swa . . . swa . . . swell day." Stub said.

The phone rang.

It was Loyal Williams for Earl. The conversation was brief and to the point. Loyal had come by as promised. The sight of the union picketers had told him that this was not the place, or time, for a black man to be challenging the status-quo. He wished Earl well, promising that he would bring two bus loads of jazz lovers right to their front door, when this union problem straightened itself out.

Earl said that he understood, and that as soon as things calmed down, they would get together and exchange a few notes; musical notes.

It was Sam who spoke next, somehow putting everything all together. When he was done everyone was in agreement. They were in a tough spot, but if they didn't stick to Earl's plan, things could get a lot worse.

The police had other calls to respond to, but they would put the word out and the next few days there would be at least one patrol car with two officers on scene as often as possible. Just keep the coffee and donuts coming and half the police force will find their way there. A few officers might even drop into the cafe, when they opened, just to let Cambria know he was being watched. Night patrols would increase in the neighborhood, but that was as far as they could go. The retired cops knew other retired cops, and promised to increase their number as soon as the old men could find matching socks.

Thaddeus made a note that he needed to call Beulah at the Cafe. The hotel's kitchen was all but empty. The union would stop all deliveries, and they might be hunkered down here for some time. The union occupied the cafe. If she was caught delivering orders to the hotel, they would shut her down. Thaddeus had known Beulah for almost twenty years. She wouldn't let him down, even if it meant losing the cafe. He couldn't ask her to take that big a risk; but somehow they'd find a way.

Beulah had closed the cafe. She kept one light on in the kitchen busying herself with some clean up, and a hot cup of tea, as she remained inside keeping an eye on the place.

With everything in place there was one thing left—that was for Earl to let everyone in on his plan. He hadn't told anyone his whole plan, not even Stella.

He edged Oscar over on the piano bench where he accompanied his old rival with a few cheerful ditties. Oscar mimicked, or added his own teasing musical comments, as the two old belligerents had their own conversation. When done, everyone laughed in support of Earl's creative brilliance. Buried within all the banter was Earl's plan finally made clear.

"I'll be damned, so that's why you sent Stella knocking on my door," Oscar said. "If I had any sense, I'd tell you to go to hell. Earl, you've been telling me since the first day we met, that I haven't a whiff of common sense, and now are asking me to do this. Well, if we are going to the dance, we might as well dance with the devil," Oscar added. "Sounds like fun."

Stella just shook her head in wonder. Her two blind men we're about to take on the toughest union in town, and she was a fool for believing they could do it.

She leaned in and gave each a kiss on the cheek. Stella's was no one's fool; that was love.

THIRTY-SEVEN

BRONX CHEER

NIGHT SLIPPED AWAY INTO DAY, THEN BACK TO NIGHT AGAIN, while the union roughnecks kept their edgy but respectful distance; respectful of Cambria's rules of order. Their eyes and ears were focused on the hotel's lounge, where everyone seemed to have gathered, where the music emanated from.

Oscar played, trading off now and then with Mollie. Rosemary brought up her bass. Stella sang, not often, but often enough to keep them company. Imogene had wanted to stay with them in the lounge. Earl cut her plea short, saying that he wanted to keep her and Les in a low profile.

Part of Earl's plan was for Oscar to appear as something he was not. Stella made him a new silk mask, all brown in color. When you added light brown gloves, anyone looking in from the outside could easily mistake Oscar for being colored. Earl wanted the picketers, and in particular Frank Cambria, to get all riled up, thinking that there was a colored musician playing in the lounge. True, Les and Imogene were colored, but it was Oscar Earl wanted everyone to center their attention on; especially the press. God bless the press, if they get the story right.

There were plenty of police officers coming, and going.

While it was cold outside the front door was wide open, the music flowing out enticingly to the picket line outside. The curtains had been swept wide open allowing everyone on the outside to see, and hear, Michael O'Dea—Beauty—playing alongside a masked pianist who the picketers had already determined was a nigger hiding his face; flaunting his being there. The union had a long term closed door policy baring blacks from membership, and performing in almost all public entities within the great golden city by the bay.

Eleven o'clock came, and everyone was tired. The number of police dwindled. It was time to close for more than one reason. The music quieted until only Oscar was left playing. He would play until Stella came back to take him to his room. One officer stayed, having a report to write, that could have been done just as easily as the precinct.

The retired volunteer cops grew to seven in all. Stella called them Ivory's lucky seven. Ivory's lucky seven had the night watch.

Detective Hoyt had gone home for the night, saying that he would be back in the morning. He would be early, liked his coffee black, eggs scrambled soft, and bacon crisp: with the cafe closed there wasn't much chance of that.

Stella raided the hotel's kitchen, finding little, doing the same to Thaddeus's suite. There wasn't much to be had by the night shift except for coffee and some stale biscuits. Their food situation would have to take top priority in the morning.

The clock ticked to twenty past eleven as the last police officer left.

Stella finally took Oscar up to his room. She brought with

her a tall whiskey. Brooks had earned it. Brooks thanked her, and gave it back, saying that he did not need it anymore.

After a tour of the building Ivory crept unwillingly to his room behind the reservation counter for a few hours sleep. Sleep tonight would be like sleeping in a foxhole, where you tried to find a dry spot, unlaced your shoes, your subconscious aware of the tinniest sound around you. Ivory lay on his bed, closed his eyes, rested but never slept, knowing that danger was all around them waiting for the right moment to strike.

No one expected trouble so soon after their earlier confrontation, which was all the reason why trouble would come knocking when they least expected it. While the others slept, Ivory waited and listens. For the night watch there were two of the lucky seven camped out in the lounge, two in the lobby, and two who wandered the halls, while the last of the seven kept his eyes on the street from the roof. It was cold outside, the roof watch would alternate every forty-five minutes.

The cafe was closed, as was most everything else downtown, the night quiet, as if everyone was holding their breath waiting for the hammer to slam down. The picketers settled in for a long cold night.

The silence was not long lasting.

At 12.36 AM, the building was rocked by a thunderous explosion. Everyone heard it. The night watch on the roof saw the first flash, followed by two thundering booms, mixed with towering flames. Jolted awake, Ivory didn't waste any time getting to the roof. The night watch didn't need to point towards the obvious. The explosion had come from a parking lot located two blocks away. "Damn it!" Ivory was pretty sure

306

he knew the cause of the explosions, but didn't say anything.

Instead, he scurried on his wooden leg along the perimeter of the roof, searching the darkened streets below for any signs of malicious activity. He found nothing. The picketers below seemed as confused and surprised as everyone. Lights came on across the city as the sirens of fire engines and police began their shrill; beware there is danger this night. More explosions echoed across the city as the sounds of the sirens suggested this was a four alarm fire at the minimum.

Earl and Oscar stayed in their rooms waiting to be told what had happened and what to do. Each calm, in his own way, there was little they could do about the explosions. Earl's plan, their moment of fame, was near.

The lucky seven remained at their posts while everyone else found their way to the roof, where the flickering flames from the fire lit up the neighborhood, the rising smoke mixing with the brooding marshmallow like bank of fog creeping in. One gigantic explosion echoed across the city as the gas station that was located on the street level of the two story garage blew, sending up flame and debris, collapsing most of the building into a twisted caldera of cement and burning vehicles. Exploding gas tanks continued to add dull booms that now kept much of the city awake.

Ivory looked at Stella. Astonished and tight lipped, she nodded, it was the garage where she kept her car.

It was too soon for the police to know if there was any connection between the devastated garage and the events building around the Honeysuckle Rose Hotel. They were not taking any chances, as two patrol cars took up position at each end of the street.

The picketers backed up into the dark shadows of nearby doorways.

Six of the officers set up traffic barricades as fire engines, and the early morning curious, headed towards the spectacular fire. The two remaining officers gave the strikers a hard look as they slunk back into the night shadows the best they could. The men looked more cold and confused, than guilty. The officers left them alone knocking on the hotel's front doors. The lobby guards from the lucky seven let them in.

"Okay, everyone, if you are up to it, we're back to coffee and music down in the lounge." Stella said. "Let's all get dressed. Mollie, would you play us some night music with a little swagger, while I get Brooks and Earl up?" If Stella ever had one of those *wow* moments, this was it. It occurred to her that this might be that moment that just might change everything. Earl had been adamant that at the right moment we needed to get the press on our side: the good guys standing up against the tyranny of a union gone bad. This was the moment Earl was waiting for, and if all went well, they would be handing the union back its power hungry greed, and testosterone fueled bravado, on a silver platter. If this were a play, the characters would all be rag-tag and quirky, and the leading man, who must get a standing ovation would be Oscar: not Earl. Oscar and Earl must work together as a well rehearsed team. She shook her head with with incredulity of the moment. Now she understood. It was a long shot, but the only one they had.

"Les, Imogene, Michael, Molly, Rosemary, let's make that old fog horn slip into tune with us as we serenade the stars. Ivory, you and some of your lucky seven officers, go down and bring the second piano up to the lounge. I'll get Earl and

Oscar, and meet you in the lounge."

Thaddeus marveled at Stella in command. *Did I say ditzy, couldn't have, not me. Play, to who, at this hour of the night?*

Everyone had the same question on their minds.

"Go on, we haven't a moment to lose." Stella clapped her hands as she would with a gaggle of school children.

Thaddeus, still dressed in his night gown, went down to put on more coffee.

Raymond Lafferty, the Precinct Police Captain, had told the night shift sergeant to call him if anything serious developed around the hotel. Anything. He had been wanting to get the goods on Frank Cambria for years, and had so far come up with nothing that would hold up in court. He suspected that half the judges in town were on Cambria's payroll, which was why most of his henchmen had also avoided jail time. Something had happened regarding the Honeysuckle Rose Hotel that had gotten under Cambria's skin. Captain Lafferty was growing concerned that this time someone was going to get hurt, or worse. While there was no known connection between the garage fire and the hotel, Captain Lafferty was now taking a special interest in the case. At least one officer was to be assigned from each shift to stand watch over the hotel. If the picketers were to do anything unlawful, including littering, they were to be arrested. He couldn't order his officers to take their coffee breaks in any particular location, but he wanted the word put out that he would appreciate it if they took their breaks at the Honeysuckle Rose Hotel.

The explosions woke Cambria as it had most of the city.

One phone call told him that it was not the hotel. He didn't know what was on fire, the explosions still echoing and jarring nerves across the city. His boys had nothing to do with it was all that mattered. That his boys didn't have anything to do with it didn't mean that whatever was being blown to hell out there wasn't his problem. Down deep Cambria was nursing a disturbing thought. His man undercover marched to his own drummer. Would he be stupid enough to torch a neighborhood to hide the arson that Cambria had ordered to finish the Honeysuckle Rose Hotel? On the other hand, the SOB might have just done it to draw attention away from the hotel. Cambria picked up the phone, if he wasn't going to get any more sleep tonight, neither would Al Louis.

Stella was right, this might very well be the moment when everything would reverse itself in their favor. When told, Earl was so excited he put on a fresh shirt Stella laid out for him, socks, shoes, and counted his steps to the elevator. Stella had gone to fetch Oscar insisting that Earl wait in their room until they came back. He did not.

Down in the lobby the great wise Mr. C got a good laugh at his own expense as he appeared sans trousers. "Well, just thank god, I had enough sense to wear my shorts." He responded.

Mollie gave him a table cloth to cover himself with as he sat at the piano.

"Okay, friends and family, this is it." Earl said, his hands nowhere bar the piano keys. "The whole city is awake and looking at the fire that destroyed Stella's car and the garage about two blocks from here. That fire is working something like a spot light and that spotlight is about to put us center stage. It's early in the morning, since everyone seems to be awake we are going to make some music and put all our cards on the table. It's time to let everyone know that we are here. Les, Imogene, I want you center stage. I want you to be proud of the color of your skin, and even prouder of your music. Michael, it's asking a lot of you to stand center stage with us because I have no doubt that there is a contract out on your head. If you want to sit this one out no one will think any less of you."

"Mr. Crier, Earl, I'll stand with you, if it's the last thing I do."

Stella appeared with Oscar about the same time as the second piano arrived.

Earl stood, the table cloth slipping to the floor, as he tried to explain where he wanted both piano's positioned.

"Earl," Stella had to cover her mouth to quiet her laughter. Mollie gathered up the cloth and wrapped it around him again.

The police interrupted saying that they could not put the pianos out on the sidewalk without a permit, especially at this time of night.

Earl answered by cupping his ears, the noise of a passing fire engine's shrill painfully loud. "I don't think we're going to wake anyone up officer. On the other hand, we might just wake up more of the union boys. They have a point to prove, and so do we. There will be only one winner. I'd appreciate it if you would stick around because things are about to get very interesting around here."

Stella rushed to get Earl his pants.

Everything was to happen at once. The two pianos were to be rolled out onto the sidewalk, one on each side of the doorway; timing was everything. As soon as Earl and Oscar were seated the rest of the musicians were to move between the two pianos. It would be a tight fit, but having Michael O'Dea—Beauty—and two black musician's center stage was as good as telling the union to go to hell. Mollie and Stella were to stand near Oscar and Earl to pull them out of harm's way if things got ugly. The lucky seven were to stay just inside the lounge, available if needed, but not threatening. Earl wanted the press to look as vulnerable as possible; a David and Goliath story. This time the fire hose on the roof wouldn't be of much use, it did not reach far enough to provide cover above the lounge. The lucky seven were their buffer should the union thugs decide they were worth a bad rap in the newspaper.

Thaddeus was to cautiously mingle with the developing crowd keeping an eye out for the press, and make sure they got the best street side view of events as they unfolded. Ivory's job was to make sure none of the union picketers went after Thaddeus.

At first, Earl had a hard time thinking of Brooks as Oscar. For the first time in their contentious relationship he needed Brooks; Oscar. Oscar was to take the lead, and this time everything depended on him. When Cambria's goons showed, and they would, Oscar was to return jeer for jeer, and insult for insult. This was the dangerous part because he had to be careful not to push them too far. Earl wanted them to think that Oscar was colored. The union thugs were not going to take that kind of crap from a black man. Oscar's surprise would come at the end. There had to be plenty of police around, and enough of an audience applauding to their night music, to draw the attention of the press. Tomorrow mornings newspapers needed to headline their musical challenge against injustice, and threat from the union, even the fires needed to take second place; that was a tall order.

Stella helped Earl into his trousers while Mollie helped Oscar put on a pair of thin dark brown gloves. The gloves would hamper his piano playing, but he wasn't going to be playing much. The gloves were a necessary part of the act. "Brooks, I mean Oscar," Earl said, "if those gloves get in the way just whistle."

"Are we ready?" Earl said. It wasn't really a question. "Les, you take the lead. We'll play in the same order as we have rehearsed in the Grotto. Michael, jump in when and where you can, and keep your eyes open. Stella, you keep an eye out for anyone paying too much attention to Michael here."

Stella shivered. *Are we ready? No, but here we go anyway.*

Earl let out a long slow breath. Just out there on the other side of those doors his dragon lurked. The dragon be damned, it was just a small lizard compared to what the union could do.

The lucky seven rolled the pianos out onto the street.

There wasn't an explosion, but rather a whooshing sound, mixed with the crackle and chime of shattering glass, as everyone's attention was drawn towards an abandoned six story tenement hotel a block to the northwest of the garage fire. Flames burst through multiple sixth floor windows, the shattering glass, a wind chime preceding disaster.

The reflection of yet a third fire glimmered off windows

and roof tops still a further block away; its origin unknown. While small compared to the bigger fires burning, its meaning was ominous."Damn, damn . . . damn!" Earl swore, The media would now swarm the neighborhood with little interest in the events developing around the Honeysuckle Rose Hotel.

"What do you think, Sarge, are these fires being set to draw attention away from us? While we're out here playing musical chairs, whose protecting our rear?" Ivory spoke aloud his concerns to the ghost of Sergeant Ware. The old Sarge, who had been mostly silent since Ivory left the hospital, reported for duty. *You are a Marine. You are our last man standing. We know where the enemy is out front, but we've got no eyes or ears to our rear. Get one of your lucky seven to volunteer and reconnoiter the hotel. If your hunch is right, it won't be long until the blaze intended gets its spark.*

Thaddeus was too busy brewing the coffee to hear Ivory's conversation with his lost Marine Sergeant.

Ivory called on Marty for his recon patrol. They had worked together before, and Marty, at least knew his way around the hotel.

As Earl and Oscar took their seats at the pianos the picketers stepped out of the night shadows. If they could have seen their faces they would have seen angry men with hard hearts.

"Cops or no cops the idiots across the way aren't going to just play some music," the picket leader said, "their trying to castrate us here for the whole world can see. I for one will not be gelded by a blind man and a bunch of niggers. He borrowed a dime from one of the other picketers, then went around the corner to the pay phone. They had strict orders not to cross the street or take any action against the hotel without Cambria's direct say so. The SOB's weren't in the hotel now.

Vocals were going to be tough, no one had thought to bring a mike and a sound system. Everyone in place Earl, made the introduction. The fire engines and street noises were loud enough he practically had to yell in order to be heard. He had no idea if there was any audience other than the union goons. "Okay, Stella, here we go." He took a deep breath. "Ladies and gentlemen *String of Pearls*. But first, here's a little something for our musician union friends." Only Earl knew what Oscar was going to do. He played as Oscar began:

'When der fuehrer says we is de master race

We heil heil right in . . .'

Brooks held his hooded head high, his voice clear, with a bad actor's British accent. Earl's fingers danced across the piano keys, careful not to upstage Oscar's words. The rest joined in with a rousing bronx cheer, aimed right where it belonged.

"Now that's what we're talking about," Earl chortled.

"String of Pearls," interrupted Oscar.

Michael stepped forward with the first notes.

This brought out an angry grumble.

THIRTY-EIGHT

SLOW NEWS DAY

HUGO CASSINELLI, REPORTER FOR THE SAN FRANCISCO Chronicle, was the first reporter on the scene of the garage fire. The fire was hot, the smoke heavy, with cars still exploding within the massive blaze. The pictures might make the front page, if it was a slow news day. There really wasn't much of a story here; unless the fire spread. San Francisco had more than its share of fires, few worth front page headlines.

The area was closed to traffic, even his press pass would not get him within a block of the fire. He spotted a parking place near a fire hydrant. A car parked too close had both side windows broken out with a fire hose run through it. Was the illegal parking spot worth broken windows, and an expensive tow? The tenement fire was the newest, so he opted to go there—with any luck he might even beat the firemen. Abandoned hotels were never really abandoned, the fleeing squatters were always good for a bleeding-heart story: *Helpless poor flee for their lives from building owned by heartless slum lord.*

He backed his '47 Mercury Coupe to the nearest cross street and parked it behind a police car. He put a copy of his press credential on the dash and followed his reporter's instinct.

It was a little after one in the morning, two, maybe three, major fires were burning in the Tenderloin, explosions rocking the night, and there was a picket line stirring angrily across the street from a hotel. Picketers rarely worked this late into the night, unless the issue was big. If there was something big brewing he should have heard something about it from one of his union snitches. The story was right in front of his nose, and it wasn't the fires. There was some kind of a jazz sextet, with two pianos, setting up to play in the street of all places. He started walking towards the union pickets, when he was stopped with his own drop dead laugh, as one of the pianists did a quick ditty from *'Der Fuehrer's Face', finished with a* group Bronx cheer directed at the picketers. This was followed by a quick lead into 'String of Pearls'.

The hell with the picketers, they get paid to repeat slogans and wave signs. He turned his attention towards the musicians. It was their eclectic mix that caught his reporter's eye. *Colored musician's playing outside of the Fillmore was practically unheard of. Maybe that is what the picketers are upset about? I've got to admit the guy on the trombone is pretty damn good. The saxophonist isn't bad either, although, the face behind the saxophone will be hard to describe. If he was an animal, other than human, he would have been put down as a mercy killing a long time ago. The group needs a drummer. There's a pretty female bass player. Two pianists, one blind and one . . . what's this . . . one wearing some kind of a hood. He might be colored? Hey, give the mask over to the guy on the saxophonist, and give us all a break.* He thought as he moved closer to the musicians. While there was a small audience growing, the musicians' were directing their efforts towards the picketers, deliberately taunting them.

A series of noisy fire engines raced down the next street over heading towards the tenement fire, momentarily drowning the music out. *Now here is a hell of a story,* he thought, as he pulled out his reporter's notebook. He carried a camera bag slung across his shoulder. He needed to get in closer, the lighting bad. He noted the name of the hotel: The Honeysuckle Rose Hotel. He'd been on the beat sixteen years, and had not heard of this one.

Ivory and Marty agreed, that if anyone wanted to start a fire, the basement would be the best place, or perhaps the service elevator shaft in the rear of the kitchen. The elevator shaft would spread the fire the fastest, and right now it wasn't used by anyone except housekeeping, which for now was all but non-existent. The elevator was located near the storage and pantry rooms behind the lounge. Downstairs, it was located in a kitchen hallway off the Grotto. They looked at each other with mutual alarm. *BINGO,* now if only they were not too late?

Ivory thought about saying something to Thaddeus, but decided there wasn't enough time. Marty was ten steps ahead of him as they hurried towards the rear of the lounge towards the service hallway and elevator.

The multiple fires are too convenient, Marty thought as he unsnapped his handgun from the belt holster covered by his coat. *Whew.* He needed to remember that he was no longer a cop. He had a gun permit, but the finger behind the trigger was civilian. The service corridor was dark. He searched for a light switch as he turned the corner, slamming into a man of greater size and girth than his own. "God damn it, Hoyt, you nearly scared me to death. You ought to know better when you see a guy coming your way with a loaded weapon."

"It works two ways," Hoyt replied as he patted his coat breast pocket where his own weapon was holstered.

"You see anything?" Marty asked as he peered down the dark hallway.

"I just got here. Before I join everyone out front, I needed to take a pee. I thought I heard something, so I came back to check it out. Nothing back here but a kitchen rat or two. The door to the alley is locked and barred from the inside. The elevator is locked off on one of the upper floors. Nothing is coming, or going back here, unless it first came through the front door."

Why would the elevator be locked off? I didn't do it. Ivory thought, as he overheard Hoyt's report. His survivor's instinct, backed by old Sarge, told him not to trust anyone. He stepped around the detective and double tapped the elevator door button. He stepped back, puzzled, eyeing the rest of the corridor, as he thought things through. *Why would it be locked off on an upper floor?* He found the light switch and tried it, with no result.

Hoyt edged an open storage room door closed with his foot. "The storage room is nothing but an oversized pantry filled with assorted bottles and cans," he said. "The light is burned out in there too." He directed their attention to a closed door just down the hall and across from the elevator. "That door there leads into the small kitchen area behind the bar. Nobody is getting through there in the dark without making a lot of clatter and noise. Light is out in there to. My guess is that it's a fuse."

Something wasn't right. Ivory could not quite put a finger on it. *Wait a moment, if you were to load the elevator with flammables and park it half way up the shaft, the fire would spread both up and down . . .* "Oh shit! Come on Marty, we'll take the stairs."

"Still got to take that piss," Hoyt said. "Be right behind you guys."

Marty and Ivory ran for the stairs. Marty wished he was twenty years younger and thirty pounds lighter. Ivory's artificial leg slowed him down, making him unsteady on the stairs.

Hoyt waited until the sounds of their hurried footsteps reached the second landing before he returned to the storage closet. He reached up and screwed the lightbulb tight until the light came back on. He then pushed aside the bottles and cans that blocked the obscure door hidden there, making sure his escape route was unlocked. He then rechecked the corridor outside before closing the door to the storage room behind him. The first moment he arrived at the hotel he had asked Thaddeus Mohler if there were any blueprints of the building. There were; that was how he found the secret doorway that led down to a passage that went beneath the alley into the building across the way.

From his window Cambria could see that there was more than one fire lighting up the Tenderloin—all three near the Honeysuckle Rose Hotel. He squinted to see if there were anymore, but couldn't tell. He ordered a cab and paid double the fare to bust every stop light and stop sign to get him to the Honeysuckle Rose Hotel as soon as the cabbie could get him there.

The lead picketer missed Cambria by seconds. He knew he would catch hell for it later. He took it upon himself to call Harry the Hammer, who was playing an all night game of poker, with the goon squad in case they were needed. There were eight in all. These were the toughest men Cambria had.

Harry answered the phone on the second ring. Their pick-up truck was parked just outside the apartment they were hold up in. It would be a five minute ride back to the hotel.

Al Louis had told his boss that he would be right there. That was not quite true, his car was in the shop, and there were rarely any free cabs running through his neighborhood at this hour of the morning. He had told his boss that he'd be there in about twenty minutes, knowing that he would be a lot longer than that. Late again. If he had told Cambria the truth he would have been in trouble for piss poor planning, as well as being late. If given a chance he would quit this god-damned job in a heartbeat, but that wasn't going to happen, because in this town he was too well known as Cambria's lieutenant.

The elevator was locked off on the third floor.

The first tinge of fear touched Ivory when he found that the elevators doors could only be unlocked with an operator's key. No one ever locked the elevator doors with the key. You did not need a key to lock it, but you needed one to get it back open. The hair went up on the back of his neck when he realized that if the arsonist had gotten this far the elevator might be bobby-trapped.

Marty urged that they wait, let the fire department handle it, there were plenty in the neighborhood.

"Marty, if I'm right about this, there isn't enough time. We've had two, three fires in the neighborhood in less than an hour. If the arsonist got in, and damned if I can guess how, he's wanting this place to go up like a grain silo . . . and Marty he doesn't give a god-damn who gets hurt in the process." With slightly trembling fingers he found the elevator key on the hotel's master key chain which he now carried with him. Their breath held, both men stepped to the side of the door as Ivory turned the key.

There was no explosion as the elevator door slid open. The elevator was loaded with newspapers, rags, and painters equipment, including four open cans of paint thinner, and two of kerosene. A fifth can lay on its side empty, the fumes of the kerosene thick, as it had been poured over the papers and rags, and splashed across the wooden elevator walls. A WWII Navy delayed action fuse rested in the center of the pile. It had been set for thirty minutes, half of that time now gone. The fuse was an explosive device used in sabotage, once started it could only be stopped by defusing it, which was a risky process in itself. "We had some of these in China," Ivory said, "but we never got a chance to use any. You ever handle anything like this?"

Marty shook his head, saying "no," as he backed away.

They couldn't leave it there, and there might be more ticking away elsewhere in the hotel. Ivory carefully wrapped the device in the cleanest rags he could find; one with the least amount of kerosene on it. "Marty, I'm not sure how safe this thing is to carry. Go down the hall and open up the fire escape window. We'll pitch it down into the alley where it can do the least amount of harm." *If it takes out a couple of the union goons, so be it.*

Hugo got several good shots of the pickets lines and the building crowd as he pushed his way closer to the musicians. The pianist with the cloth hood over his head intrigued him. There did not appear to be any eye holes cut through the cloth. From what he could see it looked like the guy was black. *There were two other colored musicians, so why hide this one's face, unless he was well known. Great headline: 'Well Known Colored Musician Stands Up To All White Musician's Union.' The Ku Klux Klan would go after him like a bunch of angry hornets.* He studied the faces of the musicians. *These guys are putting themselves at considerable risk, not from being beaten and dragged through the streets tonight, but from a quiet but deadly retaliation list you just don't want to be on.*

Brooks introduced the next number, which Imogene sang:

'Who do you think you are kidding, Mr Union Man

If you think we are on the run?

We are the boys, and girls, who will stop your game

We are the ones who will make you think again

Cus' who do you think you're kidding, Mr. Union Man

If you think the old Honeysuckle Rose is done.[1]

It had been agreed that when, and if, Cambria showed up, Michael would let everyone know by doing a short flirtatious saxophone solo taken from 'I've Got A Lovely Bunch Of Coconuts.'

A cab pulled up in front of the cafe. An agitated Frank

---

[1] Taken from: 'Who Do You Think You're Kidding, Mr Hitler', by Perry & Taverner

Cambria stepped out. He took a quick glance towards the cafe, it was closed, he turned his attention to everything that was happening on the street. He arrived not one minute too soon. The pick-up loaded with eight union goons pulled up at the end of the block nearest where the musicians stood their ground.

Anticipating trouble the police had put up their own traffic barricade preventing anyone from getting near the front of the lounge, or to cross the street there and join the picketers already in place. To join the picket line the goons would have to drop back half a block and go through the alley, then back up to where Cambria stood.

Three cars pulled up and parked illegally in front of the alley. Union goons stormed out of one and marched up the street to meet up with Cambria. The second and third car contained the night reporters from KGO-FM and KOIT-FM. They had followed the goons to the story. There were now more reporters covering what was happening in front of the Honeysuckle Rose Hotel than the fires that burned a few blocks nearby. The reporters from the radio stations could go live if they wanted to.

Hoyt knew that once Ivory and Marty found the elevator it wouldn't take much to put two and two together. He had five detonators left, and planned to use them all. During the war he had worked as a civilian contractor in the Quartermaster's Department with the naval magazine at the Navy's Port Chicago Department at the far end of San Francisco Bay. That was where he had learned about munitions. As a civilian contractor he had found it easy to steal from the supply depot, and resell whatever he had on the black market. That was what had landed him in Frank Cambria's hands. Selling munitions on the black market was something the government frowned upon, and Cambria had enough information to send Hoyt to a federal prison for a long time.

On more than one occasion Hoyt had borne false witness to Cambria's so called self defense shooting. He was tired of being on the hook to Cambria, and, now, if convicted of arson—perhaps murder—he would go down for a long time. Cambria had paid him enough to take the risk, and he wasn't going to screw it up. He planned on finishing the job, then skipping town to a more friendly climate.

He had three quick stops to make before he returned to the storage room to make his exit from the hotel. He guessed that once Ivory found the timer he had placed in the elevator, he would either defuse it, or remove it. The timer he placed at the bottom of the elevator shaft would sever the pulley system. When it dropped to the bottom of the shaft there should be enough of a fire to ignite the rags and kerosene. If that didn't work, than he had set himself up for a long jail term for nothing.

Time was running out as he placed explosives on the outside of the two stairwell doors. When opened from the inside the explosion would kill anyone within five feet.

Hoyt looked at his watch. He had just enough time to get to the roof, from there he could drop a contact fuse down the elevator shaft, which would guarantee that the explosion in the shaft would be enough to spread the fire so hot and fast the firemen could do little to stop it.

Ivory was at the wrong window. If he pitched the fuse out

there it would land among the crowd that had now gathered in front of the hotel. It would take longer to get back to an alleyway window than to take the stairs to the roof. He chose the stairs. If it went off early he would join the Sarge; better to have it go off prematurely on the roof than in the hotel.

They both knew in their guts that Hoyt was the arsonist. They might be wrong, but the odds there were pretty slim. "Marty, I'm taking this to the roof. You find Hoyt," Ivory said as he headed towards the stairs.

"You armed?" Marty asked.

His eyes touched on the explosive. "What do you think I'm carrying?"

"Tell me what you see, Michael, brief and to the point, don't leave anything out," Earl asked?

"Cambria just arrived, he's outside the cafe, and is now headed our way with eight tough monkeys each with short pieces of pipe, or rubber hose. There are an equal number of picketers straight across the street. They don't look to anxious to get involved with a fight, leave it to the goons, but if ordered to, they will. The police have everything locked off with barricades to our left. Wait a moment, something is happening with the police."

"What?"

Thaddeus pushed his way through the crowd to settle in nervously behind the band. "Earl, you have a reporter from the Chronicle, and two from radio stations. I sure as hell hope this works?"

"Don't we all." Earl said, his own voice showing the all or nothing stress of the moment. "You ready Oscar?" He played loud enough to drown out their voices and to give Oscar one last chance to back out.

"The police are pulling out," Michael said. "What do we do now?"

"I have not thought about suicide for awhile. Drinking one's self to death sounds like a lot more fun than being beaten to a pulp. But, what the hell, let's go for broke." Oscar's laugh was dry and hollow.

"Earl," Sam said, "Sergeant Cooney just showed up. He's our precinct rep with the police union. He's pulling our officers out before a crime is committed . . . and they are forced to have a showdown with Cambria's union. Cooney has been on Cambria's payroll for some time now. You want to rethink this thing?"

"How about you Sam, and the rest of the lucky seven, are you pulling out too?"

"We haven't the muscle to win this thing, but we are not about to throw you to those buzzards without a fight."

"OK, everyone, we're going to 'When the Saint's Go Marching In', ramp up the volume as you slowly back into the hotel. Imogene, you sing it girl. Stella, you go with them. It's up to Oscar, Michael, and me, from here on out."

Stella started to say no, but was stopped by a terse 'no' from Earl.

"Oh When the Saints go . . ."

"What's the matter, nigger, you afraid that your true color

327

is showing. Yellow!" Cambria was moving in at an equal speed as the cops moved out. He now saw that the piano player he had thought to be black was wearing a hood. He was still convinced the man was a coon with a big mouth. Right now his target was beauty. It was a personal score, the blind bastards would be easy enough.

"How about singing a little more for us?" One of his goons shouted from right behind Cambria. "Perhaps something fitting for a funeral."

Earl played while Oscar did the talking.

Michael did the watching.

Six of the lucky seven pulled back just inside the doorway. They remained ready to do what they could to rescue Earl, Oscar, and Michael, if they could.

Marty wasn't about to waste his time searching for Hoyt, the hotel was too big, and time too short. There could be more explosives just about anywhere. He used the hotel hall phone to call the lounge which rang four times before Thaddeus answered. "Listen carefully," Marty said. "The elevator has been shut off on the third floor with a bomb on it. There most likely are others planted around the hotel. Call the fire department. Tell them that Detective Gavin Hoyt is the suspected arsonist. He is somewhere in the hotel, armed and dangerous. Then, get everyone out of the hotel."

"Would you repeat that?" Thaddeus said, not sure if he had heard everything correctly.

"No. I've got to help Ivory who is carrying a live bomb up to the roof." Marty hung up.

Thaddeus stood there, mouth open and dumb-founded, as he put together what he had just heard.

"Well, Mr. Union man," Oscar crowed. "One of the reasons I've never joined your musician's union is that I don't sing. I can't carry a tune. I used to whistle, but that is a whole other story. I'm a poet you see. Ask Earl here, he's been telling me for years that I'm a poet, and not a singer. Do you have any poets in your union? Hmm, I thought not. So, if you are upset about me not being a card carrying union man, there you have it. I'm a poet, not a singer, and as far as my piano playing goes. . ."

"I own this place," Earl said, "and it will be a cold day in hell before I pay this so called poet one thin dime for his piano playing. No one pays me. I wish someone would. We are all just friends and family here, playing for the sheer joy of it. Last I heard there is no union rule on that."

Cambria was now too close for comfort.

"Easy." Michael said. Scared to death, as he held his ground.

"Fine," Cambria answered back, "as a private citizen I'll press charges for making a public disturbance. It's rather late at night to make all this noise. Folks aren't going to take it too kindly to find out that their sleep has been interrupted by a bunch of niggers, and a bunch of nigger lovers." Cambria's temper was as hot as the fires raging nearby.

Oscar pushed him a little farther. "Did you say that someone here is colored?"

"That's news to me." Earl responded. "What color?"

329

Cambria's arm came up, finger pointing at the open lounge doors. "There are two in there, and one wise-assed black son-of-a-bitch hiding behind a mask sitting right there at that piano. Niggers are not allowed to play anywhere this side of Van Ness. The union represents all bonafide musicians in San Francisco, and we stand by our closed door policy regarding niggers. And it's going to be my pleasure to kick your black ass clean into the Pacific Ocean."

The union goons grinned and started to move forward.

"Hold it right there, little Marine," Hoyt said as he came out of the stairwell to find Ivory on the roof holding one of his explosive fuses. "I don't know how you figured it out, but that doesn't matter much now, does it." He pulled out his gun.

"Hand it over," His free hand motioning for the activated explosive fuse.

Ivory slowly moved towards the front of the hotel hoping that someone below might see them. Two fires burned bright into the night, with emergency fire engine lights blinking brightly around them. "You started those fires to draw suspicion away from the Honeysuckle Hotel, didn't you? How many more of these fuses are there?"

Hoyt nodded towards the smaller fire burning a few blocks away. "The car fire can be just as disruptive as a building fire on a night like this. There will be another one in about ten minutes in the parking garage at the St. Francis Hotel. It shouldn't do much damage, but the smoke and the panic should draw most able fireman away from your precious hotel."

Hoyt worked his way in front of Ivory preventing him from getting anywhere near the edge of the roof. He glanced down and curled a smile when he saw Cambria just below. Hoyt had been under Cambria's thumb too long, and he remained as one more witness that could testify against him. He assumed that Ivory had disarmed the fuse. He would rearm it, drop it on Cambria, shoot Ivory, and disappear into the night. He glanced back and forth from Ivory, and down to Cambria. "That SOB still owes me some money, but sometimes it's not about the money. Cambia is about to join you in hell, and that will make my day."

Marty heard enough as he stepped out of the stairwell. "Drop it, Hoyt."

Hoyt fired.

Marty was hit, falling back into the stairwell.

Ivory had not disarmed the explosive fuse, he didn't know how. The timer showed five seconds. "Here," he shouted as he tossed the fuse to Hoyt. He then dropped, and rolled away.

Hoyt tried to shoot, but couldn't because he had to catch the fuse.

He did.

He had no chance to fire his gun. The explosive shredded his hand, blowing him off his feet, and over the brick roof guard.

Al Louis showed up just as Cambria ordered his goons to bust up the piano and the nigger behind it. "Boss, don't?"

The explosion along with Hoyt's surprised death scream was lost in the din coming from the street below.

The flash of Hugo's camera momentarily blinded Al and any goons nearby, as something large and heavy knocked Cambria to the ground.

"Boss." Al hurried over to help his boss up.

The goons had been stopped by the sudden appearance of Detective Hoyt's body.

All eyes looked up as Ivory appeared over the edge of the roof. "There is your arsonist, bought and paid for by Frank Cambria, President of the musician's union." He shouted down."

Few heard what Ivory said.

Hugo did.

As did Earl.

"Mr. C, there are still some cops on the side street just to our left," Michael said. He played three long shrill notes on his sax to get their attention.

"Officer," Earl cried out. "There is your arsonist, bought and paid for by the union."

A last fuse that was still in Hoyt's pocket blew, lifting his body, stunning Cambria, knocking him back to the ground again, preventing his escape.

Two policemen raced in, guns drawn.

Earl played the background music as Oscar showed his poetic side as he quoted, with a fair Scottish accent:

'Should auld acquaintance be forgot,

And auld lang syne . . .'

Cambria was handcuffed, arrested, and taken away'.

Al Lewis, at least for the moment, was now head of the musician's union. He waved the goons back and called off the picket line. The press was going to have a field day with this.

Marty, nursing a shoulder wound, appeared next to Ivory at the roof's edge. "I think you had better get down to the basement before that asshole's last fuse goes off in the elevator shaft."

Ivory, realizing that was where Hoyt would have planted it, bolted.

"Be careful, I suspect he might have booby-trapped the stairwells as well." Marty yelled after him, his face grimacing as he felt the bullet that was still in him.

Ivory stopped in place, turned and looked knowingly at Marty. "That is what I would have done."

Marty yelled down to Sam that there were more bombs in the building.

"Oh Mr. Union Man," Oscar called after Cambria. The police, Cambria, the press, and everyone else nearby turned towards Oscar. "Earl asked you if anyone here was colored. He's not. Michael—Beauty—isn't. Me . . . ?" Oscar slipped the silk hood up and off his brutally scared head, his face mostly non-existent. "Lately, I've been wondering, what color am I, and considering everything . . . does it matter?

Hugo got the best picture that would run center page in the morning edition. It wasn't of Oscar, but of Cambria's agonized and astonished face. Other camera's flashed, the pictures taken, telling the story of the battle to save the Honeysuckle Rose Hotel, to the world.

"Poets can't sing," Earl added with a flourish, "but they sure can tell a story."

THIRTY-NINE

WHERE BLUEBIRDS SING

TWO WEEKS PAST, AND ON A THURSDAY NIGHT THE HOTEL'S doors were wide open, with Ivory and Sam dressed in full tux and top hats as the doormen.

The picketers across the street were quiet, respectful, and carried no threatening signs. This time they were not trying to stop anybody from doing anything. They wanted inclusion. For the time being no card carrying union members were allowed to sit in at the Grotto, not even gratis. They watched silently as car after car, mostly cabs, pulled up to the front doors discharging their passengers, who all hurried to get the best seats they could at Stella's Grotto. The hotel's rooms were mostly booked with no reservations regarding the color of a musician's skin.

Loyal William Jones kept his promise delivering most of his patrons from The Alley Cat, as well as an assortment of musicians who wanted to sit in with the Earl Crier Band. A drummer, Ray Rexwinkle, out of Los Angeles, brought the missing beat the band needed.

The kitchen help were mostly colored, as were the house-keeping staff. Loyal William Jones was a man good for his word. He, in turn, had discovered that Earl was as good for his.

Oscar was more than content to have his own place in the lounge. Mollie sat in at the second piano. The press had given him notoriety, and an audience of the curious, of which many were to become regulars. His piano was fair. The scar tissue around his mouth had tightened making it now all but impossible to whistle. Earl's original jest, that Brooks was a poet who could not sing, now fit Oscar like a comfortable old glove. It was the poetry that he recited that endeared him within the San Francisco music scene as the poet that would not sing.

Stub served as head bartender, his hands flying as food and drink were being served.

When Oscar had suggested to Earl that they perform together Stella had to leave the room in tears. Earl and Brooks, when they first met back at the Veteran's Hospital, could not stand to be in the same room together. Their personalities grated on the other, but most importantly, neither had come to terms with their own blindness. Neither wanted sympathy, nor pity. But each in their own way demanded it. Each reminded the other of their devastating disability. It did not help that Earl was a musical genius, and Brooks a failed musician who wished that he could only stand in Earl's shadow. Their separation allowed each to mature and heal enough that now they could talk about it with each other— and to their audience. Earl and Oscar were beginning to actually like each other.

The lights dimmed as Earl was escorted to his piano by Stella.

"Ladies and gentlemen," she said, "my partner, my love, and one fine musician . . . Earl Crier." Earl played the first stanza of Stella's theme song, then quieted the notes as he introduced, Rosemary, Les, Michael, Ray their new drummer, and Imogene; each added their instrument to Stella's song.

Oscar entered, guided by Mollie, and took his place at the second piano, his hands held back from the keyboard. "Ladies and gentlemen," Earl said as he nodded with a smile in Oscar's direction, Mr. Oscar Katz, our resident poet. Folks, please allow me to explain something to you. I am a lyricist, not a songwriter.

Oscar is a poet, not a lyricist, nor a songwriter. If that confuses you, I'll explain a little bit about the difference between a poem and a song. Poetry is meant to be expressed with words and words alone. Poetry doesn't have to have a rhythm structure or a pattern." His fingers brought a light melody to the conversation. "You can write a love letter, and call it poetry if you want, but that doesn't mean that it could ever become a love song. A poem is designed to make you think. A lyric is made to make you sing."

"Did you ever notice that you can think about something else while you are singing or listening to a song—while it's almost impossible to think about something else while listening to or reading a poem. A song can set the mood, and take you to places and times that have nothing to do with the song you are listening to. A poem takes you to places and times too, but usually to only the places and times that are the subject of the poem.

"A lyricist . . . a crooner," Earl shared a rich deep chuckle, "brings to the song feelings that come from his life experience. The words remain the same, but the heart of the song is forever changed. So you see most poets can't sing. Brooks here can't, but listen to the poetry within the man."

All music stopped as Oscar, with a haunting, if not melodic voice, spoke. His mask rippling slightly with each carefully placed breath:

> *'Somewhere over the rainbow*
>
> *Way up high,*
>
> *And the dreams that you dreamed of*
>
> *once in a lullaby.'*

Oscar's poetic interpretation made the song a poem; a poetic soulful prayer.

When finished he fell silent as the first piano notes changed the poem into a song sung my Imogene. This was one of those rare moments when Billy Holiday could take notes from a lesser known, but intoxicating newer artist. The drum, saxophone, trombone, and base, brought the audience to a different place *somewhere over the rainbow, where the dreams that are dreamed of, really do come true.*

The song finished, Oscar the poet spoke again.

The musicians silent, you could hear a penny drop as the crowded room listened to the poet Oscar Katz:

> *'Someday I'll wish upon a star*
>
> *And wake up where the clouds are far behind me.*
>
> *Where trouble melts like lemon drops . . .*

This time he spoke to the crowd as a poet would, sharing each phrase until the poem was complete.

Earl's fingers caressed the piano as he began to sing the same song, the drum and bass sliding in. Then, for just a

338

moment, he paused in a place unexpected. The other musicians quieted as a brilliant clarinet turned every eye misty completing the song as a brilliant solo.

Stella's eyes grew misty with happiness, not from the crowd's applause, but because of the man behind the clarinet—Henry Akita—who after reading about the battle to save the Honeysuckle Rose Hotel had come back to his odd-ball musical family.

Earl sang the last words as Henry's clarinet faded away.

Oh, somewhere over the rainbow bluebirds sing

And the dream that you dared to

My, oh my, they can become true.

—Henry, welcome home.

A warm Amen resonated across the room from Oscar Katz.

The End.

CPSIA information can be obtained
at www.ICGtesting.com
Printed in the USA
FSOW01n2228250615
8273FS